CVC
6

CVC

Carter V. Cooper

SHORT FICTION ANTHOLOGY SERIES

BOOK SIX

SELECTED BY AND WITH A PREFACE BY

Gloria Vanderbilt

EXILE
editions

Carter V. Cooper Short Fiction Anthology Series, Book Six.
Issued in print and electronic formats.

ISSN 2371-3968 (Print)
ISSN 2371-3976 (Online)

ISBN 978-1-55096-633-6 (paperback). ISBN 978-1-55096-645-9 (epub).
ISBN 978-1-55096-647-3 (mobi). ISBN 978-1-55096-649-7 (pdf).

Short stories, Canadian (English). Canadian fiction (English) 21st century.
Vanderbilt, Gloria, 1924-, editor.
Series: Carter V. Cooper short fiction anthology series, book 6.

Published by Exile Editions Ltd ~ www.ExileEditions.com
144483 Southgate Road 14-GD, Holstein, Ontario, N0G 2A0
Printed and Bound in Canada in 2016, by Marquis

We gratefully acknowledge, for their support toward our publishing activities,
the Canada Council for the Arts, the Government of Canada,
the Ontario Arts Council, and the Ontario Media Development Corporation.

Canadian sales: The Canadian Manda Group, 664 Annette Street,
Toronto ON M6S 2C8 www.mandagroup.com 416 516 0911

North American and international distribution, and U.S. sales:
Independent Publishers Group, 814 North Franklin Street,
Chicago IL 60610 www.ipgbook.com toll free: 1 800 888 4741

In memory of

Carter V. Cooper

The Winners for Year Six

Best Story by an Emerging Writer
≈ $10,000 ≈
Matthew Heiti

Best Story by a Writer at Any Point of Career
≈ $5,000 ≈
Helen Marshall

CVC
Book Six

PREFACE

I founded the Carter V. Cooper short fiction competition in memory of my son, and to champion literature, which he had loved.

It is one of the great joys of parenthood to behold, in astonishment and surprise, the depth and complexity of your children as they emerge into themselves. In that spirit, I cannot help but admire the writers who comprise *Book Six* of the *Carter V. Cooper Short Fiction Anthology* series.

Open to all Canadian writers, this annual short fiction competition awards two prizes: $10,000 for the best story by an emerging writer, and $5,000 for the best story by an established writer.

If all writing is borne of a singular yearning, these stories – in genre, range, tone and interest – are utterly their own. Together, they form our most diverse and striking collection to date.

About the winners, I have this to say: "Tilting at Windmills" – by emerging writer Matthew Heiti – is a brash, volatile story of excess and high melancholy. I was stunned by its ferocity and deep forlornness. The winner of the established category, Helen Marshall's "The Gold Leaf Executions," is at once exquisite and deft. Beyond its precision in craftsmanship, it pierces the heart without remorse. It is a marvellous story from a writer who also appeared in both our 2013 and 2014 collections while an emerging writer.

In these two winners, and indeed in all of the stories gathered here, there is no doubting the intensity of their passions. It is a privilege to witness.

I would also like to give a big thank you to the readers who adjudicated this competition: the judge in charge, storyteller Matt Shaw, magazine and books editor Jerry Tutunjian, storyteller, poet and anthologies editor Colleen Anderson, and Barry Callaghan, Editor-in-chief of *ELQ/ Exile Quarterly* and Exile Editions – all of whom have played their own special roles in the development and support of emerging writers.

Gloria Vanderbilt
July 2016

Helen Marshall

THE GOLD LEAF EXECUTIONS

1.

There was a way of executing people you told me about. You found it in a book, an old one: gilded edges and a cracked spine, boards that had warped like the hull of a ship. The book, you were telling me, claimed they did it with gold leaf.

"Who?" I asked.

"The Romans," you said. Or maybe I'm misremembering here, thinking of the Romans because the Romans are the kind of people I think about when I think about things like this.

We were washing dishes in the kitchen. "That's ridiculous," I told you. "Impossible."

You put a matching set of luncheon plates in the rack, paused. Autumn light sliced across your knuckles. "But beautiful too, isn't it?"

I wanted to know how it would've worked, but you laughed and said you couldn't remember. Didn't want the details, just the thought of it. "It's better, I think, without knowing," you said.

2.

I met you on a bus to Siena, which is why I always think about the Romans when I think about that story.

I was supposed to be at conference, so were you. Post-graduation, the same hustle. You had just finished at Birmingham while I was taking my first post in Newfoundland where it snowed until May. We were supposed to be staying at the Università per Stranieri di Siena. It translated literally as the University for Strangers, which made me laugh. I'd been expecting the typical thing: dormitories and plastic sheets, the kind that made your hair stand up with static. I pictured us in the heat, frazzled and bored, electrocuting each other when we tried to shake hands.

So then this happens a week before the conference: the roof collapses. A stroke of luck?

Maybe. They organizers divided us into two groups. Half were sent out to the Tuscan countryside while the others were put up in a nunnery. It was Shakespearean, you joked. You were lucky. You'd never have made a good Ophelia.

3.

That reminds me of another story. There was a man named Simonides of Ceos, and he was a poet.

One day he gets invited to a party – a fancy one, very important – so Simonides of Ceos puts on his best toga, cleans himself up proper. But he doesn't trust these people. He wants them to love him, but he knows deep down that he'll never be one of them. They ask him for a poem, but they're laughing. He suspects they hate poetry.

But Simonides of Ceos lacks a sense of self-preservation. He gives them a poem, a good one, too. There are rhythms in it that Homer would've been proud of. And the smiles get sharper, so he does what he always does. He turns to the twins: Castor and Pollux. Everyone has their muse, and his were glorious. The golden boys. But his host is unimpressed. He'd hoped for a little amusement, a little flattery. "You can collect half your fee from them," he grunts, "if you want to be so pious."

Now Simonides of Ceos feels too drunk, angry. "Gold comes as an evil guest," he thinks, and the words come out like a curse.

So what happens? There's a knock at the door. Two gentlemen are asking for him but its dark out there, and cold. Simonides of Ceos can't see anyone. He suspects they've done all this to hurt him. He's used to childish pranks. "Hey!" he yells. "What gives?"

Then bang!

Behind him the roof collapses. He is caught by the sight of the dust rising into the air like a mushroom cloud. An act of God, he thinks.

That's not the end of it though.

Now they have to bury the bodies. That's how it was in those days: they have to bury the bodies, but the bodies have been flattened. Unrecognizable. Insects crushed against the skin of the earth.

"Simonides of Ceos," they say, "who was there? You must know."

And the funny thing is that he *does* know. He remembers perfectly. In his mind he can see them stretched out on their couches, he remembers their names. He walks through the ruins and he points at the stains: "Yes, there, Scopas was resting his head. I remember. He was lolling backwards, he was *laughing* at me."

Simonides of Ceos scratches his neck. He's a poet and so he knows words, but this is different. And he knows it's different because of something to do with death.

And the people smile. And they bury the bodies, just as he said.

4.

You had long hair down to your hips. I'd never felt anything like it before, soft and somehow clinging. When it blew in the wind and it touched me it, was like someone had walked over my grave. It made me shiver. There was so much of it. It was like you were walking in a cloud.

And there we were, in the Tuscan countryside. Trapped amidst the cypresses and the hazy countryside an hour or more from the city. You were drinking from a bottle of Prosecco. Not expensive stuff. "The cheaper the better," you laughed. One euro was as much as you'd pay, and god, the hangovers were fantastic.

There was only one bus, and it ran every three hours. Neither of us knew where to buy a ticket. "A trap," you murmured, "for the Stranieri." The ticket inspectors got you on the train in. You hadn't validated your ticket, and then to make matters worse you snuck into first-class for the air conditioning. No one was there, not a soul. Everyone was sweating it out, but "Fuck it" you said. The poor junior officer might have let you get away with one violation, but not two. You pleaded with him, tried to be as English as possible, wet-eyed and saintly. But they slapped you with a fine of two hundred euros anyway.

"It was all my spending money," you told me.

Thus the Prosecco.

But now we're both trapped on this bus, ticketless, guilty as sin. So we sit together. I tell you I can make a distraction if they come for us, you can run for it. I'm half-joking, mostly not joking. Already I'm in love with you. I'd let them string me up. I'm telling you, I'd let them crucify me. It's bad taste, but you laugh like you've forgotten what taste is.

No one asks for our tickets.

I think I'm disappointed. I wanted to show you how serious I could be.

5.

There's an urban legend about gold leaf. They put it in vodka. If you drink it, they say, then it'll cut up your insides. It'll slice up your throat. It gets you drunk faster, they say.

Was that how the Romans did it? Did it cut their victims open? Did it make a thousand tiny mouths of their insides, all ready to gobble up whatever came down?

6.

We got boozy and falling down drunk together. We stripped off our clothes and dived into the pool, well past midnight. There were other people from the conference there. They must have heard us giggling, must have hated us. We didn't care. The sun had burned itself into the pavement and left everything warm and shining. When we jumped in the water there were sharp, stinging bubbles that filled our noses like lemon juice.

"God, I love this," you said, meaning everything: water, the smell of oleander and jasmine, running from the sauna, the night creeping up on us though we were thirsty for it to come.

You took my hand, and placed it on your hip. We were dancing. We were dancing and our waists were above the water and our feet wouldn't move, so we swayed. You slumped against me. Your hair was wet and tame. I took it between my fingers and squeezed it out, one lock at a time.

"What're you doing?"

I wouldn't tell you. Really, I had no idea only that touching you was all I wanted to do forever and ever.

"I'm sleepy," you said.

"Sleep here."

"I'll drown."

"People don't drown in swimming pools."

But you knew better. "People drown everywhere, dummy. Let's go to your room."

7.

Or maybe it had to do with choking. The scene when Goldfinger smothers Jill Masterson in paint? That was your favourite, wasn't it? Her lying on the bed, gleaming.

Skin suffocation. Bond claimed it used to happen to cabaret dancers.

There was a rumour that Masterson had asphyxiated during filming. Or a body-double had. It was nonsense, of course. There had been doctors on the set. They had left a six-inch strip of her stomach bare, just in case.

Still you were careful with me that first time: "You can only touch me for a little while," you said, asking me for what? Oxygen, air, room to breathe. And later: "Don't be so sad now, you. Buck up, sailor."

8.

But you came home with me from Italy, came back to St. John's. You took up teaching part-time for a little while but eventually let it go. You'd never loved it, you told me. But you loved the students, loved how they watched you, how they wrote on your evaluations: "It's so nice to be taught Shakespeare in an English accent." You kept yourself distant from them, mysterious. You spoke in a voice you never used at home where your grammar was slouchy and free.

That first year was so difficult. You needed to take long walks by yourself, exploring the hard coastline, the grey afternoon light, while I taught Intro to English Literature to bored eighteen-year-olds whose fathers had been fishermen. You wanted to understand this place. The mist in the air reminded you of home: Yorkshire dales, craggy rocks breaking out of the dirt and the thin grass of the moors. *Wuthering Heights* was your favourite book. You loved to read to me about Heathcliffe clinging to the lattice, crying out to the ghost of his beloved. And Catherine, damning:

"I gave him my heart, and he took and pinched it to death; and flung it back to me."

In spring you spotted icebergs from Signal Hill. You dragged me from my office to see them with you. Your hands were cold, ungloved, and when we kissed your nose was red to its tip.

I could tell you were making a decision about something, you had been all winter.

9.

Gold is soft but durable. Immune to decay. I wondered about that when I heard the story about the death of Aquillius. Mithradates poured molten gold down his throat.

It started a craze. That's how Marcus Licinius Crassus went. He was the richest man in Rome and the Parthians stuffed it all down his throat. They gagged him for his greed. Afterward, they carried out his skull for a wedding feast. His face was frozen solid. It glittered like a death mask.

"We bring from the mountain a wonderful prey."

The crowd was snickering. They appreciated a good joke.

10.

That summer I was terrified of my own happiness. It burst upon me like a burning continent rising out of the water: massive, red-hot, full of its own newness. Every moment I wanted you, but I was afraid to touch you.

I remember it was raining, heavy sheets of it, but you wanted to go to the shore. White sand, turning grey, swept up by the sea. Clouds boiling overhead, thick and yellow and wondrous, making a sound like *nch-nch-nch*. The wind, I guess.

You were soaked through. Your clothes were sticking to your skin, and I could see the full glorious shape of you: breasts, those narrow thighs like columns. An ankle, a foot leaving divots in the marble sand.

Then lightning, tongues of it, licking down from the sky. Bang, bang! The thunder was on top of us. Pressure sucked at our eardrums, which were thin and shaking already. But God, what was left behind? Glass – great coral branches of it where the lightning struck the sand and froze it solid. These huge bursts of light, blinding us, and then in the afterglow were heavy crystalline wreathes. You were scared but half-mad with joy, clutching at me.

"Get down!" I screamed. "We have to get down, we have to get down."

So we were lying in the sand, and the water was falling on us, and the ocean was creeping up closer and closer. You tasted like seawater. The sky was a pair of black hands clapping.

"Stay with me," I wanted to tell you. So badly. But the storm was overhead, and it was burning in the sky. And so, instead, I held your hand, and I felt it grow hot in mine, felt all of you lighting up.

And just like that, it was over.

We collected the fulgurite afterward. The pieces were smaller than I had thought they would be. As small and breakable as seashells. They cut your pockets to ribbons.

11.

Acrisius was a bitter old man who feared for his life. He kept his daughter Danae in a tower lest she bear the grandson promised to destroy him. But Zeus saw her at the window, and, oh, he was struck by the sight of her. What a clever letch! He poured himself into her lap as a golden ray of light. He fit as snugly as a key.

It wasn't long before Acrisius discovered his girl was in the family way. He locked her and the child both in a chest and set them adrift on the ocean where they bobbed along for a record-breaking sixty days. They came ashore at Seriphus, bone-tired and hungry. Danae could not stand. Her bones were brittle from confinement, her skin red and ragged, but King Polydectes loved her anyway. She was grateful to him. Maybe she loved him. What she didn't know was the babe who clung to her breast, sucking salt from her teat, would do away with him too when he came of age.

The gods are cruel: that sad sliver of prophecy buried so unlovingly inside her.

12.

Now the autumn is coming on us again. I can feel it like a thundercloud ready to burst: all that frost and heaviness, every living thing seized up inside, moving slower. And I'm paralyzed by the thought of my mother. How three years ago she noticed a spot of gold in Dad's left eye. It was perfectly round, like a coin, and just beneath the pupil. It reminded me of those science fiction movies where the sky has two suns or two moons. Unnatural, but lovely.

Uveal melanoma. Survival rates at fifty percent.

And the way she held him during that long period of recovery, carefully, as if he were weightless. It was such a tiny thing. She told me she wanted to fish it out with the tip of her tongue the way she'd fished out lashes from my eyes when I was ten.

"Make a wish," she used to tell me. I had that kind of faith in things.

There was an operation that left him blind in one eye. He stumbled into chairs. Dark continents drifting across his vision. "I'm going away," Dad told me. "Don't come after me." And then all at once we were scattering his ashes in the sunlight. Shining, heavy, black soot and dust. Like crops of mud turning to ice. Or snowflakes.

13.

Happenstance. Bad fortune. Decay.

At this time of year there is no sunset. The daylight stretches itself over the cliffs and night beats against it but never breaks through. It's three in the morning, and you and I are drinking cup after cup of espresso, trying desperately to stay awake.

"It's just a visit," you've told me a hundred times, but some kind of animal fear has lodged in my throat. I'm afraid of car accidents, the taxi ride to the airport – you won't let me drive you – and the flight to Heathrow hijacked. Or something worse: what will happen when you see your sister's house again, that worn-down cottage on the edge of the moor so familiar you could walk its halls in your sleep.

"There are so many things that go wrong in the world," I want to say, but you know you need to do this.

Laughing but tender: "I'll be home before you know it."

But the uncertainty in your voice makes you pause. Neither of us knows for sure. There are transformations and transformations: what if one glance brings you back to who you were before me?

I can imagine you standing in the kitchen staring at a yellow streaked sky, as a child with your eyes, your dimpled chin, bangs a spoon against the cracked red tiles. And in that moment you are absently scratching your neck, everything fading, everything falling away from you, trying for your life to remember what made me so beautiful.

Diana Svennes-Smith

STRANGER IN ME

By my thirteenth year, I had never seen a river. I had never seen a staircase. I looked up from the chopping block and saw a low mean sky snot-yellow in the east and I remarked to my Pa, Might that be trouble coming? The wind was so unruly it stole the breath right out of my nostrils. It was 1937, only April yet. Gophers asleep in their holes. Geese moving north. Blood moved like with like together.

Pa halted in his axe swing and looked to the east and said, That's trouble coming if I ever saw it. Don't pay him any attention. Maybe he'll pass by.

And I looked again in that direction where the wind flattened the grasses by the road and saw a stickman come limping along beside our fence. His pants flapped loose enough to scare crows. If he did pass by, where would he be going? To the west was empty prairie, then the distant Cypress Hills that made me think of Al Capone and whisky runners hid in the folds. Bones of some historic massacre white against the grass. Indian arrows and wolfers' bullets scattered about. Sitting Bull was up there too, with his thousand starving refugees. Cattle rustlers, hunters, giant lizards whose bones were collected and stored in the school basement in Wolf Willow. All concurrent in my mind. Sitting Bull, the wolfers, Al Capone amid the giant lizards, the secret cattle corrals.

I kept my head down and my hands in my pockets out of the wind. Pa looked at me with his flat eyes and he didn't have to say it for me to hear it and know it. I raised you. I couldn't afford you, but I raised you. So get ready, boy. He swung the axe stiff-armed and stiff-legged. No give in those bones. Bent only where he had to. I darted forward to catch one half of the cloven wood before it hit the ground and set it on the block for Pa to quarter. There should be some rhythm to it by now, but there wasn't. If blood moved like with like, our blood was not like enough. My shoulders jerked like the wings of a startled hen each time the axe fell. Wood flew into the mud and my fingers were stiff and cold scrambling for it. I threw the quartered pieces in the creaky wheelbarrow and pushed the wheelbarrow twenty feet to the covered porch where I filled the wood box beside the front door of the house. That house hardly more than a shack. Rough shiplap walls, no flowers to glorify the edges. Two planes meeting, simple and delineated. House and mud-cracked yard.

Stickman grew larger, developed a human aspect, turned in at our lane, making an effort to cover the limp. Yellow clouds banked behind him as though he brought them with him. A sharp gust came up and buffeted the man. I thought he must be an old cripple, but as he drew closer I could see that he was young. I remember thinking it peculiar that he carried nothing with him. He should have had a few belongings. Every drifter had some bit of food and a knife, a pot, matches. Where was his rucksack with a change of socks, a scrap of soap and dull razor? Where was his filthy blanket, his tattered dime-store novel?

Pa glanced up and stared at the stranger, keeping his expression flat, unmoved. The man was nearly in our yard. Pa said to me, Get the gun. Don't let him see it.

We had been to town the week before, Pa and I, in the wagon. I wasn't often allowed to go, and didn't want to go either, but the rains had been good that spring and Pa needed me to push if the wagon got stuck. We were not far along when a girl ran out in front of us. Spooked our horse. That girl was crying, her dress torn open in front and muddy about the skirt. Her legs muddy, too, and scratched up.

Can you take me to town? she said, sniffling and wiping at her nose and trying to hold her dress closed.

What happened to you? said Pa.

I just want to go home, she said, and she made an attempt to compose herself like nothing at all had happened.

You live in Wolf Willow?

Yes, I do, sir.

Help her in the wagon, he told me. And find her something to cover up with. Can't you see she's cold?

I got the girl in the wagon and found some sacks to wrap her with. She sat between us, shivering and trying to be unobtrusive in her crying.

Pa said, We better take you to the law.

I'll be alright if I can just get home, said the girl.

She wiped her nose and dried her eyes on the sacking and was silent the rest of the way. When we got into Wolf Willow she told us calmly where she lived and Pa took her in, and I could see her mother at the door grab the girl tight in her arms. That's home, I thought.

When Pa came back out, his face was rigid.

What do you think happened? I asked him.

Hobos got her, he said.

I saw the stranger full in our yard now, arms poking out of ratty sleeves, and I stood on the porch and leaned against the house with some pretence of surly toughness as I fingered the gun behind my back. His eyes were haggard like a man who hadn't slept in a long while. His pants were cinched tight at the waist and caked with earth as if he'd spent time on his knees. A bloody hole in one boot. The gun I held in case of mischief was only a gopher gun. I decided to aim at the other boot if it became necessary, and I hoped I wouldn't disgrace myself by missing.

The man said no word until Pa acknowledged him. You going to stand there all day?

If the wind ever stopped blowing I'd fall over.

That's an old saw. What's your business?

I saw a piece of fence broke down on that east corner. Thought I might fix it for you.

Pa looked at the stranger and I could see him take in the uncut greasy hair, ill-fitting clothes, the wounded foot. You got a bum foot?

Only a scratch. Ain't nothing at all.

Ain't ain't in the dictionary.

The man stood quiet and unsure at Pa's rudeness. Despite his ragged state he was nice enough to look upon, with a long curved nose that pointed delicately at the end, his mouth grave and serious, like a storybook knight facing his dragon with the experience of sad and brutal battles already fought and lost. His arms hung loose at his sides, hands open, a subtle implore.

Pa worked his advantage and, staring the man straight in the eye, came bluntly to the point. I don't care where you hail from, and I don't care where you're headed. But I will know this. Are you the fellow that interfered with a young girl down the road?

The stranger looked surprised and there was nothing guarded in his demeanour as he answered. I don't know what you're talking about. I wouldn't interfere with no girl.

You don't know anything about that?

Believe me when I tell you, I'm not the sort to interfere with girls.

Pa watched the man intently, and the man's eyes did not waver. I saw the knot of muscle along Pa's jaw line dissolve and I relaxed my hold on the gun. The stranger would not have to be shot after all.

Well, I can't pay you nothing, said Pa, and he spat on the ground by way of dismissal.

I've fenced before. I'll do the job right.

Are you deaf? I said I can't pay you.

I'm just looking for a place until the weather warms.

You'll work for free?

Just a room.

You don't eat?

Not much.

I got no room for hobos, said Pa, with that note of termination I knew never to argue with.

The stranger, though, was unschooled in Pa's vagaries, and he persisted. Maybe your barn?

To my surprise, Pa regarded the man with new interest. Maybe the barn.

The stranger studied the barn and said again, Just till the weather warms.

Pa hesitated, and the stranger looked over at me for the first time with his dark eyes, and on his gaze I was impaled. The blood drained from my veins. It happened so fast, it terrified me. I felt my legs want to buckle, but then he smiled in a private way and his smile transfused me with a quickening current, an essential life force so potent that it rendered all my past anaemic. Some dormant creature that had slumbered mythic and secret amid the dim confusions of my boyish heart awakened and possessed me with a new and different nature. It had the focus of a prey animal and the ardour of a lover. Through the windows of his eyes I saw his soul respond in kind and, in that moment, I put away childish things. Ignorant though I was, I understood the stranger could not leave.

He looked back at Pa, who hesitated still, and without warning he rolled his eyes skyward and swooned and fell on his knees. Then he toppled sideways and lay still on the ground. I ran to him, but Pa held me back, said he might have some sort of disease. We watched the stranger reclined on the dirt. Get water, said

Pa, and I ran to the pump and got a bucket of well water. Pa said, throw it on his head and see what he does. I poured water over that pitiful, weary face and the stranger began to sputter and moan and his eyes fluttered open.

Are you sick? demanded Pa.

No, it's just… I haven't eaten… The hobo staggered to his feet. I'll be on my way, he said.

I was drowning in his hunger. I was swallowed by it, consumed by it. I was in agony. Pa, we got leftover porridge. Couldn't he have that? And eggs, I think there's enough.

The stranger waited for Pa's invitation, but only as long as dignity would allow. Then he turned and limped off toward the road.

Pa, I said, and gave him my most pleading, blaming look. I saw the doubt cross his face and I kept my pleading eyes on his doubt until I had it pegged, and Pa turned his face toward the man and hollered, You'll work for it!

I will, said the stranger, and his expression about the mouth was glad, but a little smug, too, like he knew all along. I forgave him that look because I had more than he did of material wealth and I was willing to share it with him. And I had peace with my Maker and something about him told me he was a stranger even to his Maker, and didn't have any peace.

Pa turned to me without shaking the man's offered hand. Put him in the loft, Peter. Show him the tools.

But, Pa, I said, looking to those yellow clouds that billowed thick over the fields. It's going to storm for sure.

This man wants to fix my fence. Show him what tools we got and let him do it.

But, Pa—

Do like I tell you.

Thirteen years in my father's house. I'd seen drought and storm. And worse drought. I'd seen rainstorms and snowstorms and dust storms. I'd seen a storm of locusts so thick they darkened the sun, devoured the crop as they moved across the sky, like with like, a demon horde. I'd seen many things and imagined many more, but I never saw my Pa change his mind twice in a row. So I went in the house and put the gun back on its rack above the door. Then I walked the stranger into the barn, watching the way he tried not to favour that tender foot, the way his back carried him erect despite the pain. A friendly moo and a chorus of clucks and squawks greeted us in the warm dimness. The pungent, acrid odour of hay and manure enveloped us. Jersey milk cow in a stall at the back, stall beside it empty. Chicken stoop along the right wall, some white hens and Banti hens, a rooster. Hay stacked to the left. Open rafters, ladder to a loft. Drafty but warmer than outside.

I rummaged in my mind for something reasonable to say. Where you from, if you don't mind my asking?

Hell.

You're from hell?

Just a devil from hell.

Where you headed now?

Straight back to hell, I expect.

What's hell like? I asked, excited by his way of talking, which told me nothing definite but felt so intimate. I sensed the code in his words, that hell was a real location he had visited, mysterious and difficult.

Hell's a watery place, kid. Where it rains and snows and you can't get warm. I like heat on my back. That would be heaven.

I was deeply honoured. This man, a grownup, was willing to converse with me, joke with me, make an effort to be entertaining. It irked me, though, when he called me kid. I wanted to be his equal, to be worthy of that look he gave me in the yard, of his attention, his teasing banter now that we were alone together.

The temperature had dropped and the wind made a clatter of the frozen grasses around the barn. Yellow clouds boiled up beyond the frame of the wide door. Hens clucked against the draft and pecked around our feet. They were leery of strangers, but not this one. They treated him like a familiar.

I glanced at the stranger's bloody boot. Looks like you had some bad luck.

The stranger drew back his suspect boot as if to pull it from my attention. You make your own luck, he said. In fact, the harder I work, the luckier I get. So why don't you show me those tools? I got something to prove to your old man.

Then, as if to override his abrupt tone, he reached out his finger and tapped me lightly on the chest.

The touch of his finger. So incidental, so casual. To my inflamed senses it was confirmation that he longed in the same way I longed, for touch to connect us further than gaze, further than speech.

I'll help you, I said to him.

No, you're not, he protested, as if afraid that he had gone too far and would cancel it out, that touch, retract the small advance, sidestep what was between us. Our bond. Our simpatico. Our friendship. I didn't know what to call it.

His seesaw confused me. It was a poor attempt to gain back the upper hand that he had already forfeited with one light touch of a finger on my breastbone. But then I realized that he was in the vulnerable position. He had come into my yard. It was my Pa that owned this place. The stranger was only a hired man here who had no rights to the big house, such as it was. I had held a loaded gun behind my back, ready to shoot him in the foot if he took a misstep. I could push my own tiny advantage, shift the balance of power in my direction.

Yes, I will, said I, trying to stand as he did, erect and confident.

The stranger cupped an ear. I hear your mama calling you in for your cocoa.

My mama's dead, I informed him.

We locked eyes and the stranger backed down, though he was older than me, taller than me, more assured even in the ragged coat that was too small, maybe a cast-off or theft from someone's clothesline. A desperate act to keep the rain and snow off his back.

You got a name? I asked him.

Name's Jackie, kid. Jackie O'Dell.

My name's not kid. It's Peter.

I know it, he said. Kid.

And then he smiled and what could I do but let him call me what he wanted? Any power I laid claim to became as dust when he looked at me in that kindred way. I coveted his sickle nose, his grave mouth, the fine creases in his cheeks, lines of experience, of joys and sorrows untold. The small mole under his left eye. Eyes like rain-soaked clay. Or even darker, like the rich chocolate I had once at Christmas. I would be his kid. I would turn it into something interesting. Like the Sundance Kid who worked the Bar U in Alberta for a time. Or Billy the Kid, another legend. Peter the Kid. Why not? I would choose it. Childe Roland to the dark tower came.

I banged open the door to the tool room under the loft, trying to be obnoxious, trying to regain some equilibrium. I succeeded only in startling the cow and the hens. Jackie, unruffled, gathered what implements he needed: hammer, nails, crowbar, hatchet. Then he limped toward the barn door. Tripped over a hen in the dim light, got his legs tangled up trying not to crush it with his big feet. Went down with a clatter of tools and nails on the wood floor. The cow lowed and the hens collected their wits, came over to peck at the straw on his coat.

I stood a moment, then walked over and put my hand out to Jackie, helped him to his feet. We rounded up the scattered implements, found every nail by feeling around in the cracks of the boards with our fingers. I followed him outside without a word, carrying my share of the tools.

We went along the road past hummocky swamp grass, stands of dried bulrushes like cornstalks, the swollen sloughs. Pushing all the time against a wind that still had winter teeth. Past the small coulee with thorny old bushes, don't know the name. Grey spikes an inch long and every branch ended in such a spine. It was starting to grow its little yellow bead clusters. The smaller willows forming buds. There were last year's flowers still on their plants, dried and withered. Little ones like sunflowers in miniature. Yellow wolf willow flowers. It looked to be a good year. Pa said it had to happen eventually. We'd suffered seven years of drought. It seemed to me that I was seeing everything anew, noticing every detail through Jackie's eyes, and though we walked in silence my mind chattered all the while as his tour guide. See there? Deer prints in the clay, their soft brown pebbles in clusters everywhere. Some patches of clay-dyed ochre, some dyed rust. Patches of whitemud clay. Twisted little trees only a foot tall with sage-smelling leaves. The tiny curled lichens of lime green, bright orange velvety rings on the rocks. Carpet of low juniper. Cactus patches. So many shades of grasses, reddish gold, wheat gold, pale dull gold. It looked like the hide of an animal, the hide moving in the wind like when an animal shudders to get rid of an itch. Wind all the time shoving us along. A length of rusty old barbed wire twisted in the ditch. Magpies, did they ever leave? The little sparrows didn't. Sparrows stayed all winter The wind wouldn't let them sing. The wind snatched the song right out of their throats. Such was my world. I wanted to share it all with him. In my mind I told him how I once saw a sharp-shinned hawk eat a sparrow in neat shreds. I went to that spot later and saw a pile of feathers, nothing else. I looked for claws, bones, beak. Nothing but the feathers. Isn't that something?

Boiling clouds, avalanche of clouds, clouds like the surface of a warped piece of tin. We got out to the east corner where the fence was leaning. I took the role of tool holder and helper. He was bigger, stronger, and he seemed to know what he was doing, and I let him boss me and it worked out okay.

The storm hit just as we were finishing with the fence. Snow began lightly, then heavy and thick. It blew straight across the field, a whiteout. Should have been alright but the wind came up harder and the temperature dropped fast. Neither of us had hats and the wind near froze my brains. Our hands fumbled with cold. I could see white in Jackie's cheeks and his nose.

Let's call it a day, said Jackie.

You're getting frostbit, I told him. Come to the house and warm up.

Which way?

I looked and could see nothing but whiteness all around. We'll cut across the field, I said. We stood and shook snow off our clothes, out of our hair. Put our hands over our ears for a minute, could feel neither hands nor ears. Jackie nodded to me, turned and disappeared into the whiteness.

After some time we hit the fence and I couldn't figure it out. We must have got turned around. We'll hang onto the fence, I told him. I put my right hand on the fence and hurried after Jackie, stumbling through loose drifts with a nauseating sensation that I was walking upside down, feet thrashing through the sky. Disorientation. Liquid fear in my stomach. My heart drummed in my head, brought back some circulation. I broke into a run. My hand began to burn as it skimmed along the fence wire.

Ice pellets and sleet blasted from all sides as the wind swirled up snow to throw under our coats, up sleeves, down necks. There was not a building nor hill nor solitary tree for shelter. We stopped to rest, huddled low to the ground covering our heads with bare hands. Air, ground, and sky were a shapeless cloud enclosing us inside, our bodies layered in a sheet of snow. This was the weather farmers lost their way in, struck off in the opposite direction of home or went the right way and missed it by feet, never knew. Bodies found weeks later in a thaw. We got up and ran again.

And we went along like that, our hands near frozen to the wire until we came to a corner and I knew by the left turn that we were going the right way. I bumped into Jackie waiting at the corner of the fence, which veered away at a right angle, west toward the hills. This was as close as the fence would bring us to the house.

Jackie yelled above the shrieking wind, I'm about froze.

You better hold onto my coat, I told Jackie. He didn't argue. His lips were bloodless, his brows fringed with frost, his hair a brittle cap of ice. I guessed I must look about the same. I felt his hand grip the side of my coat. If we struck off in the same direction we had been travelling, we would walk right between house and barn and on into the next field, and the next, toward the American border. I had to lead at a forty-five degree angle southeast. We started out, my hand in front, groping my way through an erased world. I could feel the bunched coat at my side where Jackie had a grip. Even in my fear I was aware.

It was taking too long, we should have reached the porch by now. I pulled him in the direction I knew the house must be, but we went quite a while and I thought about all that prairie in between our house and the next, and nothing to stop us if we kept walking past that house, too. I inched forward, Jackie close behind. My foot struck something hard and I looked down at the chopping block. I grabbed Jackie and pulled him forward.

We stumbled onto the porch, tried to get in the door. Pa got his stout body between us, shoved me into the house and slammed the door, leaving Jackie on the other side.

I pleaded for him.

Vagrant, was all Pa would say as he hung the gas lamp on its hook above the table. His toothless jaw worked as I fumbled to remove my coat and boots by the wood stove.

Then he began to holler and scold. Where's your God-given sense to stay out of a blizzard, you blockhead little fuck!

I did not see it coming, knew it only as a whistle like a boiling kettle and a thin sting across my neck. I winced, felt the blood spring up, and steeled myself for another. It did not occur to me to take that old cracked belt, throw it down the outhouse pit, bury it somewhere. This was my life, unchangeable as the flat land, the bitter cold and burning heat. But already Pa was hitching the belt up under his slack belly.

While he snored all night behind the curtain, I fussed about Jackie out in the blizzard, didn't think he could survive. Felt responsible. I crept through the snow to the barn at first light before Pa was up, found Jackie lying with the cow in her stall, asleep. Nearly collapsed with relief. I went back to the house and got a quilt, some whisky and rags for Jackie's wounded foot, a heel of bread. When I returned to the barn, Jackie was in the loft with his boot off. Loft door open to the paling sky.

I dropped the quilt in a heap on the hay. Guess you could use this. Blood crept up my face as I saw the clean pinkness of Jackie's bare foot. I noted the bloody gash under the ankle and opened the whisky bottle like I knew what I was doing, spilled it on a rag, handed the rag to Jackie. How'd it happen?

Jackie accepted the rag with a nod. Took a wrong step, I guess. He wiped at the blood, drew in his breath with a hiss.

I could see it was swollen and tender. I sat down on the quilt, bottle tucked in my crotch, and made binoculars out of my hands. Watched the sun sweep over the shoulder of the hills, lighting them with purple and gold fire.

Cypress Hills is full of outlaws, I said.

Jackie started to laugh and then he said with a raw note in his voice, I tell you, kid, anybody living in them hills is just like you and me, except they can't go home, one reason or other.

You been there?

Few times. One of the sweetest spots I know is this side of the hills. Tucked into the bottom there's a stand of cottonwoods. Leaves appear silver in sunlight.

I screwed the cap back on the whisky and unfolded my legs, preparing to stand. I could feel Jackie's eyes on me.

Haven't you been to school?

Sure I have. Lots of times. I sat back, unscrewed the whisky again, took a sip and coughed it down. I'd never had whisky in the morning. My body warmed with the tingle. Yourself? I passed the bottle to Jackie, tossed him the bread.

Self-taught. Every place I go has got a couple books lying about. Jackie chewed the bread, washed it down with whisky.

Not here. My ma used to read to me, though.

Jackie's eyes roamed my face for a moment, dropped to the wound in his foot. Little young for drinking, ain't ya, kid?

Going on fourteen. Old enough. I pulled strands of hay, rolled them into chafe between my finger and thumb. Ma died two years ago, just so you know.

I'm sure sorry. Jackie passed me back the bottle, tied the alcohol-soaked rag around his ankle and pulled on his boot.

You got a home, Jackie?

He stood and aligned four hay bales in two rows in front of the loft door. Placed a fifth bale across one end, making a horse-shoe with the open end facing the view of the hills. Opened a sixth bale and spread the loose hay inside the horseshoe, then pulled the quilt out from under me and laid it on top of the sweet-smelling mound. Now I do. He winked at me, his mouth tugged up in that grin I liked, then he stretched and yawned, palmed his hair a few times and smoothed it to one side. Fine morning, he said, closing the loft door and fastening it shut. He walked over to me and messed the back of my hair like he was playing with a pup. Come on. Let's find those tools we left out there. Make your Pa happy.

Jackie mended the fence, fixed a wagon axle, repaired the barn roof. When the outside was in order, he showed his worth indoors, boiling kettles of water for the big tub and helping me agitate blankets, twist the water out, hang them to drip on the porch railing. Taught me how to roast grain for coffee when the last of the real deal was used up. He took over the bread baking from Pa, pounding out beautiful loaves on the unfinished pine table in the middle of the room. Wasn't much more than that table, four rickety chairs, shelving for pots and dishes, and a stove in that room. And my bed at the far end by the stove, with some hooks above for extra clothes. Pa slept in a small bedroom off the main room with a quilt hanging over the doorway. Anything in the house that could be sold was already sold. But we had enough.

As Jackie spent more time working in the house, waiting for spring planting to begin, he fell naturally into taking his meals indoors. After a hard day, the three of us would combine our efforts to prepare a supper – usually winter turnip, a few shrivelled spuds, some canned deer meat or salted pork, thick slabs of Jackie's bread with chokecherry jam – and Pa would light the gas lamp over the table. Pa was standoffish, but when we all sat down together and ate, talking over chores for the next day, the bare, aged wood walls, the nickel-plating on the cast-iron stove, the sounds and smells of eating gave the room a homely warmth.

One day Pa gave us a pot of grease and some rags, told us to oil the tack down. He would take it to town to trade for seed. The weather was warm for May. We shed our coats in the barn, rolled up our shirtsleeves. Sat down on the floorboards in the tool room among the hoes and rakes, shovels and sacks, saws, hatchets, hammers, nails and shingles. We spread out the tack and greased up the rags, rubbed down the halter and bridle first. Worked together on the saddle. Air pleasantly thick with the smells of the barn, the greased leather. We hadn't been alone since the morning after the storm. I felt shy and didn't know what to say.

Got a girl in town? Jackie asked, casual-like.

Not too many girls I'd be that keen on. Had one once, next farm over. Farm went belly up, though, and they moved to Swift Current.

We worked our way up each a saddle fender toward the skirt, rubbing the carved leather to a dull glow, polishing the tooled curly cues of oak leaves and bursting dogwood blooms. Paid careful attention to the stitching. It was relaxing work. We stretched our legs and reclined on our sides, each with an arm bent up and a hand cupped to support our heads, the other hand rubbing the grease in a circular motion along the skirt and cantle.

Got any other friends? asked Jackie. He dipped his rag in the grease pot, worked his way around the back of the skirt.

There's a bunch in town I used to chum with. They're not that friendly anymore. Fact is, they'd as soon break my face as look at it. I'm no coward but there's three of them, one of me.

I swiped my rag in the pot and continued rubbing around the curve of the skirt.

Jackie pushed his hair out of his eyes with an oily hand. You do something particular to bend their noses out of shape?

Guess they don't like the way I look is all.

It was true. You only had to look a little less ugly than your pals and one day a switch flipped and they were pounding your face in the dirt. *Eat this, faggot, fairy, nancy boy.* As if mashing your looks would fix something inside them. My hand was moving close to Jackie's along the back of the cantle. A tremor went through my muscles and I kept my eyes down, watched the slow rub of Jackie's hand near my own. The breath hitched in my throat. Our fingers touched, two live wires coming together. A judder of lightning passed through my body. Jackie jerked back, moved his hand around to the gullet and up the horn. He cleared his throat, sat up, threw his rag on the saddle seat. Watched me continue to rub the leather.

You got to have some strategy for dealing with it is all, said Jackie.

Sure, don't go to town. Best idea I come up with so far.

Know any boxing? Wrestling? I got a few wrestling moves might help in a pinch.

Yeah? Like what?

We stood and shook out the kinks, rubbed our hands down the thighs of our jeans.

Shirts off, case they get ripped.

My heart galloped as he removed his shirt and threw it down. I thought sure he could see the vibrations in my chest, my trembling limbs. I unbuttoned my shirt and slid it off, folded it, laid it in a corner of the tool room, ashamed of my own small torso, thin arms. Trying not to stare at Jackie, so finely muscled even with his ribs showing. His stomach was hard and lean and rippled. I was thinking all the while, This is not love. This is not love. I would not call it love. But what is love? What does love feel like? This feels more like thrill, like fear, like danger. We are here together half-naked, man and boy. But Jackie was my friend. We had fun together, we helped each other. He would never do anything to hurt me.

Jackie looked about for an open spot, stepped out into the barn area, surveyed the straw caked with chicken shit. Loft's bigger; hay's cleaner, he said.

We climbed the ladder.

With the loft door closed, there were only bars of light slanting through the grey boards. Hay bales were stacked to the roof on the right, Jackie's bed was in the middle, and to the left was open floor strewn with hay. I went over to the wall on the left, studied my finger in a chink of light. A fresh breeze blew through the cracks, stirred the chafe. I could feel Jackie's eyes on me.

Something the matter?

Sliver. Fingernails is too short to grab it.

My nails is stubby, too, said Jackie. Show you what I do, though.

He stood shivering in front of me, his nipples so soft and pink they made my insides twist with pity. I wanted to cover them with my hands to warm them. He took my finger and felt with the pad of his thumb to find the sliver. The chickens clucked below, the cow shifted her weight with a creak. Jackie found the woody point protruding from the skin on the underside of the finger, put it to his mouth and found it again with his tongue. His mouth felt hot on my finger and the feel of it went right through me. He bit gently till he got the end of the sliver in his teeth, pulled the sliver out.

Then he let go of my finger and put his hands against the wall on either side of me, and when he looked into my eyes I could tell he was seeing all that was inside me, all the things I didn't want anyone to know. He stood close and slid his hands onto my hips and backed me against the wall, breathing hard. I smelled saddle oil and leather. He pressed his groin into mine and I didn't know what to do. This was more than I wanted, more than I was ready for. I strained and contorted, got my hands in between, pushed Jackie away.

Thought you was a friend! I spat the words at Jackie.

It was in rain that I first knew I was in love with Jackie O'Dell. After the incident in the loft, I feigned gut ache. While Pa went to town with the tack, I stayed in the house, checked the windows before going outside to pump water or bring in an armful of wood. Jackie did not appear until Pa came home with the seed. Then I watched through a windowpane as Jackie helped Pa unload the sacks and carry them in the barn, shirt on and buttoned to the neck. I noted with satisfaction that Jackie didn't limp now. The foot had healed without infection, due in small part to my ministrations.

When Pa and Jackie entered the house to start dinner, I stayed in my cot near the stove. I kept my eyes lightly closed, watched

Jackie through the slits as he chopped turnip and potato. Jackie put the pot on the stove with a bang, glanced at me. I would not flinch. Would not get up to eat with them. Moaned I'd puke if I tried. Best not waste food. The longer I avoided Jackie, the harder it was to face him again. I didn't understand why it was *my* stomach writhing with shame when it should be Jackie's. I, the innocent one, should be going about my everyday business while the guilty one suffered. But somehow it had flipped around and I stayed in bed for two days with the blankets over my head, heart palpitating whenever I heard the door open. Pa left water beside the bed, and a chamber pot. Went out into the fields with Jackie to plant the wheat. Jackie would come in at midday, make three chokecherry jam sandwiches with hardly a sound, put one by my bed, and take the other two with him back to the fields.

On the third day, I got up and dressed, ate breakfast at the table, would not look at Jackie. Pa shifted his gaze from one to the other, kept up a rattle of conversation. He knew there was something sour between us. And I knew he wouldn't have it because hard feelings would interfere with the work.

Here's what we do, he announced. Today we finish planting. Tonight we celebrate with a glass or two, play cards. Jackie and I shrugged, summoned smiles for the old man, dropped them when his back was turned.

Planting went quickly as everyone kept their hands busy and their tongues silent. I watched Jackie out of the corner of my eye, resented the awkwardness of being around him. Resolved to confront him, tell Jackie where I stood on the matter so we could be friends again. I saw that Jackie might have been confused about what we were doing in the loft with no shirts on, my letting Jackie take the sliver out with his teeth.

The days had been fair and hot. The dry dirt of the fields got down my neck, under my shirt, crept up my pant legs and coated my skin. Made me itchy and uncomfortable. Pa pointed to dark clouds building on the western edge of the horizon. I knew it, he chuckled. Rheumatism smarting in all my joints. Bodes well for the seed.

We walked back to the yard, put tools away. As Pa left the barn, I cornered Jackie. You were out of order and owe me an apology.

Jackie leaned against the doorway of the tool room, rubbed his chin, tried to keep the corners of his mouth from creeping up. Alright, I apologize. Now will you grow up, God damn it? What I done's not that bad. Hell, I don't see you marching up to those that beat you, demanding an apology.

What you done was unnatural.

Let me tell you about unnatural. I slept in more barns than you can count on your fingers and toes, kid. I seen unnatural.

Like what?

Like fornication with chickens is what. I seen boys do it with a knothole in a board when they can't find nothing else. Tell me what *I* done was unnatural. At least you're a human being.

Chickens! I stared at the chickens on the stoop, shook my head in wonderment. They're butt ugly!

We laughed, not at the joke but for how good it made us feel after all the tension and the heat, the dirt and the day's labour.

That evening in the house, supper eaten and the dishes cleared, Pa poured whisky while I shuffled cards. Cut, I said to Pa, who had his eye down to the level of the shot glasses, making adjustments.

Jackie cut, I'm busy.

Jackie and I bumped hands, spilled the cards. I gathered them up and set them on the table. Jackie cut.

Acey, deucy, one-eyed jacks, I called, and dealt five cards each. Jackie won that hand, straight flush. He stretched his feet out under the table, bumped mine, pulled back. We clinked glasses and swallowed. Pa poured again. He became quite sociable when he drank, and I wished he drank all the time. It could be a fun life.

Five card stud, called Jackie, and took the cards from me, our fingers getting hung up, cards fluttering to the table. Jackie collected the cards and dealt. Won again, pair of kings. Pa poured.

Jackie and I took turns dealing, calling the games. We second-guessed every movement, changed direction at the last minute, bumped and knocked. Hands and legs found every way in which to collide. Chairs scraped, cards fluttered, glasses clinked.

Pa grew boisterous, clapped my shoulder over the table when he heard the thunder. Rain coming! He pushed his chair back and stood, hitting his head on the gas lamp. It swung crazily and he tried to steady it with a wavering hand. Like to propose a toast to a fair crop, God willing, amen.

Jackie and I stood and clinked glasses with Pa, tossed back whisky. The first fat drops of rain hit the window, dirty streaks on the pane. Jackie put his glass on the table, said he'd make his exit. The door snapped shut behind him.

Pa tottered off through the curtain. I gathered the cards and put them away on top of the shelf, wiped the glasses and put them on the shelf, too. Wiped the table and tucked in the chairs. Turned the lamp down low. Laid on my bed listening to the rain drum on the shingles, feeling dreamy with liquor, thinking over the day, the distance I'd travelled since morning. Satisfied with how I'd handled things. Wasn't even speaking to Jackie, now everything alright. I was glad, too. Glad having Jackie around, someone to talk to. Maybe Jackie was lying up in the loft thinking about me right now, how good it was to be back to normal. I figured I'd just go out and see if Jackie wanted to talk some more, have another drink, tell those outlandish stories about what he'd seen. Wondered if Jackie was still up, wondered if I'd be disturbing him.

I rose from my bed and went to the window. It was washed clean but was still opaque with rain. I put my head out the door, then stepped onto the porch. Rain pelted the hard-packed clay in the yard. The air was warm, smelled of iron and wood chips. Fresh and watery. It was raining too hard and I didn't want to get my clothes soaked. I'd go back inside, see Jackie in the morning. I turned toward the door, but a whiteness near the barn caught my eye. I strained to see through the rain. There was Jackie under the downspout, stripped naked, rubbing his arms and chest, washing himself.

I stepped out from under the porch, put my face up to the splash. Let it run into my eyes, my mouth, down my neck. Trembling in my stomach. Tongue dry as the underside of a wolf willow leaf. Heat all over my body, like the rain was burning me. I walked across the yard to where Jackie was standing, let myself look. Noted the lanky legs, pointed hips, penis blind as a turnip. I reached out and turned Jackie around to face away from me. Put my hands on the thin, long back, moved them slow and solemn over his skin. Jackie turned again to face me. Go on in the house now, he said. Water dripping off his nose, his hair, his lashes.

I tilted my face up to Jackie. Just shut up about it, I said.

Look, I got something to tell you, kid. That bad foot I limped in here with? I had a situation at a farm way other side of Wolf Willow. Took a liking to the farmer's boy of fifteen. He was a lonely kid like you and I was trying to make him feel better, I guess. Farmer caught us at it, chased me off his property with a pistol, fired a shot on the ground to hurry me along. Hit my foot by accident or design. I heard later he whipped that boy to within half an inch of his life. Sent him to a sort of sanitarium over in Saskatoon. I was wrong to pressure you in the barn. I thought you wanted me to, I thought you were waiting for me. It's the boys that need comfort. I've seen it before, all these lonely boys who can't find any comfort anywhere. But we won't do anything you don't want to do.

Shut the hell up, I said, because I didn't know what I wanted us to do and I was ashamed of this. I didn't want him to suspect my innocence, my fear, my wonder. I, that creature he had woke and called to him, craved only to be near him. He had done this before, called another boy to him, did things with him that I could only imagine, and it shocked me. Now he was manoeuvring me, making me the one to decide so he could remain blameless. But I forgave him because I understood that he was a stranger to the whole wide world and would never find a home. I forgave him as I forgave myself because I was a stranger, too. Homeless like him, shut out by my very own nature. I wanted a home. I wanted it so badly I was willing to risk being beaten for it, or shot for it, or sent to a sanatorium for it. I wanted love, or what felt like love or the hope of love. It didn't really matter what it was, as long as it felt like love when he touched me. As long as it felt like home. I wanted him to kiss me in the way my mother had kissed me after I was fished out of the well half drowned when I was little. Passionately, like she cared if I lived or died. I was just a naive kid and Jackie was a grown man of uncertain scruples. But I will have you know this. You, who would judge me and Jackie O'Dell. What I did, I chose to do. I closed my eyes and opened my mouth, let the stranger in.

KIMCHI

At the kitchen counter, she is looking a little more desperate after the first bite. About the cabbage, her mother would say: *Be generous with the salt.* But there was nothing to be done about a chile's shortcomings. This time, she dips the stalky end of the nappa leaf into the pounded flakes and bites into it. No, it is not the cabbage – it is definitely the chile. She hurls the leaf into the sink. That *fool*!

Earlier in the day, the boy – Jeem or Jahn or whatever his silly anglicized name was – had bullied her into buying last year's crop of dried Korean chile peppers. He assured her they were as good as the current year's, which had failed to arrive as promised. Ever since the deacon passed away the previous winter without too much fuss or ceremony, his grocery store, now in the hands of his half-witted son, was in shambles. It didn't take long before some of the deacon's most devoted parishioners took their money across the street. The competitor, a Presbyterian, ran an adequate and – it was grudgingly admitted – honest business.

"Korean chiles never go bad," the boy said, shrugging his shoulders and holding his hands up like a criminal. "But if you want to wait, the new shipment should arrive in another week or so…*Halmonee.*" The grovelling "grandmother" designation did little to endear him to her. She pursed her lips, shoved the chiles in with the other purchases, and hastily left the store without so much as saying goodbye. Besides, she could not wait "another week or so." Her daughter Sera was due to arrive the following day with her Mexican fiancé, Miguel, to observe *Gije* with her – and the kimchi needed to be finished, like it had been on time every year for the past nineteen years. The deacon made sure the arrival of the new crop of chiles from Korea always coincided with the commemoration of her dead mother, and so, without them, she was left feeling unhinged.

Outside, the drop in air pressure ahead of the coming storm and the gusty October breeze rushed to her head. She put the grocery bag down on the sidewalk and propped herself up against the wall. In the store's darkening window, she was not surprised to see the ghostly pallor of her skin and the dark bags under her eyes. She had always been the plain-looking one compared to her five older sisters, but knew her present appearance had something to do with the recent diagnosis of arrhythmia and all those damn pills. Her condition had taken a turn for the worse when Sera left Toronto in the summer to join Miguel in Ottawa, where he was a chef at some new "fusion" restaurant. The heart attack happened in her suite three years before, within weeks of burying her husband, and Mrs. Cho, her neighbour, will never let her forget that if she hadn't come barging in at just that moment, poor Sera would have been left an orphan.

She watched her face in the window slowly metamorphose into that of her mother's during those final days – serene in the ambient light of the bedside lamp. She blinked two or three times and tried to focus, but her mother gazed back at her with moist searching eyes.

"*Halmonee*, are you okay?" It was the boy again, holding out a tissue in his grimy hand. She waved it away, picked up her bag, and shuffled unsteadily toward the subway.

The day she saw Sera off at Union Station, she held on to the bannister in the stairwell until the flutters passed.

"I told you to stay home," Sera said. "Doctor Kim wants you to slow down."

"What does a doctor know?"

On the platform, after the final boarding call, her daughter held her for too long and sobbed on her shoulder. "Sera-yah, enough," she said. "People are watching." She shoved the *doshi-rak* into her arms, wrapped in the same embroidered silk her mother had passed down to her on her wedding day. It was filled with Sera's favourite dishes: pan-fried tofu, spicy dried squid, seaweed rice rolls with canned tuna, and a side of kimchi.

"*Ohm-ma...*" Sera blubbered.

"Go, before you cry again. You're too much like your father."

"If you need me," she said, "I'm just one train ride away."

"Yes, yes, if I need you."

Now, pacing back and forth in her kitchen, she curses the boy again under her breath. What is missing from the chiles is that smarting sweet linger that never failed to transport her back to the family farm in Andong. There, under a poplar grove aquiver with leaf shadows and the nippy breath of the late autumn breeze, she and her sisters would gather around their mother to make kimchi together. There was the usual gossip, blushing banter that only her married sisters could decode, and, of course, their mother's exacting instructions. When the kimchi was finally put away into clay jars, and darkness had set in, they moved to the inner courtyard of the *hanok* and told ghost stories. Against the crackling light of the hearth, her sisters' shadows mimed the movements of female *gwishins* – legless spirits with scraggly black hair and tattered smocks – that wandered the countryside to complete unfinished business before entering the underworld. By the end of it, she found herself clinging to her mother's neck, so spooked that she vowed never to speak to her sisters again.

She dumps the rest of the infuriating chiles into the stone mortar and pounds the pestle harder than she should. When her heart starts to race, she stops. "*Ohm-ma,*" she mutters, "what now?" She slides open the kitchen door and steps onto the balcony to consider her options. She pulls the dead leaves off the chrysanthemums shivering on the railing. The wind has picked up and rain is falling in sheets over St. Joseph Church. The cemetery, where a prepaid plot awaits her between her parents and her husband, slopes like a giant camel hump behind it. She picks up the stainless steel bowl with the remaining quartered nappa cabbages and returns to the kitchen. Over the sink, she gently wrings the salt water from each leaf and rubs sea salt on them. *You feel that? It's much thicker here near the root. It needs more salt.* Her mother's voice hovers in the air behind her and by force of habit, without turning around, she responds: "*Neh, Ohm-ma!*"

Her mother's love of salt came second only to her love of chile, and its over-consumption was attributed by her doctor as the cause of the stroke and kidney failure in that final year. And while her sisters agreed with him, she knew better. It wasn't the salt that killed her mother, but the death of Yong-su, her firstborn, who, at the age of six months and fourteen days, died in her mother's arms. He was left in her parents' care soon after he was born so she and her husband could continue working in the city. It was a simple abdominal infection gone horribly wrong, misdiagnosed from the beginning, and her mother never recovered from it – blaming herself for not taking him to the hospital sooner. He would be almost four years older than Sera now.

A loud knock on the door startles her. She stands as still as possible, stretching out the seconds in her head. She hopes Mrs. Cho will think she is not home and move on.

"I know you're back," she calls through the mail slot. "I saw you walking past the rec room." She dries her hands on a towel and walks to the hallway. After unlocking the door, she walks away, and says over her shoulder, "It's open." Mrs. Cho is wearing lime-green aerobic tights, a pink T-shirt with a Playboy bunny on it, and white sneakers. Wrapped around her ankles are one-pound weights. Suddenly she is self-conscious about the nightgown and bedroom slippers she has on and silently accuses her for making her feel this way. Mrs. Cho is holding a glass casserole pan wrapped in tinfoil. Recently, she has been experimenting with strange foods from around the world. She can no longer endure eating three Korean meals a day from room trays while watching Korean soap operas with the others. "Slow death by distasteful food and dishonest feelings," she calls it. So, after the Sunday afternoon Cooking Basics class, taught by a peppy student from the nearby culinary college, Mrs. Cho makes the same dish every day until the residents on her floor grow sick of it. This week it is Indian food.

"I thought Sera would like to try my butter chicken. I would also like Mikhail's opinion on it, too."

"His name is Miguel."

"Oh, right." She puts the dish down on the coffee table. "My grandchildren couldn't finish it yesterday." She knows the truth, that like so many other times in the past, Mrs. Cho's three children, in particular her divorced eldest son and his ten year-old twins, did not actually visit, but she asks anyway because she is annoyed by the intrusion: "How are the twins?" As soon as the words leave her mouth, she is ashamed of herself. She avoids eye contact and returns to the kitchen. Mrs. Cho follows behind and stands by the kitchen doorway. "Oh, they're fine. Very good kids. I don't think they like the smell of Indian food." She quickly changes the subject. "So Mr. Kwak's sister came by this morning. The crazy man thought it was his wife returning from the dead and locked himself in the mop room. Poor girl – the look on her face. They really should move him to the Rose of Sharon. I heard they recently built a special ward there for" – and here she twirls her index finger near her temple – "people like that. Everybody knows his mind is mushier than congee." They burst out laughing at this. She knows that despite the trivial lies and loose-lipped personality, the lonely widow has a good heart.

"Would you like some tea, Mrs. Cho?"

"Can't. I have ping-pong date with Park Jung-ho." She is standing at the makeshift shrine, lighting a joss stick. "Looks lovely."

"I think Mr. Park is in love with you."

"He falls in love with anyone who will play ping-pong with him."

"No, I mean it. He's told me he thinks you are pretty."

"Really?" She pauses, then with girlish coyness: "He never said that."

"He did. At Karaoke Night last week. When you sang "Soldier of My Heart." And he's right, you know. You look so pretty when you're up on stage." Mrs. Cho stands at attention, salutes with her right hand, then goose-steps toward the hallway, breathing in sync with her raised ankles. At the door, she says in a near whisper: "I will say a prayer for you and your mother tonight."

"Thank you. Come by tomorrow. I know Sera will be very happy to see you."

Back at the kitchen counter, she finishes salting the cabbages and lays them out on a large baking tray. Time is running out and she has to move on to the anchovy paste. She empties a package of dried baby anchovies into a pot of simmering water. As a child, following behind her along the aisles of Geumnam Market, she was never certain which vendor would be the next casualty of her mother's plucky words. *Fish with no heads – what a waste. And you see that – yellow bellies are no good. So careless of these people to keep them out in the sun so long.* With chopsticks, she picks out the headless and yellow-bellied ones from the pot and throws them into the organics bin. When the water rises to a boil, she pours the anchovy stock through a cheesecloth and into another pot holding the rice flour. She picks up a wooden spatula and exhales deeply. Even now, almost twenty years to the day of her mother's passing, a debilitating anxiety comes over her during this part. *Quick! Keep stirring! Don't let it stick to the pot. Put it over here, on the counter.* It was the family secret, passed down through generations, a process overlooked by the other mothers in the village. How many times had she and her sisters been told that the difference between a good kimchi and a great one lies in the consistency of the anchovy paste?

In Andong, they liked their kimchi the way they liked their men, in three distinct phases: fiery in their youth; vigorous through middle age; and a touch of acceptable sourness when they reached their prime. There was no mystery to how it was done well: local cabbage, fresh sun-dried chile peppers, a hardy sea salt, and a perfectly executed anchovy paste. In the cities, where they preferred their kimchi crisp as collared shirts and without the depth that anchovies gave it, her sisters referred to it as "Peter Pan kimchi" – immature and without lasting character. Afterward, they forced the kimchi to ripen in clay jars through a long and bitter winter, allowing it to achieve something close to the ideals of arranged marriage, and its only objective: family – each ingredient imparting its better qualities to become something more than itself.

In the living room, she lights the candles on the shrine. There is a framed black-and-white portrait of her mother, taken weeks after her wedding. Her hair is pulled back and bundled behind her neck with a long silver pin. She looks regal in her traditional silk *hanbok*, seated in front of a folding screen featuring some famous Korean landscapes. Her gaze is directed inward as though she is attending to some tiny movement in an uncharted part of her body.

She reads out her mother's name, then kneels twice, her forehead touching overlapped hands on the floor. Each year she has had to remove yet another step in the ritual to simplify matters for

Sera. From twelve steps for each dead ancestor, there is now just the kneeling and the burning of the paper tablet. She knows that when she too has passed from this world, Sera will have forgotten to teach her own children even these steps.

The phone rings on the sofa end table and it's Sera.

"*Ohm-ma*, we'll be on the last train out tonight," she says. "We should arrive around breakfast time."

"Sera-yah, it's too early."

"Miguel wants to help." She could hear his Latin-inflected baritone voice in the background, encouraging her. "It's too much for you."

"Tell him I'm fine." She scans the shrine, stacked with plates of dried fish, rainbow-coloured rice cakes, and apples. "Everything is finished."

"Well, we're coming anyway," then after a pause, "*Ohm-ma, Meehan-hae.*"

"For what?"

"We should be visiting more," she says, then sprightly, "And I miss you." Sera, her sentimental daughter, who has never seen her mother shed a single tear, created in her father's image.

"Yes, yes, goodbye. I still have much to do."

The winter they began dating, Sera wanted to teach herself how to make her own Korean dishes to impress Miguel. Her mother looked up frequently from the armchair, where she pretended to be knitting, and waited for a plea for help that never came. When Sera was in the bathroom, she snuck a peek into the kitchen. There was a cookbook open on the counter, written by some second-generation Korean-American housewife. It saddened her to see a scale and all those measuring cups. Hadn't her daughter been paying attention all these years? Didn't she know that recipes were inscribed on the tongue, that portioning was a matter of taste, and that no cookbook could teach you this? That night, in bed, she worried about what would happen when Sera and Miguel were married. However, her anxieties were dispelled at Korean Thanksgiving when Miguel prepared a five-course dinner for the three of them – Mexican dishes he grew up eating on a farm with his family and other migrant workers in Caledon – and she saw there was a beacon of hope for her daughter. Here was this hulking stranger, whose accent made his sentences difficult for her to follow, navigating through her kitchen with so much self-assurance – dipping his finger into bowls, wafting fumes from a steaming pot into his nostrils. It pleased her to think that they shared at least this common language. *Attention must always be paid to the ingredients available around you, as long as they are the best quality.* She rises from the sofa, puts on her slippers, and shuffles back to the kitchen. In the spice cabinet above the sink, there is a bag of dried ancho chiles, recently purchased at *Las Americas*. It was intended for a pot of beef and kidney bean stew for Miguel and Sera to take back with them, but she sees now that they could be put to better use. Ever since that dinner, she wondered about the chiles he used to make his mole. She liked the taste of them – they were pliable and slightly fruity, with surprising depth of flavour; not quite like fresh Korean ones, of course, but close enough. She hesitates, then adds a handful into the mortar. Through searing eyes, she pounds them and mixes them together with the stale Korean ones. When she is done, she adds the blended chiles into the anchovy paste with a cup full of shucked oysters.

On the eve of her wedding, before she left her home for good to join her husband's family, her mother lead her behind the miso and soy sauce shed, and into her private alcove. Like her sisters before her, she would be taught how to make kimchi properly. They said very little to each other, working silently in unison, keeping their tremulous emotions at bay. After all the ingredients had been prepared and laid out on the table, her mother brought out something else, something she had never seen before – a plate of Miyagi oysters. Where her in-laws lived, along the coast that faced Japan, the locals put oysters in their kimchi. And although she had no taste for it herself, she knew that necessary small adjustments had to be made to please her new family. The next day, when her husband and her in-laws arrived in the village to take her with them, her mother handed her a small clay jar of kimchi wrapped in embroidered silk, to be shared with her new family. When the kimchi was finished later that week – quicker than anticipated – she woke the next morning and before sunrise went alone to the shore to wait for the first oyster boats to dock. Oysters have been used in her kimchi ever since, and both Sera and her husband could not abide any other kind.

In the final stage, she adds the minced garlic and ginger, julienned daikon radish, Korean chives, and scallions into the oyster-anchovy marinade. She mixes everything together with her bare hands, tasting as she goes along. It is smokier and sweeter than she is used to, but the ancho chiles have done their job. She stuffs the ingredients in between the leaves of the cabbage and packs them tightly into three large plastic tubs. Sera will want to eat them right away, but Miguel will know better, will insist on letting the kimchi sit through the winter, fermenting in its own juices, until it is just right.

She looks up at the clock on the wall: fifteen minutes past midnight. They will be here in five hours. She wraps a wool blanket over her shoulder and steps out on to the balcony. Mist-like rain drifts obliquely under a streetlamp and the blue tendrils of lightning in the distance bring to mind images on an electrocardiogram monitor. At the corner, four stories below, an amber light flickers on the slick surface of the street. When she hears light tapping behind her, she is expecting it, and turns around slowly.

"*Ohm-ma…*" She suppresses a sob in her throat. On the sliding glass door is a strange look from her own exhausted face and her outstretched palms. There is a rustling like poplar leaves in the breeze and a vague longing seizes her. Over time, when she imagined her mother was still alive and the inevitable sadness set in, she found ways to cope by accepting her losses in the same way she accepted the gift of her daughter. She had no way of knowing how she found the strength, except when the deacon occasionally reminded her that it was never a question of "how" but of "where," as he turned his gaze to the heavens.

She closes her eyes and envisions a cab pulling up to the residence lobby. Sera leaps out of the back seat and waves wildly at her from the sidewalk. Within minutes, her daughter is catapulting through the front door, squealing with delight after seeing the tubs of kimchi on the hallway floor, and rushes at her, arms flung wide. Behind her, Miguel, her future son-in-law, covers the doorway, a basket of dried dates for the shrine in one arm; in the other, a bouquet of flowers – a good man. She sees all this playing out on the inner screen of her eyelids, and when that is over, it is replaced by cumulus clouds – thick tufts against a blue-black sky, flecked here and there with small cold stars. They are bunched together to resemble a cave, then a camel's hump, then a rabbit standing on its hind legs. It all appears random, odd things that take shape in her head at this time of year. Only the wandering spirits seem to know what to do, where they are going. Her chest feels heavy and her temples throb, so she grips the balcony railing, gathering every will in her body to beat back some nameless need rising up in her. She turns her face eastward toward the lonely churchyard, and past it toward the horizon, waiting now, waiting for the first rays of light to break over it.

A.L. Bishop

HOSPITALITY

It takes forever for the sun to set in the north in June. When Violet looked up to turn on the banker's lamp near her elbow, she saw by the clock on the wall that it was already an hour past closing, but she was loath to shut the door on the breeze. She rubbed her eyes but stopped when she heard a car on the highway slow down, pull into the gravel lot, kill the engine. She had been hoping for a quiet night.

The screen door opened and he was there – Victor, in the doorway, with some filthy, ragged girl beside him. Violet flattened her face, her voice, her breath.

The man – not Victor – strode across the lobby, the pine floorboards letting out giddy shrieks as he passed over them. He came up to the counter and leaned on a mottled forearm, just a few inches from Violet's face. "Need a room."

His jaw didn't sit properly. After he spoke, a small bead of spittle under his lip caught the greenish light from the lamp.

"Got any?" When she didn't respond, he explained his joke. "No cars out front."

Violet looked over at the girl, who had a bandaged hand. The girl wouldn't look at her.

"You slow, or what?" His wispy hair lifted and fell in the breeze from the screen door.

"Welcome to the Sunset Inn," Violet said.

He snorted. "Where'd they find you?"

Violet pulled out the register and slid it across the counter. It bumped his arm, and there it was – a small flash across the eyes, the mildest baring of teeth. "Sign in here."

Maybe he didn't want to give his name, or maybe he didn't know how to write it, but some imperceptible command passed between the man and the girl, the kind of command that anyone outside a couple like this one could never hope to understand. The girl lurched forward to scribble in the book. The pen kept slipping on her bandages. Jenna Marchand.

Violet tucked the register back onto its shelf. "Cash up front. Sixty-five."

"Sixty-five? For this hole? Give her forty," he told Jenna Marchand. "Probably can't even count."

"Next motel is 178 kilometres north," said Violet, still flat. "210, going south. Careful of moose this time of night." It was Victor's spiel, and there was theatre to accompany it – Violet took out the register again, always kept open on its shelf, and picked up a pen. The man gripped the counter with both hands.

"You're lying."

She waited, pen hovering over Jenna Marchand's childish printing, for the man to remember whether or not they had passed any other motels in the last two hours.

After a moment, he said, "Fifty, then."

Violet laid the pen down. They both watched as the girl dug around in a grubby change purse. The third of the twenties she pulled out caught on the zipper, and she struggled to disengage it. When she dropped the last mangled bill on the counter, Violet swept up the money in one hand and took down a key from the pegboard behind her.

The man leaned over the counter. "I said, fifty."

"Slow night. No change. Rather pay by credit?"

His stare had embers behind it. She held out the key on its sticky orange paddle to the girl instead of him. "Ms. Marchand."

He yanked it out of her hand, twisting her thumb hard before he released it. "You here all by yourself tonight?"

He left the threat there, on the counter, as the girl followed him outside. Violet listened to his muttering until it got swallowed up by the vast quiet of night on the highway in the forest. Once their cabin door slammed shut, she came out from behind the counter and used Victor's keys, heavy on her hip, to lock the main entrance. She turned off the motel sign with the switch on the wall before unlocking the door to Victor's apartment behind the office.

Putting the earnings, such as they were, in the safe, she imagined Victor and this guy, a bottle or six, maybe a knife fight in the end. She crossed the small bedroom to the window and slid it open to let out some more of the smell. Nicotine, bourbon, waste. It would rain soon – it always rained soon here – and the rain would pelt the stench down into the sand that gave way to the long grasses at the edge of the woods behind the motel, where paper and other trash were always snarled up among the weeds.

At the doorway to the kitchen, she stopped and stood in the dark. The room yawned black before her, and she could feel Victor there, waiting. But when she reached out and turned on the light, the only person she saw was herself, reflected in the cracked windowpane in the door that led out back. The kitchen was empty, clean, everything just where she'd left it.

She left the light on as she went out through the kitchen door into the still warm night. Out back, in the shed, she got to work.

⌁

The shouting started almost right away, but the true commotion took a few hours to cook up. When she thought she heard something land hard on their car, the only one in the lot, Violet left the shed, locking it behind her, and went around the side of the motel to check on it. A flicker at the window of their room showed that the TV was on. It had fallen quiet. Under the yellow light of the parking lot, the car looked unharmed.

Rounding the corner on her way back, Violet tripped over something she couldn't see, something that made a small, injured sound, rustling on the ground. Raccoons often scavenged and shat here, next to the dumpster. She stopped. "It was you, that hit the car."

The girl, Jenna, stepped out of the building's shadow.

"Looking for a place to sit?"

"Looking for the ice machine." The light caught the side of Jenna's face, already starting to swell.

Violet nodded. "I've got a freezer full of ice. Follow me."

She didn't, not at first. When Violet looked back at her, she was almost pouting. "You sure wound him up."

"Couldn't help myself," Violet conceded. "Never can, with his type. You coming or not?"

They went past the dumpster, past the shed, into the kitchen. Violet held open the door for Jenna, who kept her face tilted toward the linoleum as she sat heavily at the greasy wooden table. Violet pulled a tea towel from a drawer to rub the sweat and dirt from her face and arms, leaning against the counter where the sink was, across from Jenna.

"I thought it was always cold up north," Jenna said, looking past her. "Could you turn that on?"

Violet turned to glance at the dented air-conditioning unit in the kitchen window over the sink. For just an instant, she could feel Victor's meaty hand darting around her again. "It's broke." She sat in the other chair at the table. "I was chopping an onion. He came up behind me, all pressed against me, you know, like a wall, and grabbed the knife while it was still in my hand. He brought it up, like this, to my throat, but when I tried to push his arm away, it cut him, his other arm. He dropped the knife, spun me around, went to bash me. I should have just let him. Don't know why I didn't. But I ducked. He hit the A/C instead."

When he'd finished yowling, Victor had gone at her with the bloody knife again, pointing it at her sternum. She didn't resist that time. She melted right into it, so that he was the one who had to stop it from going deep enough to really hurt her. He hadn't liked that, either.

Violet shrugged. "Never worked that good to begin with. And it usually is a lot cooler, so it don't matter much, except on days like today." She stood up and took a glass from the drying rack, turning her back on Jenna to run the tap. Over her shoulder, she said, "You wanted ice." She nodded at the chest freezer by the door.

Jenna moved slowly, like she was suspended in liquid, but when she lifted the freezer's lid with both thin arms, looking for an ice cube tray, and found something else, she swore and jumped back quickly enough. The lid thudded closed.

Violet put the glass of water onto the table and went to the freezer on top of the fridge. She pulled out the tray, working it back and forth until it coughed up a few bouncing chunks of ice, and tore some paper towel off a roll.

Jenna stared at the chest freezer.

Violet held out the bundle of ice. When Jenna still wouldn't take it, Violet put it into her bandaged hand and pushed it up to her face, knocking the red curve of her cheekbone.

"Sit."

Jenna went back to the table.

"Where you two headed?" Violet leaned against the sink again. "Victor brought me out here, to nowhere. No one to look in on me, no place to run away to. No one to come check on us. No one would have stopped him, even if they had."

Just then, a distant bellowing caused them both to start, squirrels in the grass. A faint pounding and roaring moved around the front of the motel for a few moments, then got closer and clearer. Jenna lowered the ice from her face.

"If you want, you can go around the way we came in, around the side. Lock's broke on room six. Use the phone. Call for help. Stay out of sight."

In the front office, the metal storm door whined as its frame gave way.

"If you want." Violet opened the breadbox on the counter near the freezer and pulled out Victor's pistol, which she placed on the table in front of Jenna. Shattering glass meant he had broken the window on the door between the office and the apartment. Violet dropped the muddy tea towel over the top of the gun just before he loomed up out of the dark in the kitchen doorway.

"What's all this now?" His dull eyes swung back and forth between them. "A little girl talk? Little chinwag?"

"With the OPP." Violet stepped closer, getting between him and Jenna. "Just got off the phone. Detachment's ten minutes up the highway. Here in no time."

He planted both hands on her shoulders and shoved her back and down, sending her crashing into the counter, sprawling across the floor. Then he lifted Jenna by her neck from the chair and pinned her against the wall, wedging his forearm under her chin so that her dirty sneakers dangled over the floor. He cocked his head to one side, as though he were considering the height at which he wanted to hang a picture.

He ignored Violet until he heard the hammer on the pistol click into place, a few feet away from his head.

"Now, just a minute." He caught Jenna under the arms and slid her back down the wall, almost tenderly. She gasped and wheezed and fell against the back of the chair. He reached out to steady her. Violet glanced at her, trying to meet her eyes.

He snatched up the tea towel from the table and wrapped it hard around Jenna's neck, pulling him against her, keeping his head behind hers.

Jenna, already on the edge of passing out, wilted in the space between him and Violet's gun.

Violet flattened herself again. "Not too tight. Soon as she's done, no reason for me not to shoot."

The man started backing out of the kitchen, loosening his grip on Jenna just enough to keep her breathing.

"Last chance," Violet said, not to him.

Jenna, clutching at the tea towel, drew in a gulp of air and kicked backward into the man's left knee, twice. As he faltered, she crumpled away from him. He lost time turning to run, trying to make it to the darkness. Violet took the shot.

—)ı(—

"You can go," Violet said. Jenna's colour had gone completely, apart from the streaks of red and mud on her neck and the shadows taking hold over her now swollen-shut eye. Huddled in the corner next to the doorway, she couldn't take her good eye off the dead man.

Violet knelt down next to him and dug around in his pockets.

"Is he dead?" Jenna's voice came out in tatters.

Violet fished out his wallet and car keys and waved them at her. "Yeah. Here."

"Are you sure?"

Violet made a show of feeling for a pulse. "Yes. You should go."

"Where?"

Violet sighed, putting the man's things on the floor beside Jenna. This was the worst time, when freedom looked you in the face. "Anywhere. Go back to the room. Take a shower. Take the car. Drive away. Leave it in a parking lot somewhere, as far from here as you can manage. Then hitch, or buy a bus ticket, or do whatever you like."

Jenna touched the keys lightly. "Is the OPP really as close as you said?"

Violet hauled herself up off the floor. "You should go."

"You only did it to save me," Jenna argued. "They'll believe us."

"They never do. It's OK. I know what to do. You go on."

"You saved me," Jenna said. "I'll help."

"Don't need help."

"What are you going to do? Put him in the freezer? You can't do that on your own."

Violet opened the broom closet and pulled out some dirty yellow nylon rope and a pulley she had rigged up out of an old clothesline wheel. "Isn't room for both of them in there."

Jenna frowned at the pulley from the floor. Violet took Victor's keys off her belt. "You want to help, fine. Go out front, to the last door, the one with no number. It's the supply room. Empty off the housekeeping cart, top and bottom, and then roll it around back."

Jenna stood and rubbed her neck before taking the keys. She went out through the kitchen door, instead of stepping over the man's body to go through the apartment. Once she was gone, Violet pulled a stick out from beside the freezer and propped open the lid. When the ropes were knotted, she anchored the pulley over the open kitchen door. She had the frozen body on the floor by the time Jenna had reappeared with the empty cart.

Together, they dragged him out the door using the ropes, angling him onto the lower level of the cart, and wheeled the cart over to the shed in the moonlight. Violet unlocked the wooden door and swung it open. The smell of the damp earthen floor poured out around them. "The cart won't go over the threshold," Violet said. "Just have to tip it off."

They pushed the cart forward against the wooden threshold and then lifted the back wheels. Violet used her foot to send the ice block sliding forward to disappear into the black stillness of the windowless shed.

Violet untangled the rope from the cart and tossed it in after him. Then she rolled back the cart and closed the shed door, dragging it over the dirt, putting her shoulder into it to close it up. She started back toward the kitchen door.

"Wait," said Jenna. "You can't leave him like that."

"I want to get that floor wiped down while the blood's still wet, so we need to get the other one up off the floor. Now, bring this cart back and fill it up the way it was."

"But it's so hot. He'll start to—"

"I'll take care of it," Violet said over her. "Just now, we have to get your fella into the freezer and get that floor wiped up."

Jenna didn't move. "I don't think I can touch him."

"Then go take a shower, like I said. Get in the car and—"

"No! I'm helping. I'll bury Victor." Jenna tugged on the shed door.

"Leave it," Violet told her.

The door swung wide. "Is there a light?" Jenna stepped over the threshold and out of sight. "Where's there a shovel?"

"Don't—"

Jenna screamed.

"Quiet! Stay still."

Jenna continued to struggle and whimper as Violet closed the shed door behind them and switched on the 40-watt bulb overhead. She looked down into the pit where Jenna had fallen in the dark. "Are you hurt?" She reached over and pulled a short stepladder down from a nail on the wall, which she lowered into the hole. Jenna climbed up and sat in the dirt next to the frozen corpse. It still had yellow rope tied around it. She didn't seem to know where to look – at the empty grave, at the block of ice, at Violet.

"You're all right, aren't you? You didn't hurt yourself. I told you I'd take care of it. Now, let's get moving. I need you to put away that maid's cart."

Violet tried to help Jenna to her feet, but the girl stayed put, surveying the six covered mounds beyond the open pit, one after another, going all the way to the shed's back wall, through one eye.

"Come on, now. Up you get."

"You already dug the hole?"

Violet hesitated. "Wasn't going to leave him in there forever."

"For Victor? That's why you were so dirty before?"

Violet crouched down. "I know you've had a shock, but we have work to do. You're helping, or you're leaving, but you can't stay here."

Jenna's eye ran over the dirt floor, the gaping hole, the lumps, all six of them, all different shades of brownish grey. "You did that tonight? It's so hot out. And we were here. What if we'd seen what you were doing?"

Violet stood and put her hands on her hips.

"You made him so mad," Jenna said at last.

Violet went flat. "When I leave this shed, I'm locking it behind me."

That got Jenna moving, and faster than Violet would have expected from a girl who had just been strangled nearly to death, twice. The girl ran from the shed to the kitchen, from the kitchen to someplace else.

Violet watched her go. Then, no longer in a rush, she used the ropes to pull the body into the pit. She hopped down to untie them, used the ladder to climb out. She threw a few shovelfuls of dirt in, just enough to cover him, and pulled a blue tarp across the pit. Good enough for now.

In the kitchen, she rigged up the ropes and pulley again to wrestle the dead man into freezer. Jenna, in all her shock and horror, had remembered to take the wallet and keys. So she wouldn't know his name. No matter – she never could remember them afterward, anyhow.

Katherine Govier

ELEGY: VIXEN, SWAN, EMU

VIXEN

I first saw her three years ago early in the morning in Mount Pleasant Cemetery. She had her warren near the fountain on the east side of the park. It was fall and in the mornings we walked, a group of women, talking about our divorces. The fox came like a slow leak out of the rocks, paused to catch my eye, and then fled into the trees.

I was smitten. She was beautiful, she was wild, she was angry, she was arrogant. Every day I would pause in our conversation as we came near the spot. I narrowed my eyes and jutted my head in that direction, but I did not see her again. Not there.

Later, up north, at a friend's chalet, a red fox – male? I think so – crossed the lake ice before my eyes at dusk. He was big, with thick fur, his tail held high, stalking, and again so arrogant. It could not be the same fox, but to me it was a reminder of fox. This was a fox sent by foxes to keep me in thrall.

I often drove down the Rosedale Valley Road at night to meet my lover in the east end. Once, in the dark, I saw the fox. She stood electric in the headlights at the side of the road, just where it curves to its deepest point between ranks of trees. My breath was gone, suddenly. Please don't run. I did not want to hit her. She seemed to bid me. Then she vanished.

Who was she? Was she the lover, or someone else calling me home? I knew the love affair would pass.

When people leave their marriages, the next affair is called transitional. It felt that way only in the sense of the pain of birth. Remember, ladies, I said to the walkers, when the labour gets impossible and the pain is so intense and getting stronger, they say you're in transition.

The night we ended it, I lay on the bed of all our protestations and heard foxes crying below. In that part of the city they come out of the big expanse that used to be a race track and is now a housing development: they have nowhere to live. Those foxes are not truly wild; they're city dwellers and they've been displaced. They give tongue, as hunters say; I heard vulnerability in their cry. But I did not go to them.

Since then, I have kept company with this fox or skulk of foxes over what seemed a long time. Sometimes it seems she is the same red fox, sometimes clearly another one. She would be on the roads I drove, or near the beach, mysterious, obdurate, and waiting. Then she would be gone. I kept company with her through difficult times. She was difficult, but she was also for me a solace, a comfort and a promise. I began to expect her appearance but I knew I would not be lucky forever. I suppose I became complacent. It seemed my due, to have this fox in my life. And then she went away.

I drive miles across the city. Wondering if I have failed in some way. Wanting the wild. Wishing I could have made a place for the fox in my life, wishing I could throw my life over and be with the fox, wishing the fox would stay with me. Wanting the fox, the sleek body, the fierce gaze, all her disguises and foolish pride and guile. But how? On the one hand there is fox; on the other memory, family, home, everything I have hitherto considered to be my life.

I try to put the fox out of mind. I do not look for her but she manifests. I moved from my old house. I don't walk in the cemetery with those women any more. I am seldom in the east end and never in the country. But I go out with my dog late at night.

Only two weeks ago, in my new neighbourhood, I saw the fox again. She was trotting northward in the empty night street. Bitch! Her tail was streaming flat out behind her, bushy and the colour of autumn, as if she were flying. She stopped and gave me her fox smile. My dog lifted one paw and ceased to breathe. I ceased to breathe. There was nothing to say. I was full of joy. Then the fox was gone. Sometimes I think this was the only time I ever felt love. Sometimes I think it was all just mad.

SWAN

She is tailored and white, a life going on, smartly stepping to her taxi. I stand on the sidewalk and hold the door. Or it holds me. She gives her address, the one I'm not privy to, but she doesn't look up so I send all the tenderness I can muster into the back of her neck. And then I slam it – the door, I mean. Lucky girl. She has twenty-five years to go on that meter before she catches up to me.

I drive alone to the farm, I and the Bach cello concertos, strangely contained in window glare, floating northward. Some missed turnoff takes me out of my way. That and the heat and my wet eyes turn the pavement to glass. I drive blind.

I wouldn't say I was lost. I did find all the promised markings: concession roads, turnoffs, gravel driveways, chained gates. But not where they were supposed to be, or in the right order. I arrive at the place from an unexpected direction, having pushed some new way through the usual grid. Here is the key hidden behind the third post. I know these friends' fields, this borrowed house, much too beautiful for my already ravished eye.

Someone in my life predicted I'd never be happy, one of those other lovers I've long ago got over. The truth is, I feel good, often. Even today. There's no accounting for it, for I am a displaced person in mid-life who has lost her child. I find it exhilarating, actually. But this. This hit me.

I watch the silent phone. No doubt you miss me. And regret the ridiculous scene. I miss you too. There is however no chance of your following me here, especially considering my evasive tactics. But then comes the knock. It is not you at the door, of course it isn't.

It is the damn swan.

I'm not kidding, he knocks. With his beak when he is hungry. We'd been through it before. They have a pond, my friends. Pretentious.

Aren't you a sight for sore eyes? I say, opening the door a sliver. He advances with his sinewy insinuating neck. Muscles the crack open farther. He is close to me. So close and presuming.

Disappointment crushes me. It enrages me. Already I have felt the richness, you in my arms like a great bird grounded, black-browed, white-chested. You must have been made of air, no marrow in those bones. Like Nijinsky, who jumped so high. He was a prince before he was changed to a swan. You cannot do this to me, I said, gripping your sad shoulders. My angry angel messenger with the pinned wings. I know I know. We wept.

But.

This one was a beggar. Rude, raucous, hard-nosed. I was not giving that bird a thing. I shut the door on his beak. Went to look out the window, a prisoner in this log castle. The swan wagged off. How did they ever get that idea for the ballet? Take away the water and they are the most graceless creatures you ever saw.

EMU

I saw a mound of grey feathers and sticks on the side of the road. Then we flew past.

What was that?

Dunno. Something big enough to do serious damage to a windshield.

A few more seconds and I knew. Four emus stood at the edge of the highway, tall as men, small heads with big beaks on snake necks. They were close together, bustles of salt and pepper feathers, stalky legs akimbo. Looking confused. In shock. I seemed to catch a pair of deep brown eyes. In them I saw puzzlement, grief.

We were travelling. I went unwillingly. People urged me – go, go, your daughter will be fine. So there I was, as far away from home as one can get on this globe, which in its roundness takes you away in order to bring you back.

And I had been diverted, it was true, by the animals down under. A beach-going owl that barks like a dog. The stoned koalas that dangle chubby legs from the crutches of eucalyptus trees as they slowly strip them of leaves. Three sizes of kangaroo: the horsey kind, the mid-size wallabies who scratch with tiny front paws at the skin of their stomach until the head of a baby pops out, and the tiny quakka, first taken for rats. Flying foxes that hang all day by a thumb, wrapped in vampire-style wings, and fly out in their thousands at night. Kneeling birds that look like stones. Snakes in the vineyards. Stingrays lying like downed kites in the shallows.

But the emus brought me up. It was the way they looked at me. In that moment I understood what had happened.

The first emu, the now mound of feathers and sticks, was young. Impetuous, defiant, she had gone to the edge of the highway, flirting with death. Her elders craned around, trying to talk her out of it. But no, she knew what she was doing. She turned her back and began her dance. Faced the wind of traffic, the soft distant roar. The blank thump every minute or so of a car passing.

She judged it, timed it, figured she was faster. Emus run like fire. They like to race. Or was she, as my friend Elizabeth used to ask, in any kind of despair? Perhaps. Consider the future of her kind. Low cholesterol meat. Leather purses, anti-aging cream.

In any case, she sprints out from the shoulder and there looms a car, just that second, out of nowhere. What to do? The secret of the emu is this: it cannot go backward. The same is true of a kangaroo. This is why the two species face off on the Australian coin. It is an attitude. Never retreat, that sort of thing. And a tragic flaw, especially if you have stepped into the speeding traffic.

What they can do is a karate-style flying jump kick. And take nine-foot strides. She tries one, then the other. Crack of windshield. Shriek from inside the car. Wail of brakes. Flight of the flightless bird some distance ahead to where it crumples, dead.

Meanwhile the emu family has faded back into the shadowy bush. The car stops, the driver emerges, puts his hands on his hips and walks in a circle, vomits, drinks water out of his canteen, splashes his face, and in a gingerly fashion grabs one of the huge three-toed feet and drags the thing to the shoulder and inspects the damage to his car. Cursing, gets back in and drives off only moments before we approach.

As the others return to the roadside, that's when I see them and we have that brief moment of contact which I cannot call human. They signal their grief, I mine. Do they know she is not coming back? How long will they wait there?

Sheila McClarty

THE DIAMOND SPECIAL

Larry and I have been driving through the black flatness of Saskatchewan all night. Both of us bleary-eyed and stinking of lack of sleep. We're hauling a two-horse trailer, lopsided with the weight of the Appaloosa stallion on the left side. Every time the spotted horse sits down on its haunches the front end of the pick-up hydroplanes, strains forward, and Larry lets out one of his raw-throated guffaws, slaps his hands on the rim of the steering wheel and says, *Damn, Brett, you trained that spotted horse good.* And then he rants on about how I should get back into the business of showing trick horses and he shouldn't be selling the Appaloosa to stand at stud for a Pregnant Mares' Urine farm.

Larry's voice is like a hot spike driven into my forehead. He's wrong on two accounts. First, the only trick I ever taught the spotted horse was to sit on its arse and, second, he doesn't own the stallion anymore. I hunker into the worn plush of the passenger seat, chew on Larry's stupidity and try not to think about Francine. And of course, once you set your mind to not thinking about something, it's all you can think about.

All my white lies to Francine are clotting into a dark gooey mess inside my mind. When I pick out one lie to ponder, stuck onto it is another lie and on and on. If I call Francine to tell her I am on the road with Larry (leaving out the horse part of the story), she is going to ask why I am not at work, which leads into that I told my boss at the steel factory to stick his job where the sun doesn't shine because he wouldn't give me the day off, which leads to my boss saying my final pay cheque wouldn't be seeing the light of day either, which leaves me without the thousand dollars to make the final payment on Francine's engagement ring. Shit. What possessed me to listen to Larry in the first place? Francine had just left for the hair show in Moose Jaw when Larry showed up with a six-pack under his arm. He was all gung ho, ranting on about how he'd found a buyer for the Appaloosa and he wanted me to have a slice of his good fortune. Promised me seven hundred dollars for the use of my truck and trailer, and could I come along as a second driver. It would be like the good old days. After two beers, the plan seemed foolproof. We would be back before Francine returned home and I would have an extra seven hundred dollars. I could buy Francine flowers, dinner and a night at an expensive hotel; make the occasion I slipped the ring on her finger extra special.

Larry punches me in the shoulder and points to the green highway sign, WELCOME TO MANITOBA. He lets out a war whoop and brags about how he's beaten the Mounties, that they can't touch him now. I just shake my head in disbelief. Larry is convinced he has pulled off a spectacular heist and that the RCMP have him on their most wanted list. Larry's ex-wife has probably not even noticed the Appaloosa is missing from her pasture. She is a lot like a barn cat, wanders all night and sleeps all day. I reach for my cold cup of coffee and stare out the windshield.

The sun is sitting on the horizon, all bright orange, yellow and purple around the edges. We haven't pulled over since the outskirts of Regina and I am thinking it's time to stop and let the stallion out of the trailer for a piss and a few minutes grazing on some ditch grass.

Larry turns off the highway onto a gravel side road. The truck and trailer rattle along the washboard surface. After half a mile, Larry pulls over and stops the truck. Along the edges of the fields there are still patches of snow, which sparkle, in the early light. Shit. Now I can see the sparkle in Francine's eyes when she saw the engagement ring at the jewelry store. She thought it was too much money, but I insisted that after nine years of waiting it was the ring she deserved. For once, I was on the straight and narrow, my longest clean spell out of the horse business, one solid year of nine to five-ing it at the factory.

Larry turns off the ignition and flashes me a wide yellow-toothed grin.

"What are you grinning at?" I ask, trying to keep the snarl out of my tone.

"Just thinking of the last time the two of us were hauling horses in this neck of the woods."

Larry is referring to us hauling my two trick white mustangs to the Brandon Winter Fair a year and a half ago. It was my last performance with them and the crowd went nuts over the grand finale of the two mustangs sitting down, side by side, on a concrete bench set up inside the arena. There wasn't anything those two horses wouldn't try to do for me. Smart and beautiful to boot. But it was them or Francine. I sold them right after the performance. Two trick horses which paid for a used house trailer on five acres of land to woo Francine back and show her I had changed for real.

"Those two white horses were smart," Larry says. "Money machines. I heard the guy is showing them in Toronto this year."

"Fuck you," I say, opening the door of the truck. As I step out I can hear Larry part laughing, part snorting. Just like when we would be sitting outside the principal's office in high school, waiting to be suspended for one asshole act or another. Larry would be all brag-postured and I would be studying my shoes, praying

Francine wouldn't walk past and see me. I fell hard for Francine in grade six but didn't have the guts to ask her out until the last year of school. Prom night, Francine's silver-blue chiffon dress, white rose corsage, perfumed shoulders, and me the luckiest guy in the school gymnasium.

I unlatch the horse trailer's door and step inside. The warm smell of horseflesh, straw and fresh manure awaits me. I inhale deeply and some of the worry inside me disappears. The Appaloosa nickers softly. I step forward and pat his shoulder and the animal turns his big head toward me. I hold my open palm under his mouth and feel the warmth of his exhalation. I crouch down and run my hand along his left hind leg and then his right. The stallion has stocked up from standing in the trailer for so long. I should have bandaged his legs. In the gooseneck of the trailer there might be my old tack box and, hopefully, inside are some leg wraps. If so, I will wrap the Appaloosa's legs and walk him around before letting him graze. We are meeting the farmer at the Diamond Café in Austin, which is only another hour and a half away. I don't understand why we aren't taking the horse directly to the farmer's place, but Larry has reassured me numerous times the buyer just wants to make sure the horse is sound before taking him to his barn.

I untie the horse's lead rope. Backing out of a two-horse is a bit tricky and the last thing I want is for the Appaloosa to fall out the back door and hurt himself. I back him up a few steps, the muscles of his neck tense. I pat his shoulder. He is a sensible horse and just needs to trust me to unload. I discovered when I trained him to sit down that once he understands the signal he obeys. I swing the lead rope over the horse's wither and knot it under his throat. I press my right hand into his chest, pick up the rope and gently tug it. Right away the stallion remembers this cue – this was the beginning step in teaching him to sit down, so he knows to step back slowly. He takes a step. I wish I had a treat to give him because he turns his muzzle to ask for one. Instead, I whistle softly. The stallion steps back, one hoof, then the other. He lowers his right hoof onto the ground and then his left. For a second he stands with his front legs in the trailer and his back ones on the ground. I lift the lead rope and he steps out. I lead him to the side of the trailer and tie him up.

I crawl up into the gooseneck and find my tack box in the corner. I open the lid and the sweet stink of horse sweat, my mustangs' fragrance, hits me smack in the face. Two sets of show wraps are right on top and I bury my face into them and feel the scratch of sequins. Sequins, Francine hand-stitched, one by one, transforming each navy wrap into a mass of glitter. When those stallions entered the ring, the crowd would gasp at their magnificence. Francine groomed their long manes and floor-length tails into floating white silk. I bite down on my bottom lip. Man up, Brett, I tell myself. It's over. I lift my head and take two wraps in each hand. With my elbow, I bump the lid. It slams shut.

I wrap the stallion's legs and untie the lead rope. The stallion follows me, lifting each glittering leg high into the air and tentatively placing it on the ground until he becomes accustomed to the sensation of wrapped legs. After a few minutes I stop and the Appaloosa leans forward, collapses his haunches, drops his dick, and takes a good long pee.

Larry has the window unrolled and the radio turned up. Blake Shelton is singing his new hit, "She Wouldn't Be Gone," a love-sorry song. I hurry past the truck and down the side of the road. The fresh cool air clears my mind. I can call my boss and beg for my job back. I am a good worker, I like hard work. It's rules that get me in trouble. If my boss agrees, then I wouldn't have to tell Francine about being fired. I don't want to worry Francine with the truth. Besides, Francine is so happy now. She's graduated hairdressing school with flying colours, and is crazy about her job in town. Cripes, she's away at a classy hair show right now. What would be the point in bringing her down? I turn around and head back to the truck.

I tap on the driver's window and Larry turns to me. I hold up the lead rope and ask him to take the horse to graze. He gets slowly out of the truck. Neither of us have slept for twenty-four hours. Once I am inside the truck, I open up the glove compartment and take out my cellphone. I turned it off because my battery was getting low and there is no outlet in the truck for a charger. There is a text from Francine. *Learning so much about applying streaks, a new method from France where you hand paint in the colour. Miss you.* I answer with three heart-shaped icons.I start to dial my work number and then a low battery warning beeps on my phone, so I start composing an I-am-sorry text. I really pour it on. Finally, I press send, turn off the cellphone to save the battery, and put it back into the glove compartment.

The stallion is grazing in the ditch. I lean back in the seat. I hear the gurgling sound of a diesel engine. A blue pickup passes by and slows down. The truck pulls over to the edge of the road. A guy wearing a big silver buckle gets out and walks over to Larry. He is probably a quarter horse guy judging by his belt buckle. I can tell from his hand gestures that he is admiring the stallion. Larry's lips are moving with great speed, spurting out bullshit. I pull down the sun visor and close my eyes.

I wake up to the sound of a trailer rattling on the gravel road. At first, I think Larry has loaded the horse and we are back on the road, but when I look over to the driver's seat it is empty. And then I turn to the windshield. What the hell! There is a horse trailer pulling in front of my truck. Larry is holding onto the stallion in the ditch. The Appaloosa holds his head high and dances on the end of the lead rope. The guy with the buckle gets out of his truck and walks to the back of his horse trailer. A sound of horse hooves clunking on the floor of the trailer and a high-pitched whinny comes from the trailer. The stallion responds with a deep throaty nicker and paws the ground. What has Larry been up to while I was sleeping? Now the buckle guy is unloading a horse from the trailer. He must have gone and picked up a horse while I was sleeping. A tall weedy bay horse scrambles out of the trailer and almost lifts the buckle guy off his feet. Good Lord, I know what Larry is up to.

I get out of the truck and slam the door. Larry stares at me with that go-along-with-me look that fifty-fifty split grin, I have seen so many times in the past. I cut down into the ditch.

"Hey, Brett, good sleep?" Larry doesn't wait for me to answer. "We're giving Jim here a discount on our stud fee. Four hundred bucks, right, Jim?" he yells.

Jim reaches into the pocket of his jean jacket and holds up a wad of cash. Larry winks at me. I walk up the ditch toward Jim. The mare is dragging him so hard his cowboy boots' heels tunnel grooves into the gravel. When I reach Jim, I see the mare is taller than I first thought. All legs and jug-headed. Urine runs down her hind legs.

Jim hands me the cash as I dodge the mare's swinging hind end. "Shit, your mare must be seventeen hands," I say, leaving the word "ugly" inside my head. The Appaloosa is barely fifteen hands. The cash warms my palm. Larry starts shouting orders to Jim, to bring the mare over to the stallion. But the mare is such a handful, dragging Jim behind her, making it look like he is water-skiing on dry land. I stuff the cash in my pocket, run over and take the mare off his hands. The Appaloosa screeches and lunges forward to the end of the lead rope. Larry reels in the stallion.

The mare kicks out and I yank her head hard. She gets the message. This mare is too tall for the stallion to breed on level ground. I will back her to the edge of the ditch and Larry will position the stallion on the higher ground so the horse can mount the mare. Larry knows the plan without me saying a word. Jim is all smiles now that I have taken over the mare. Probably dreaming of the nice foal he will have, thinking the good attributes of the mare and stallion will combine. For some reason, people never consider how the faults of the parents can just as easily mix. I imagine a gangly spotted homely foal. I tighten my grip high up on the lead rope's snap, and lean my shoulder into the mare's. Her trembling skin is warm and damp. One eager mare.

I take the mare down into the ditch and back her up to the ledge. Larry stands on the high ground with the stallion. Both horses are screaming. As soon as the mare is positioned, Larry walks the stallion over. I warn him to be careful. The mare has proven she likes to double boot. Larry gives the stallion the full length of the lead and stands to the side of the horse's shoulder. The mare grinds her teeth and shakes her head. The stallion mounts the mare, his glittering forelegs draped over the mare's back. In a few minutes the breeding is finished.

I lead the mare, quiet now, up the ditch and back to her owner. Jim takes the lead from my hand. He asks, "What if she didn't take?"

Larry shouts from the ditch it is a live foal guarantee even with the generous discounted stud fee. I flash Larry a dirty look. In an hour the stallion will be the property of the farmer. Larry yells to Jim that once both horses are loaded he will give him his business card. Business card...what a lark.

I walk over to Larry and take the stallion from him. The horse nickers softly as we walk past Jim's trailer. I open the door to my trailer, loop the rope over the stallion neck, pat his butt and he jumps into the trailer. I get in and tie him up. As I am coming around the trailer, I watch Larry take a card from his wallet and hand it to Jim. Without looking at the card, Jim slides it into the breast pocket of his jean jacket. The two of them shake hands. I slide into the driver's seat of the truck and start the engine.

Larry jumps into the passenger seat. "They never look at the card," he says.

"You bastard," I say. "What card did you give him?"

"I think it was an expired Costco card," Larry says. And then he laughs and snorts.

I laugh too, thinking about how the two hundred compliments of the Appaloosa added onto the seven hundred makes me only one hundred short of a diamond ring. Larry's not all stupid; sometimes the guy's a genius. I step on the gas.

I yield off the highway and turn onto the main drag of Austin. I chuckle to myself, big name, small town. Larry's snoring and drooling in the passenger seat. I lean over and slap his chest. He squirms and groans. Up ahead a blue weathered sign reads, The Diamond Café.

As I pull into the parking lot, Larry rouses, blinks a few times, stretches his arms over his head, and announces he is starving. We are thirty minutes early and decide to have a quick breakfast before the farmer arrives. I park the truck and trailer lengthwise outside of the restaurant. I want to keep my eye on the trailer while having breakfast.

The café is empty except for a table of two old guys drinking coffee. They give us a good look over as we sit down at a window seat facing the truck and trailer. The smell of bacon and eggs makes me realize how hungry I am. The waitress comes over and pours us each a cup of coffee. She tells us our choice of breakfast is the Diamond special or the Diamond special. Larry laughs, leans over and punches my shoulder. We both order.

I take the cash out of my pocket and count out two hundred dollars and pass it to Larry. He doesn't even look up from his eggs, just reaches out his hand, takes the money and stuffs it into the pocket of his jean jacket. I finish my eggs, drain my coffee and push back my chair. I want to take the wraps off the stallion before the farmer arrives. I offer Larry a ten-dollar bill to pay for my breakfast but he shakes his head and, with his mouth full of toast, waves me off.

The stallion unloads without a hitch. I tie him to the side of the trailer and unwrap his front left leg, walk around and do the same to his right. I toss the two unfurled wraps over my shoulder. Just as I am unwrapping the horse's hind leg, a shiny one-ton Dodge Ram steers into the parking lot. If this is the farmer, the PMU business must be good. Maybe I should have taken up harvesting pregnant mare's urine for the big drug companies instead of training trick horses, steady salary, predictable costs. I was paid well for the trick horses' shows, but the cost of travelling and hotels ate a huge chunk of the salary. I turn back and unwrap the stallion's other leg. Behind me I can hear Larry talking to the farmer. I stand up and throw the leg wrap over my shoulder.

The farmer comes over to the stallion places his hands on his wither, leans over and peers between the horse's two hind legs, checking to make sure there are two balls hanging between them. It wouldn't be the first time someone tried to sell a stallion with an undescended testicle. The farmer reappears and asks to see the stallion trot out.

I undo the lead and run with the horse across the parking lot. The stallion trots at my side. I turn around and trot the horse back to the farmer. He lifts the stallion's lip and checks his teeth. I hope Larry didn't lie about the age of the horse. The farmer steps back, nods to Larry and tells him to follow his truck back to his farm for the cash. I try not to smile. Deal is done. Don't get cocky until the money is in your hands, I warn myself.

The farmer stops his truck in front of a stud corral. At the end of the laneway a massive red and white metal barn dominates the yard. Larry and I look at look at each other and vow not to blow this sale. The farmer walks toward us. I get out of the truck and head to the back of the trailer. As I am unlatching the door I can hear Larry complimenting the farmer's barn.

The stallion unloads, raises his head in the air and inhales the scent of mares. A good life awaits the Appaloosa. Judging by the size of the barn, a large herd of mares need his service. I am glad for the Appaloosa.

I walk around the corner of the trailer with the stallion. The farmer is counting out cash. The stallion whinnies loudly, a chorus of mares answer. The stallion paws the ground and I tug forward. The stallion trots beside me, picks up his pace and tries to cut in front of me. I turn in a circle to slow him down. We walk forward past the farmer and Larry. I clearly hear the farmer say thirty-five hundred as he places the last bill into Larry's hand. Larry told me three thousand, but it is really his business. The seven hundred he offered me is fair. I unlatch the stud gate, lead in the stallion and remove the halter. The stallion bursts forward and gallops around the perimeter of the corral. I close the gate.

Larry and the farmer are walking toward me. When they get close, Larry tells me we are about to have a tour of the PMU barn. I nod, even though I want to get back on the road. It is unforgivable to refuse a man's offer to see his stock after you have just sold him a horse. I tell Larry and the farmer that I will meet them in the barn. I hurry back to the truck.

I open the glove compartment and take out my cellphone. I turn it on. There are no messages. I toss it back into the compartment. Damn. But it is still early, maybe the boss hasn't seen my text yet. Besides, Larry will spot me an extra hundred dollars. He's packing more cash than he has had in ages.

I stop at the entrance to the barn and savour the earthy scent of straw, manure and horseflesh. I open the door. Stall after stall after stall line each side of the barn. Each stall holds a fat, shiny pregnant mare. They are bar stalls so it looks like there is no separation between the horses, as if their bodies meld into each other.

Each mare is tethered to her feed box. The stalls are set up with an alleyway in front of the horse's head to make it easy and fast to drop hay into each feed box. I walk down along the horses' heads; most of them are heavy horses, Percherons and Belgians, gentle giants chewing on their hay.

At the last horse in the row, I walk around the corner. The horses' rumps face the main alleyway. Each mare has a black rubber urine bag harnessed between their legs and attached to the base of their tail with a leather ring. Straps attached to the urine catching bag run along the outside and inside of their legs, and join in the air above their rumps onto what looks like a pulley system. This holds the bag in place when the horse moves inside the stall, although the narrow standing stalls don't have enough room for much movement. The farmer is resting his elbow on a mare's butt and explaining to Larry how the urine bladders operate. He lifts the mare's tail and pulls the bag out and shows the large cup at the top which, I assume, is for pouring out the urine. The farmer replaces the bag and gives the horse a pat. On the other side of the barn there is another row of full stalls. The horses on this side are more like quarter horse crosses – bays, chestnuts, a few paints. The farmer obviously wants the Appaloosa stud for these mares. I overhear him telling Larry he wants to produce riding horse types because they are easier to sell. I can hear the pride in the farmer's voice. In a roundabout way, he is telling Larry he does every thing possible not to ship horses for meat, but at the same time he has to make a living.

I walk down the heads of the mares on the other side of the barn. There is a pretty dished-faced chestnut and I stroke her forehead. When I come to the end of the alleyway, a white-faced mare pins her ears flat and bares her teeth at me. I stand back from the mare so as not to antagonize her. I know how the mare feels – as well taken care of as the horses are, this place is still a factory, a prison, spending half of your time incarcerated in a narrow stall.

My eyes start to water, from the ammonia smell of all the urine, I tell myself. I can't stand it in here another minute.

I push open the barn door and step outside into a small grassed paddock with an open gate leading onto a large pasture. This is where the mares will be turned out when it is time for them to foal. It can't be too soon for the white-faced mare.

In the distance I can see two chestnuts grazing. One of them raises its head and sniffs the air. A second later, both horses are galloping toward me. They run through the open gate into the paddock. I lean against the fence. They brake into a trot, their heads down approaching me. They are yearlings, good lookers too. I feign disinterest as they walk tentatively toward me. They are carbon copies of each other, red chestnuts with the only markings of identical white diamonds on their foreheads. The two yearlings are glued to each other's sides. Both are wearing leather halters so they have probably been handled, which is a sign of good upbringing. I kneel down on the back of my heels, pretend I am fascinated with the ground and wait.

I can sense the yearlings' presence, smell their scent. They are standing about a foot from me. One walks forward and drops its head. I blow gently into its nostrils and it blows back. Now the other chestnut muzzle drops to my face and I blow into its nostrils. I stand slowly up. The yearlings don't move. I let them sniff my pant legs. Tingles run up my spine and down my arms. I whisper nonsense to them and then reach out, gently cup my hand over one's muzzle and with other hand stroke its shoulder. The other yearling pushes in and I do the same to him. They are colts, uncut. What a pair. I raise my hand and shoo them away. They know this is a game, and they lean back on their haunches, turn on a dime and gallop, one down one side of the fence and the other on the other side. When they come to the end of the pasture, they turn down the centre and run side by side toward me. I trained my mustangs to do this in an open arena as part of their opening act. As the yearlings canter toward me, I see them in my mind's eyes as glossy, muscled three-year-olds, show stoppers. They come to a stop in front of me and wait for another pat. They are curious, but respectful, each already has an innate sense of boundaries, a good sign for training. I lean back into the fence, one yearling on one side, one on another. These two are special. It is a blessing neither of them are gelded. Stallions are the easiest to train to rear up on command. Voices break through my thoughts.

Larry and the farmer are standing in the doorway. "Ready to roll?" Larry asks.

I push off the fence and walk toward the barn. The yearlings follow me.

"Like those two?" the farmer asks, pointing at the yearlings. "They are twins, from the same sac."

I nod my head.

"You can take both home for eleven hundred. Two for the price of one."

I stop and the yearlings stop beside me. Just to see what happens, I take a step forward. So do the yearlings. Damn. There is no way. These two are gems, but my horse days are over. It's time for Francine to live her dreams – marriage, children and a home.

Larry walks over to the fence, rests his arms along the top rail and squints into the sun.

"Your friend here told me about your mustangs," the farmer says. "A few years back, I saw them perform at the Brandon Fair. What you trained them horses to do! I bet you could work magic with these yearlings."

Some magic, watch Francine disappear. I stub my toe into the ground. One of the yearlings nudges me and then the other one follows suit. I look down at the two white diamonds. No way, I repeat inside my head. These aren't the type of babies Francine pines for. It's too bad because these colts are a steal and have what it takes. No, I am going to be at the jewelry store before closing time, and if my boss won't give me back my job, I'll find another one. I gently tug one of the yearlings' ears.

"One grand. My bottom line," the farmer says.

Larry spins around and gives me a look. Funny thing about Larry, he thinks we are alike, cut from the same cloth. But I don't want to end up like Larry. No wife, no job, scratching through life, living off half-baked hare-brained deals day in and day out. He can wipe that big grin off his face. See, Larry, I am not like you. I am ready to settle down. Problem is, my heart can't catch up to my brain. "Nine hundred," I whisper.

"Deal," the farmer says.

Larry digs into his pocket for my share of the cash. I take each colt by its halter and walk forward, past Larry and the farmer, through the alleyway of the barn, out the door and down the lane toward the horse trailer.

I love Francine. I really do.

Caitlin Galway

BONAVERE HOWL

A clip and a buckle, a door bouncing on its hinges: the sounds of my sister disappearing.

She vanished on a drab Saturday afternoon, while our parents monopolized the main floor with cocktails and slow jazz and a laughing coterie of guests. My two older sisters and I had barricaded ourselves in our room. Except for Fritzi, the eldest, whose energy was as spark-lit as ever, we were drained to a dreamy lethargy by the heavy Southern sun. Fans whirred in our ears, blowing pink streamers like bicycle tassels. Mere hours before Connie would lift herself from where she lounged, and a series of sounds would click together – each step in her departure fastening like ribbons through our dark halls, ending at our backdoor and the burned-yellow dusk – and beyond that, nothing.

I was busy peeling worn muslin down my sticky skin, trying to keep my sweat still. Stop my makeup from drooling down my face. Before the guests had arrived, Fritzi and I had dragged a costume trunk between our beds, savouring the breeze of the lid flying open, a whoosh of release from the spoiled New Orleans heat. We rifled all afternoon through the contents of our late grandma Gerta's wardrobe – her chemises and sashes, her endless bronze and turquoise brooches – while Connie read, sprawled on her stomach, letting us drape luxurious fabrics around her and assign her magical names.

I sat on the floor and rested my cheek against my fist, examining Connie's drowsy face. "Why are your eyes so puffy today?"

She leaned over and fiddled with the dials on our bulky myrtle-blue radio, but didn't answer.

Fritzi opened our window and leaned out to see if any guests were mingling in the driveway. She lit a cigarette and let the smoke curl from her nostrils, blowing out the window through the corner of her mouth. "*Constance*, how we *miss* you," she badgered in a big, pompous voice.

Connie turned to me. "My eyes are puffy, pet, because I stayed up all night guarding you from *le croque-mitaine*." She grabbed Fritzi's wrist and chomped the air in her direction. "If I fell asleep it'd come and eat your hands clean off the bone."

Fritzi laughed and jerked her hand free. "You child."

Already we had been trapped in our room for hours, and the sun had begun to set when the radio crackled on our bureau. *Up next, one of the hottest little ditties of 1955!*

"Ugh." Fritzi snapped it off.

"Don't be a pill, Fritz," Connie said, with a bored slope in her voice. She turned the dial until out came the listless croon of Eddie Fisher or Perry Como or some other love-kissed singer she knew Fritzi couldn't stand.

"*No*. We're not listening to that song." Fritzi tossed a thick cotton coat from our grandmother's trunk over the radio to muffle the sound.

"It's only a few minutes long," I said, in the deliberately neutral voice best used whenever it was necessary to compromise with Fritzi.

"His voice gives me a *migraine*," she said. "It's so whiny."

"Plug your ears, then." Connie said. "Better yet, wear a hat over your whole head. It'll make Mama's day."

I tried never to take sides when the two of them bickered, but for a moment I couldn't help it – I laughed. Fritzi was the spitting image of our mother and grandmother in their youth, all three of them svelte and beautiful, with soft features forever antagonized by dragon-flare temperaments, and long black-licorice waves that hung about their waists – until, to Mama's horror, Fritzi roped her own hair into one thick twist, their eyes locked in some heightened, dramatic feud, and snipped it off.

Connie slid her hand underneath the cotton coat and cranked the radio's volume. She swayed her legs back and forth to the rhythm, and itched at her collar with long, lazy swipes. "This house is suffocating," she said, rolling onto her back with a spiritless air of declaration. "We're going to lose our marbles stuffed in here."

I bit off a chunk of watermelon Popsicle. "It's not the poor house's fault we've been *quarantined*." It was a loudly spoken rule of ours not to criticize our home, the smallest, oldest, loveliest house on Toulouse and, as far as we were concerned, in all of the enchanted French Quarter. Ever since we first saw it, the walls of deep mahogany and the darkest purples and reds had called to us, their elongated lines of Victorian fashion so beautiful and unnerving. We loved the dentil-frilled arcade of powdered lavender, hung with sweeping hibiscus and milky Louisiana iris. And the ambitiously pitched roof forgotten to a state of mossy cat's claw that Daddy set out to clear, but Mama argued to keep. We were protective of it, as if it were a sentient mass of brick and vine and clapboard listening in on our every word. For it was the place to which we all came back, at the end of the day. A fixed point, like the North Star or the glint of the Mississippi River.

"You're right, Bonavere," Connie said, rolling her eyes toward our eldest sister. "It's not the *house* that's suffocating." She reached out and pinched Fritzi's waist, giving her a start. "Why are we never invited to Mama's parties, anyhow? It's our house, too."

Fritzi's eyebrow perked up. "She's worried you'll embarrass her, of course. *You* don't know how to behave at proper social events. Plus, Bonnie's only twelve. She wouldn't have any fun." She lifted her dainty chin with sharp authority, blue eyes so chilled they could crack – until a line broke across her forehead. *"What is so funny?"* she asked.

Connie laughed and rolled back onto her stomach, dipping her head into her book. "You don't think it's because of the time you ate a dozen pastries, and threw them up all over yourself? In front of *everyone*?"

Fritzi huffed. "That was years ago!" She began to shimmy into an old taffeta slip before the window, ignoring Connie's laughter.

The afternoon had begun to shed its light for the cindery dimness of early evening. I tugged the chain on our favourite yard-sale lamp, with its waltzing couple embroidered on the shade. The light fell on the window, illuminating Fritzi's figure as she adjusted a black garter on her thigh. Daddy wouldn't let us keep a mirror in the room, so we had to make due with the window's glass.

"Oh, *gorgeous*," Fritzi whispered at her reflection. "This will do just swell."

Connie watched, fiddling with the chain of her new necklace, a dire-looking piece I assumed had been bought while antiquing with Daddy. She slipped its dark, engraved stone behind her collar. "Mama wouldn't let you be caught dead in that and you know it. Remember those polka-dot shorts you tried to wear? She says you dress like a hussy."

Fritzi stiffened, mouth agape in mock surprise, her choice of fashion a favourite subject for playful bickering. She touched her fingertips to her chest. "*Pardonne moi*?"

"*She* said it. And that you reek like a chimney, too." Connie ducked her head behind her arm with a drowsy laugh.

"Oh, Mama doesn't know I smoke."

"She does!" I said.

"With *Theodore Zimmerman* of all people!"

"There's nothing wrong with Theo," Fritzi said, suddenly rather serious.

"Oh, *really?*" Connie didn't seem to notice the shift in humour, and gave a little imperial cock of her chin that lit a frosty fire in Fritzi's eyes. "*Maybe* you should be more careful who you're seen with."

"She's only teasing," I offered, but a bright red smile broke across Fritzi's face. An amused and reeling laugh as her temper rippled.

"You would certainly know how *that* goes," Fritzi said. "Sneaking out after supper. That necklace I know I've never seen before in my life. You're keeping whoever gave it to you well hidden enough. Something *wrong* with him?" She stared knowingly at Connie, and for a moment neither of them spoke. At first I assumed they were communicating in that secret silent way they had that drove me crazy, but Connie paled dust-white, and Fritzi stopped smiling.

"Connie?" Fritzi's eyes softened. "I'm sorry, it was only a joke."

Connie stood up and threw her book onto the mattress with more energy than I had seen in months. She turned slightly toward me, her profile a wan wisp clinging to endless coffee curls. "I'm going to go crazy cooped up in this room all day," she said, her voice catching like a hiccup in her throat. She started toward the door, then swung back, tearing the necklace up over her head and tossing it onto my mattress. "Keep that, Bonnie," she said. Then a sudden wash of calm dropped over her as she opened our door and stared down the empty hall.

"Where are you going?" I asked, watching after her. I listened to her footsteps hurry down the stairs and into the kitchen, until the backdoor gave a loud creak. Nobody used that door, other than Fritzi for sneaking out. It was the only way to leave the house without our mother or father seeing from the living room or den.

Fritzi shrugged. "If she's going to be that way…"

"You hurt her feelings, Fritzi."

She crossed her arms and stared for some time at her feet, until meekly she asked, "But what did I say?"

We packed our grandmother's clothing back into the trunk in silence, as gingery doo-wop boomed from the radio. Dusk came on nearly as hot as the day, the mid-sky sun pressing hard against my cheek, flat and overcooked and ringed in white like a hardboiled egg. I ignored the uneasiness in my stomach at the door squeaking open, clapping shut. I let the feeling trickle in a thin stream from my chest into my gut, like the sweat down the small of my back, or the sticky melted Popsicle between my fingers.

❧

"Hypnotized," said Abelia Fay, raising a finger. "Your sister. Maybe she was lured out in a trance. She's a little loopy anyhow, right?"

Below a squat palm tree in the shadowed courtyard of Ursuline Academy, I ate my lunch with Abelia Fay – daughter of my mother's oldest friend, Mrs. Lily Lafleur. "My sister's not loopy," I said, "and she wasn't in a *trance*." I had no desire to discuss Connie leaving, least of all at school, and especially least of all with Abelia Fay.

"You said she suddenly looked *struck*? Dazed, maybe? Seems an awful lot like a trance to me."

I brushed the bronze-blond hair out of my face. "Goodness gracious. Hypnosis isn't real, it's what magicians do."

"Yes, it *is* real. It happened during the war." Abelia Fay's crystal-grey eyes gave off a vacant sparkle. "My daddy said two girls were hypnotized and plumb disappeared."

"Then it was probably the Germans." Grandma Gerta had never stopped fearing a knock on the door, nor any hard-eyed man in her periphery, even well after the war's end and she had left her haunted Parisian arrondissement for America. "My grandma said that people would disappear all over Europe and you would know it was the Germans. The Russians, too."

"It *wasn't* the Germans," said Abelia Fay. "These girls disappeared from *here*. They were called the Bellrose sisters, you listenin'? They got hypnotized and lured by ghosts all the way out to Red Honey Swamp. That's what people said."

I coughed a little half-laugh. "What people?"

"*People*. You know. All sorts." With fair hair and skin as pale as greasepaint, Abelia Fay was a dandelion ghost of a girl. Sunlight bounced off her face as she leaned out of the shade, her eyes levelling seriously with mine. "It was a very gruesome incident, Bonnie. Mr. Latimer Bellrose has been an utter recluse since it happened." Her nose pricked upward. "They all lived in the house my daddy just bought. He says we're a part of local history now."

My head slacked. "Oh, *are* you?" Fritzi and Connie and I had been fascinated with the lore of Red Honey since we were small. The Scarecrow Witch of colonial days, or the silver-skinned oysters with eyes popping out of them like pearls, or the Blind Fisherman who lost his way one night in a blizzard of fog. We knew every spectre and ghoul, had used them to scare each other with uncanny tales and then snatch each other's ankles, running and squealing through the purple aster bushes in the yard. There had never been a breath uttered amongst us of the Bellrose sisters, and besides, none of these old stories were true.

"I've been hearin' stories about Red Honey since before I could walk," I said, "and I've never once heard of this one."

A single eyebrow pinched up Abelia Fay's forehead. "Well, you *wouldn't* have" – she sniffed – "The papers were all about the war back then. Important parts of history have to be rediscovered, sometimes. That's what my daddy's doin' with our house. Matter of fact, he said we're livin' in the most gossiped about house in all the South, and only the *most* elite even know it."

"Connie *ran away*," I said. "She'll be coming home any day now, my daddy's already said as much. Trying to scare me with some Halloween story is nothin' if not cruel, Abelia Fay."

Her nostrils scrunched, twitching like a bunny's. "It's *not* a Halloween story. It's New Orleans history, as much as my house." She flung her hair from her face and it shimmered in a sheer white spray against her shoulder. "All's I know is gator hunters found one of' 'em floatin' in the water. Her clothes caught in the trees, too. Way up high. Now the ghosts of the two sisters wander the swamps, searchin' for one another forever."

"Shut up," I said. I shook my head so I wouldn't have to look at her, and so she wouldn't see me, either, the pinch in my nerves clear as a ray of water across my face.

"Ask Miss Audet," she insisted, as if the word of our rumour-milling math teacher gave her nonsense an air of authority. "Was her daddy who saw 'em, strollin' off like sleepwalkers. Prolly hypnotized by some crazy witch doctor. You should talk to that little creep always followin' you around about *that*."

"Don't talk about Saul that way." I glanced around to see who had heard her. "And keep that voice of yours *down*. My mama will kill me if she finds out about him."

Abelia Fay rolled her eyes. "Oh, please. Nobody's goin' to find out about your little backwater beau. Just sayin' he might know about some things, his family spendin' so much time in that dirty swamp and all. People are found in Red Honey all the time. How it got its name'n all. Betcha he'll tell you the *same thing*."

I snapped my lunchbox closed. "It's called that 'cause some drunk settler thought he found Himalayan honey beehives in Louisiana. Everybody knows that story."

She pursed her lips and shook her head. "No, it ain't. It ain't named for that at all. It's 'cause if you go far enough the forest turns red. Whenever someone dies out there the blood sinks into the soil, makes the cypress seeds bloom into blackgum."

"How could anyone possibly believe that?"

Abelia Fay blinked at me, unmoved. "Fine. Believe what you want."

There was always the pinch of amusement at the corner of her mouth when she was teasing, or mocking, or telling a lie. I examined her closely as she pressed the neat folds of a napkin over the rest of her sandwich, brow cross with concentration as the corners fluttered in the breeze. There was no pinch. No trace of humour, nor satisfaction, for a finely tuned trick. She looked as blank and cold as a slab of clay.

∽

That afternoon I sat at the edge of Fritzi's bed, looking out over our street through the window. The view was largely veiled by the old live oak, its evergreen shag a mauled curtain across the glass. I had searched for Connie in every room of the house since getting home from school. I checked her favourite nooks three times over, as if she might still be sleeping in her bunk, or sitting in plain view, and somehow none of us had noticed. A lawn mower outside calmed me as I pulled my knees to my chin. It drilled and jerked its violent gurgle, and there was noise enough to chew through the queasy hush that filled our house.

If only I had done it differently. The thought played over again in my head. If I had only said to Fritzi what I felt when my nerves rustled under my skin and the backdoor sounded its curious, broken *c-click*. And I almost had. *I had almost done something.*

I slugged off the bed and onto the floor. "She couldn't be in trouble," I told myself. "You're delirious." People didn't get hypnotized, nor lured into swamps by some bayou pied piper.

I needed to speak with my mother. She knew the city, the people in it; she made costumes for the New Orleans Ballet, attended galas and fundraisers and all sorts of dreary black-tie affairs. If the Bellrose girls had in fact existed, and vanished into the gloomy tresses of Red Honey, as Abelia Fay claimed, certainly my mother would have heard.

I was surprised to find her lying in the hammock on the porch, with her arm slung over her face.

"Mama?" I let the screen door smack behind me, loud enough to wake her.

"Mm?"

"You're outside," I said. She hadn't left her bed in three days.

Her arm dragged down and away from her face until her elbow made a sharp point and her fingers nestled limp against her collarbone. "Lily came over. Said she wouldn't leave unless I" – Mama shook her languid fingers toward the sky – "got some sun."

She was wearing a beige summer dress printed in red flowers, with a button in the wrong hole around her midriff. In the sticky heat the whole front yard smelled of soot. Cotton Miller's kitchen next door had caught fire the previous week, and the scent of damp ash and debris still clung to the air, even days after they hosed it down.

I stepped toward the hammock. "Mama, I need to ask you something."

She sighed. "Not now, Bonavere."

I twisted my hand out toward the vacant lawn. "Are you *busy*? It'll only be a moment." I approached the hammock and looked down, my shadow puddling over my mother's slack form. The sun had beaten her face into a pinked mask, and her breaths were long and easy, as if she were in a deep sleep. She hadn't yet opened her eyes. "Have you ever heard of the Bellrose sisters?"

Her brow dipped at the centre.

"Somebody told me they disappeared during the war," I continued.

Her eyes opened, slowly, squinting against the sun. Over the past several days they had skimmed blindly over me, but now in the piercing afternoon light they shimmered with a trace of clarity. "What could possibly be your interest in that?"

"Well" – I felt suddenly nervous. "I heard they disappeared into Red Honey Swamp."

My mother's chin slowly rose. She stared at me with such a look of consternation that I glanced over my shoulder to see if it was directed at someone else. I found Fritzi sitting on the lawn before the porch, somewhat hidden by the tall blue shoots of delphinium, with her bare legs outstretched in front of her.

"Darling, a story like that isn't for a girl your age," Mama said.

"So you do know the story?" I asked.

She said nothing, merely stared in her stern manner, and I was certain I caught the sharp precision of look one finds when two eyes are lost in the churning of a thought. I waited several moments for her to speak, as the leafy shadows of our live oak washed across her face, moving in the breeze like dark moths.

"I know of no such story." She moved to lift herself but her elbow slipped through a gap in the hammock and she set herself rocking in a clumsy swing. Her fingers dove to her forehead. "*Bonavere*," she said, cringing.

I rushed to still the sway of the hammock. "Where's Daddy? I'll ask him."

"You will *not*, Bonavere. Your father is with the police right now, he hasn't time for this."

"The police?" Fritzi turned so quickly she knocked her shoulder against the side of the porch.

"They already told us Connie ran away. That she could come back any day now." I looked down to the yard at Fritzi, who looked up at me with an unbearable strain of fear in her face.

"Yes." My mother's fingers spread in a shaky sprawl across her temple. "But they can get her home sooner. You know your sister. She gets…very lost, sometimes."

Everything took on a sudden sickness. The scent of ash was so strong in the heavy heat that it dried out all of the jasmine in the breeze. Ash covered the porch in faint grey speckles – blown over the fence, onto the planks, down the front steps of our house. "Mama," I began, "what if Connie isn't coming back on her own? What if she can't?"

My mother's hand wrapped around a knot of rope. "Why would you say that? Why would you ever say that?" Her head lifted, hair falling forward in dark plumes, as her burned brow weighed down her ice-blue gaze. "Your father is speaking with the police *at this very moment*." With a sliding glance she rolled onto her side, leaving her back to me and her hair dripping like oil between the hammock rope.

∽

Saul Chiffree and I were crouched on a shaded stoop along an empty street in the Esplanade. The store to which the stoop led – a blue and yellow antiques shop in the last little dwindling patch of business before downtown gave into the river levee – had been abandoned for months; cardboard over the windows; plaster crumbles on the steps; a spooky warehouse look to it when you peered through a small clear space by the window's ledge.

The street was isolated enough on summer weekday afternoons that Saul and I could go unseen and cool off under a store awning's shade after biking back, tired and sun-woozy, from the gritty unused trails which stretched out toward the Mississippi. When we were younger it was easier; we would carry kitchenware and linens in our schoolbags to the densest recesses of Couterie Forest, and wear pots like a knight's armour, or tablecloths like a sorceress' cape, and duel it out amongst the slash pines. Saul as King Arthur, with his sword fashioned from cereal box cardboard; me as the evil Morgana with a twig for a wand. But the older we got the more insidious grew the fear of accusation; what would people think – or worse, say – if we were caught alone together?

It was an apricot-sky afternoon as we examined a photograph that Abelia Fay had sneaked out of her attic and slipped into my desk at school, an indignant *"See?"* scribbled on a note beside it. Her custard-brick, camellia-lined mansion sat staunchly in the middle, behind two girls in tropical-flowered skirts and sleeveless tops. The older girl had sugar-white hair, but the little one's hair was like Fritzi's – a vital black that snatched the light and slicked it around like pomade.

I told him Abelia Fay's theory and he gawked at me like I was crazy.

"You're worried about something *Abelia Fay* said?" A wash-board row of wrinkles narrowed in the centre of his forehead. He and Abelia Fay hadn't been able to stand each other ever since Saul and I met at the comic book shop four years earlier – both look-ing for the latest issue of *The Vault of Horror* – where we discov-ered a shared love of all things monstrous and make-believe.

"Whatever Abelia Fay says, best always to believe the opposite is true." Saul slung an arm around my shoulders, shook me a lit-tle. His dimples dug deep into his cheeks. "Girl's got a head full of molasses. Don't let her scare you."

"I'm not scared," I said. And I wasn't. I couldn't be.

Only – ever since I talked to Abelia Fay, an undefined appre-hension grew in the pit of my stomach. The police had told us that Connie ran away. *"Any day she could come back, sir,"* they said to Daddy, when he started to raise his voice. But a week had passed, and still she hadn't come home.

Saul leaned forward, scratching his dark, sweat-damp curls. He tapped the glass over the photograph. "So this is them? The two sisters?"

"Must be," I said. "Here, flip it over. Maybe there's something written on the back."

We unclasped the picture from its frame and found, in letters scrawled as fine as thread work, the names of the Bellrose sisters – the youngest sister Amy's name written in slightly larger, lopsided letters, presumably by her own hand.

"The younger one here, she was the only one never found."

"*Nooo, Bonnie.* Don't tell me you've been reading up on this." Saul pulled the frame away from me and poked his finger against my temple. "You're lettin' Abelia Fay get inside your head."

I swatted his hand away. "I am not."

"Then I'll keep the photograph. You won't be able to stop thinking about it if you keep it."

I ran a finger around Amy's face. She was plump and doughy as a pastry, sinking into unshed infant chub on the knee of her sister, who had her arms crossed over the much smaller body in her grip, the way Fritzi and Connie had often held me.

I pulled the picture back so that it rested between us. "I'm not saying I believe her. It's just a picture." But the sisters' faces had begun to linger in my footsteps, and scratch at the back of my skull, and I wondered if Saul could tell. I hadn't built up the nerve to explain to him my plan, or ask him for the favour he would almost certainly refuse to give.

"Wait." He leaned forward. "What's that in her hand?"

I lifted the picture and noticed an item entwined in Amy's fingers, half-hidden by her sister's hair. I peered closer: there were green beads along a silver string, with a pendant being tugged from the older girl's neck. "I've seen this before."

"Seen what?" Saul asked.

"Those are the same engravings and everything."

"What engravings?"

"Right *here*, look closely." I pointed to the centre, and as my finger landed I felt the shivery bite of an electric shock. I drew back and shook my hand, eyeing the two girls with vague discomfort.

"Oh, right, I see them," Saul said. "Gee, some necklace. How come you know it?"

I lowered the picture onto the stone step. My hands were oddly heavy as they lifted from the frame.

"Bonnie?"

"My sister," I said. "She has a necklace like that. She's been wearing it all the time lately. The other day she called it a blood-stone."

"Wonder how she got a hold of it." Saul's brow furrowed. The day was hot and clammy, and the sun skimmed his sweaty upper lip. His energy was draining; soon he would be tired, and humour-less, as he grew on any day thrown off tune, and there would be no asking for any favours. "Reckon it means something, huh?"

I stared into the picture until its lines blurred indistinct and its grey and white patches floated out of place like loose clouds. "And what if it does?"

"What's it goin' to mean?" He was dragging a twig across the pavement in listless strokes.

"Well" – I paused, preparing for the snap of his head in my direction, the look of plain disapproval – "if I went to Red Mire" – I saw him opening his mouth to interject – "if I went...I could see what kind of place it really is."

He nodded, but his lower lip pushed up a weight of exaspera-tion. "All 'cause of what some snotty brat said."

"No! Not just 'cause of that. Mama was acting awfully strange yesterday when I asked her about the Bellrose sisters. You should have seen her. She wouldn't even talk about Red Honey."

"Well, tell me this, then. How on earth do you expect to get all the way out to the swamp?"

"See, that's the thing. Your brother fishes there, doesn't he?"

Saul's eyes didn't turn but shifted toward me. "Yeah. I guess he does. So?"

"I've been thinking."

He tossed his twig down the street and began scuffing out the chalk strokes with his shoe. "You're not thinking Dalcour will let you ride along in his boat with him." I didn't answer, but he read it across my face. "You're thinking you'll go *alone*?" He laughed. "You've never been in a swamp in your life. You'll drown before a gator has the chance to eat you."

"Your brother goes into swamps all of the time."

"That's different. Dally's older, and he knows what he's doing."

"I need you to help me get into his truck before he drives to the swamp. We could borrow his boat, once he's done fishing. We'd take good care of it."

"*We'll* borrow his boat? How are *we* going to do that?"

"I can figure it out. I'll go through the swamp by foot if I have to. You don't have to come, anyhow, I don't need you to help me once I'm there."

"Do you hear how crazy you sound?"

My chest was heating up. "I'm not crazy. You weren't there, you didn't see her. Connie just walked out of the house with her eyes *fizzed out* like television static. I'd never seen her look like that before. *Anyone* look like that. And then, these two sisters from the war…" I heard the notes of my voice slipping out of place, and a springing sensation in my eyes like blood vessels popping. "When does your brother go fishing next?"

"I'm not saying." Saul held the photograph between his fingers like he meant to rip it.

"My stars, Saul!" I snatched the picture away from him.

"You should chunk that thing right in the fire."

"Help me. I don't know how else to get that far out of the city, 'cept with Dalcour. My best friend in the world and you won't help me?"

Saul lowered his head onto his fist. "Dally's behind on a shipment. He had a bad catch and needs to replace it, so…he might have to go back out this week."

"Will you find out for me?" I asked.

His dark curls wriggled about his face, masking his expression. "It could be like we said last summer, I s'pose – finding monsters." We had wanted a single shot of any number of elusive swamp monsters with Saul's new Straight Eight camera. "I could sneak the camera out, and" – his tongue poked the parched corner of his mouth, eyes hanging low around my ankles – "you could see your sister's never set foot anywhere near that swamp."

∞

On the blistering August morning when Saul and I headed to Red Honey Swamp, the heat stuck to my skin like gum. Through the window above his kitchen sink, I watched Dalcour load dip nets and mesh-wire traps into a truck that had a licence plate plucked upward like a bucktooth.

Connie had been missing for eight days.

"Finally learnin' the ropes," Saul said. He squinted at a colourful mass of thread sprouting from a tiny tin fish.

"That would be a good tassel for the rougarous costume," I said. We wanted a *rougarou* – the French werewolf – to rival another beastly creature in our movie, though the costume was far more Mardi Gras than monster, with all of the birthday streamers and patchwork we had tacked on.

"Your brother looks 'bout ready to go," I said, peeking through the sink window. Dalcour was circling the open end of the truck, fastening a stiffly billowing blue tarp over his fishing equipment and a small boat turned upside down, with sun glints sharpening against its hull.

"He's going to go into the backyard for a minute," Saul said. "Wait for the gate to make a big clang, and then we'll run."

Dalcour brushed some dirt off the tarp and kicked up a light, bouncing jog as he turned around the side of the house.

"He's loading up a cooler of cream soda." Saul's eyebrows rose. "He never goes fishing without it."

A rusty swing alarmed us of the gate door. Saul tugged my sleeve. "We've got to be quick."

The sky was a thin, greasy yellow, and the air as we stepped onto the porch tasted worn and brittle as dust. We hunched, cowering from the daylight as if shielding ourselves from a storm. I crawled onto the end of the truck and yanked up a handful of tarp. After squirming in backwards until I was waist-deep, I extended my hand to Saul. Half-climbing, half-dragged, he tumbled onto the truck and under the tarp next to me. We whipped it over our heads and flattened ourselves as best we could, pressing close against the wooden planks of the upturned boat as Dalcour's sliding footsteps hefted a cooler through the yard.

With the thump of the cooler against the passenger seat, Dalcour trailed around to the truck bed and paused, the long silhouette of his hand lingering on the tarp – but he only yanked the tarp tighter. Satisfied, he climbed into the front seat, started the engine, and with a rumble that vibrated up and down my bones we pulled out onto the road.

When we arrived in Red Honey, I knew it by the scent. Slowly, the city's colourful smoke, and the clear drinkable air of the countryside had disappeared. In its place sweltered a brothy whiff of algae. From beyond the tarp came the sounds of Dalcour stepping onto the dirt and rounding the truck bed. The ropes holding the tarp in place began to loosen, then unravel, and in a blue sweep like the sky folding in and flying off, our eyes met.

This, of course, had been the intention. The bad catch, which had prompted Dalcour back to Red Honey and pressed him so strenuously for time, made it unfeasible to drive us back to the city, then back to the swamp alone. And, naturally, two children of our age couldn't be left unattended in the truck. Realizing this, with his hands spread against the small of his back, spine bent and head thrown forward, Dalcour paced in circles for a solution that wouldn't present itself.

There was no option but to bring us on the boat.

Within thirty minutes we were floating on the Pearl River. Saul's camera peeked out from his bag, its small but lead-heavy weight balanced against his knee. Dalcour arranged us close to him, and moved with bristling caution. Shoulders raised and back stiff, never fully turning from his brother. I watched as a scaly slice, the shape of an almond, cut through the water and disappeared between spears of bald cypress.

I pointed to the ripples. "Saul, look."

"A gator," he whispered. "There are tons of them."

We glided along a smooth surface of malachite-green, below ghostly hems of Spanish moss. Carmine-bellied snakes coursed through the reeds, and made the sounds of the swamp snap.

All afternoon we settled in pools of light along the bayou, Dalcour dangling traps, passing on his knowledge to Saul who wasn't listening. Come early evening the sky purpled, and swelled with mosquitoes and the shy sparks of fireflies. In the back of my mind Dalcour's instructive low-hum voice ticked, like the dripping of a loose sink. *Tink. Tink.* A shapeless marker of time as I peered into bushes and up trees and through glassy patches of water – and found nothing. The shadows were empty but for leaves and cattail, frogs and crickets, cigarette stubs or shattered bottles whose delicate glints snapped like gator teeth.

Late afternoon, back on the mainland, Saul and I slumped down onto a cooler of empty cream soda bottles. My mood hung low. My legs were on fire with bug bites. "Where's he going?" I asked, when Dalcour chugged his last soda dry and told us to stay put.

"To find a bush." Saul pulled a bottle of calamine lotion from his backpack and squeezed a pink glob onto his palm. "I told you there was nothing going on here."

I stared at the countless bug bites pocking my legs. They were firing up, bloodying my fingers as I scrawled my nails up and down my calves. I thought of Connie all alone, scared, and scratched harder. I had been seeing her eyes at night, in the sliver of moment cushioned between consciousness and sleep. Two amber-black eyes like the darkness just above a fire. I lifted my chin to the descending nightfall, bluing the water and blackening the trees. A thought drizzled, speck by speck, into shape, until it plummeted to my stomach. "What if we looked too early in the day?" I said, straightening.

Saul looked like I had flicked him between the eyes. "What's that got to do with anything?"

"In ghost stories, everything always happens after dark."

"Yes, in *ghost stories*, I s'pose it does."

"I don't mean to suggest," I began, but Saul was giving me such a look of disapprobation that I couldn't bring myself to continue the thought. I looked over his shoulder at the boat – half on land, half on the water. Every muscle in my chest constricted as I stared at the motionless stern, dug deep into the encasing mud – and its other end, rocked and swayed by little nudging laps of water, pointing straight back into the bayou.

I never meant to drag Saul into what followed. To this day I don't remember leaping back into the boat, only a needling urge cutting through me, down to the bone of my spine, until I was flying down the muddy path to the shore. And Saul barrelling after me, fear stricken across his face, Dalcour hollering his brother's name, his frantic splashing as he chased after us. Then, the sharp jolt of a sudden drop in the water – and my stomach tangling with the realization of what I had done, as the river swept out all around us.

∞

We didn't pay attention to where the crawfish swam, or count the screech owls as they squeaked against the sky. We paddled with purpose, drifting further and further into the dense cypress dome.

"He won't tell," said Saul. "Our ma would kill him."

"I doubt Dalcour is so cowardly."

"He might as well just wait a few hours instead of getting everyone in trouble."

I leaned over the boat's edge. "Do you know where we're going?"

"No, of course not. But we'll just keep in a straight line." His eyes maintained their sterling blue calm. "That'll make it easy to find our way back."

"All right," I said, but in my gut grew a familiar unease, like mould spreading along my stomach lining. Suddenly I was caught in the memory I tried to hold off, which always found its way to me, bullying other thoughts away. The backdoor buckling with that crooked click. That bad, bad fear that sank through each layer of my nerves like acid.

The realization of an unbreakable mistake.

Overhead, massive trees extended from one side of the bank to the other, cradling us in the middle. I swallowed, heart drumming. Even if Dalcour reported our runaway boat once he hit town, it was roughly an hour's drive. By the time anyone reached the water to search for us, how deep in would we be?

Spikes of bark shot up through the water, watchful and still, like clusters of crows. I grew restive, chewed my lip. "Are we lost?"

"We're still going straight, you see?" He pointed behind us. "Right from the mainland." His eyes rolled over the scene in a glaze. "I *think* we are."

Around us was so much water. I couldn't see how anyone might know east from west. At last we reached a small clearing, where leaves grew sparser and the light leaked in. As we entered it the sky unrolled, merging with the river, a crease in the middle from the horizon's silver thread. The switchgrass rustled.

"What was that?"

"Nothing," Saul said, gripping the oar. "Just a snake or bullfrog."

I peered through the countless webbed branches. "Connie?"

"Shush."

"You said it was nothing."

Saul dipped the oar into a sheet of algae, coating the wood in clumps of putrescent green. "Shh," he eased, patiently this time. "Bon, I don't know what it is. Stay quiet."

The rustling broadened. Silhouettes were building in the trees. Birds – big, dark ones – batted their wings together with a great *fwomp*. It sounded as though they were gathering wind, balling up cyclones like twine. I couldn't see their beady eyes, but I felt them slide against me like cold marbles.

We continued along a mossy channel, yellow as a dandelion field. The moon had reached us. It was closer than I had ever seen, its glow so strong it looked tangible, a film that I could graze with my fingertips. Across the wide, watery acres, stars glided down the black-ice sky.

They fell like snow. "Saul, the stars are moving. Do you see them? They're all coming apart."

He stared at me with his eyebrows stretched halfway up his forehead. "Bonnie – don't move." His hand reached forward, pointing toward me. "Your nose," he said. His eyes were fixated on my face. I touched my fingers to it and wiped off a warm streak of blood. Saul paled, turning the spongy white of seasickness. He took my clean hand in his own, and I couldn't tell which one was shaking. "What's wrong?" he asked. "Why are you bleeding?"

My fingers gravitated toward my sister's bloodstone necklace. I had been wearing it ever since we saw it in the Bellrose photograph. I felt around my chest to find it, clutching it through the cotton of my dress as I rose to peer through the gathering mist. There was a shape. Not far from the rocking wooden pod of the boat, a drizzly film of moonlight wound into a slithering figure, like phosphor-dust that had once decorated a person, but now only hovered in the brief illusion of form. I blinked and my vision blurred, as if the dust had blown into my eyes.

"Bonnie, sit down, you're going to tip us over."

Saul, I tried to say, but I couldn't speak. The shape was moving toward us. I could feel a shriek building in my lungs. *What's happened to you, Connie? What is this place?*

Bonavere.

Whispers came to me in a dozen voices. The sound of them stung my heart, as longing and primeval as the howls of the French Quarter dogs at night, restless for one another. Barking and howling and wrestling against their chains.

I snapped straight as a bleached breeze enveloped me.

Bonavere, went the whispers.

The shape drew closer, spiralling like a cyclone, and in its eye I saw a windstorm of crumbling crystal.

"We have to follow the shape in the dust," I said. Contours affixed to nothing, they weaved in and out, then trickled downward and dissipated in the distance. "It might lead us to my sister."

"What are you talking about? What dust?" Saul asked.

We stood still in the centre of the boat, the only sound the dry whistle of dead leaves blowing from the cypress.

∞

Dawn was nearing. A yellow streak wedged itself between the overhanging night and the tops of the tallest trees.

"No way am I going any further. We're lost." Saul leaned his oar against the side of the boat and caught his chin in his hands.

I set my own oar on my lap with waning confidence. The shape had faded and not so much as a twitch ran through the water. My arms shook from exertion, my muscles were frayed, but still I gripped the oar like a weapon. I looked down the bank, in the direction the shape had gone, where a rock pinnacle shot up in giant spears.

"That's strange," Saul said. "The trees look sick."

I squinted through the darkness, and my veins chilled. "Just the leaves do." Blood-tinted tupelo spotted the bank all the way to the rocks. "They've gone all red."

I lifted the oar and sank it head-deep, my arms squeezing to a burn that bled all the way to my spine. Black ash drifted up from the trees and scattered across the sky, flapping before the bright pearl moon. In a moment I saw that I was looking at dozens of blackbirds, breaking away from the forest like burnt bark.

As we reached the rock pinnacle, a stretch of tall tupelo snuffed out any lingering light. A dull shiver ran through me at the stillness. I scanned the water, but heard only the engulfing splashes of sinking creatures not far enough away.

"There's dry land up here," I said.

Saul's oar made a thick wrinkle in the water as he quickened his pace.

The sharpened stone rose around us, and beyond its thick, grey walls the bank curved into a forest, the sight of which cut me through the middle. Bright red leaves erupted in a scarlet boom of blackgrum trees. I hadn't told Saul about the red forest, the leaves birthed of blood. He wouldn't have made anything of it. *Just stories*, I could hear him say, like I had said once, too.

We paddled the boat toward the woods and wedged the stern in the mud, resting our oars by an oyster bed. As we stepped onto the bank, the spongy peat welcomed our feet with soft hisses.

"Forget the boat," Saul said, as we tried to haul it further in. "It's not going anywhere."

I didn't want to leave it with its bulk half in the water, but my arms were like sandbags crawling with fire ants. I sat there motionless. I heard how my breaths shuddered, like they were tumbling down a staircase. *Get up, Bonavere*, I told myself. *You're here, get up and find her.*

At the forest's edge stretched stout palmetto, waving me into its girth with ghoulish green hands. "Don't move from this spot," I said.

"You can't go off on your own, Bonnie. You'll get lost."

"We *are* lost."

"You'll get lost *alone*. Big difference."

I stared into the dense darkness of trees. "Someone needs to watch the boat. I'll come back before I lose my way."

I knew that he was motioning to stop me, but I had already approached the threshold of the woods. As I walked I rubbed the mud from my eyes and swatted at clingy moss catching in my hair. My breaths were wet as if punctured, bleeding air, as I stumbled over roots and through the sinking peat. I felt how fuzzy and blank my mind had gone, everything blipping in and out with the sweep of some translucent panic. *Where am I? What am I doing out here?* I breathed Connie's name as I panted. Each syllable burned a hole inside of me, flaming through my throat.

Then, in the lilac-light of dawn, there wavered an unexpected sight. My eyes watered as the mild wind whipped against me, but I saw well enough – a small house in a clearing by a brook. Perhaps a wash-house, or a fisherman's cabin. Whatever it was, it looked bomb-blasted, post-apocalyptic, with a chimney collapsing through a torn tin roof and curtains reduced to soiled strips as browned as bandages. Part of the roof had caved in, the hole canopied with moss, and sludge was pawed across the wooden planks like a mudslide dragging its fingernails. In a story, this would have been where the witch lived, luring lost children into her candy-bricked trap. I peered over my shoulder through the forest. *How long would it take to run back?*

In front of the house, tin pots with dribbling rust stains lay toppled around a fire pit of charcoal-smeared stone. Along the twisting branches of a stately willow stretched the string of a laundry line. The clothes were dripping, freshly washed. The string sloped in the middle with heavy male clothing, but pitched tight at the ends, only lightly weighed by winter-blue blouses, the kind a girl my age might have worn.

"The Scarecrow Witch," I whispered, searching for a bedraggled stuffed figure. Only, that couldn't have been it. The Scarecrow Witch was just a story children told to spook each other. That Fritzi used to torment me, draping our mother's crushed-velvet shawl over her face and lunging at me from darkened corners. "Get a hold of yourself." I shook my head, scratched the spurs from my hair, swatted at the bloody bites on my neck.

At last I forced a firm step forward, and in that instant my skin squirmed. I felt every tiny fragment of my body as surely as I felt my elbows and knees. *Something bad happened here.* My stomach clenched. *Something horrible.* The sensation shot through my spine in a fluid sting, like liquid lightning. There was hurt in this place, I could feel it. Sadness and fear balled into fists and intertwined with fingers.

"Connie?" I continued to draw closer, my boots squelching in the mud. The sound stretched wide over the quiet and within the little house, something moved. My foot, mid-air, twitched back, as the florid face of a woman appeared in the window.

I fell over in shock through a pepper-puff of mosquitoes, palms smacking the dirt. My lungs squeezed. *A person, all alone out here?* The sky reddened in wisps, veins bursting into smoke. It matched the woman's blistered face as she emerged from a cracked wooden door.

She looked predatory. Her sight glided without focus, twitching to the side like the oscillating eyes of an old dog. She sniffed as she roamed in a tattered shirt of muddy plaid, large enough for a broad-shouldered man, which hung well past her starved, rickety-legged figure.

"Ma'am?" I called. Fear grappled at my throat.

The woman's head snapped in my direction. Her black haystack hair jerked with it in one stiff movement. "Get!" she said, shocking me with speech.

"Have you seen a girl in these parts?" I unlocked from my crouch, still cowering into my torso. I took a step backward, balled my hands to my chest. "I'm looking for my sister!"

"Get! Go away!" She swatted at the air.

"If you haven't seen her, *please* say so." It was all I needed from her, a fibre of reality. *No girl in the swamp, lost and scared. No girl but you.*

I began to approach the woman in small, wobbling steps. As I neared her the smell of the shack's panels grew, and I saw how the wood moulded in grimy fractals. The woman eyed me over her shoulder as she turned to walk away.

My heart flung forward. "Wait!" I lifted Connie's bloodstone from underneath my collar. I didn't know why, but I held it out for the woman to see.

She halted. With a slow hiss she asked, *"Where did you get that?"* She narrowed in on the talisman, her eyes like broiling tar.

"It belongs to my sister." I lowered my arm and cupped the peculiar piece to my chest. Suddenly, I didn't want her to see it.

"Give that to me, little girl..." She swung at me with fingers tipped with rash-red tines, and for a startling moment her face was clear to me, underneath the dirt and sunburn, where young skin had been dried to harsh desert rock, and bright eyes glittered in clear oases of blue. The part of her resembling any young Southern girl stepped into the trickling sunlight. Her ravages

eviscerated by a stunning show of grief. She didn't look much older than Fritzi. We stood still, staring at one another in a sudden, shimmering descent of rain.

Hardly aware of myself, I was listening to her. Lifting the bloodstone, ready to hand it over. *What has she seen? What grief brought her here?* Until her eyes widened, and her teeth chattered, and she looked about to rip my arm from my body. The stone shot back to my chest. "Daddy!" I shouted with a hurried glance through the woods. "Daddy, I'm over here!"

"No, no, give it! Give it here!" Her upper lip quivered.

"My daddy is just down by the water. He's right down there, so don't you come any closer. I'll scream." The house's mould stung my nose with a wave of revulsion. This woman was sick, I realized, as my legs and stomach weakened – and nobody knew where to find me.

All at once she lunged for the necklace, scabby-rough hands grabbing hold of me. I twisted against her, the suffocating stench, balling into myself as I squirmed out of her arms. Her caterwauling shriek following after me as I lurched back into the woods.

I ran as pine branches racked my face. Ran and ran to the pulse of my guilt, *I'm sorry, Connie, I'm failing you, I'm failing you.* But louder still was my sister's voice – and maybe it was fear distorting my senses, but it came to me in Connie's feathery timbre and it screamed at me to *keep running*.

Bleary-eyed, I tripped through endless foliage. I lost my boot in peat like sinking sand, had to tug my foot free, run it bare and bloody against the ground. My ears were so deaf with wind and my own rush of blood that it took me a long while to notice that nobody was following me. I wrapped myself around a massive root, knees burrowing into a puddle, and cried until my throat felt sandblasted.

I was out of breath by the time I reached Saul. The rain had settled and the sun, in full, emerged.

"Bonnie! What happened?" He hurried to his feet.

I collapsed before him and dragged myself onto the boat. I felt like I was dreaming; how could I explain to him what I had seen?

Spurs covered my clothes, digging through my hair and prickling my neck. "Where's your brother?" I asked, panting. "He would have told someone by now." Panic swelled in my chest. "Dalcour wouldn't just sit in the truck all night waiting. He drove back to town. He told your mama what happened." In the silence that followed an arrhythmic chill ran through my body, stirring my blood and breath out of place. "Even if he didn't, Fritzi would realize I wasn't home, wouldn't she? She would look all over the house for me, she probably didn't go to bed at all last night, she'd have been so——"

It hit me. *She'd have been so scared.* My heart slid down the back of my chest. I felt it slap through my stomach, smack against my kneecaps and burrow, filled with shame, into the peat below me.

Fritzi. I hadn't considered her. I was so immersed in the desire to find one sister, I had completely abandoned the other. I curled into myself, my head heavy. She was probably sitting alone in our bedroom at that very moment, feeling like the last person on the planet.

Countless red leaves fluttered overhead, bleeding across the sky. I lay shivering in the heat, the microscopic fibres of my nerves in tight convulsions, listening to the busy sounds of a new morning. Birds squawking, water rippling, little splashes out of sight.

I stared up into the dark, wiry blackgum. Where was Connie, if she wasn't here? The more it sank in that I didn't know, that I might never know, the more a crushing vastness collected upon me – flake by flake, like ash. *I will never see her again.* A split through my chest. *Will I ever see her again?* The vastness blew through me – grey, wide, empty rush of a wind tunnel. It was where she lived now, wasn't it? This vastness? A timeless and untraceable landscape. A place where the heart swings back and forth, between hope and fear, like a primal pendulum. And in vanishing she swept her sisters off to this place with her, where we would live forever staring out from its deep unknown. Waiting, until the pendulum stilled.

Bruce Meyer

THE SLITHY TOVES

This isn't something I can put in an academic paper, yet it is the story of how my career in academe was made. It is not something you need to take as fact; very little of what I am about to tell you about how my research evolved actually matters now that the real facts about Lewis Carroll are widely known. That said, I was the one who discovered those facts. And what truth about Lewis Carroll did I discover? He was framed.

I understand what Lewis Carroll had to endure. The very *thing* that ruined him made me a target of its destructive force. That *thing* was not scholarly jealousy or even the disputes that embroil graduate students and supervisors in a quagmire of distasteful behaviour. Far from it. What plagued the author of *Alice in Wonderland* was the same *thing* that appeared in my childhood garden and haunted me through the early decades of my life. My St. George-like struggle against the thing began one summer day when I was three.

When the petals of the blooms on the red rose trellis turned grey, my father sweated and delved to discover what was killing the bush. He idled for a moment to investigate the damage, and then plunged his spade into the brown earth. Over and over again, he turned each scoop until he had exposed the rose bush's roots. He stabbed the spade into the grass, wiped his brow, and removing his shirt, hung it on the thorns before going into the cellar to find a box of rose food for the roots. As soon as he was gone, I pulled the heavy tool from the ground and poked the soil with it. I slapped the mud and scraped the bole until small, fleshy wounds appeared. Something stirred.

A large yellow worm slithered through the muck, entwining the base of the bush, circling as if swimming in the flower bed. Its body wriggled and writhed. I poked it again and again with the spade's pointed blade but I didn't have the strength behind my parries to wound the worm. I jabbed it harder and harder, hoping to split the thing in two, driven by curiosity to understand what it was.

The puce-and-black-striped body surfaced. It sprang up at me, hissing and snarling. It stood on its haunches and shrieked into my face. I began to choke and gasp. The thing's face was that of a woman's contorted into a grimace. Its black painted eyebrows were raised in anger. Its matted black hair and red lips parted over jagged and rotten teeth.

I dropped the shovel and ran into the house sobbing and screaming.

I stuttered to my mother that *it* had stung me. My mother bent and checked my arms and legs for signs of a stinger's welt.

"Did a wasp sting you? Where did it bite?"

I pointed to my heart and sobbed.

"Nothing has stung you. You are imagining it."

It was real. I woke up screaming for nights afterwards. I saw it. It, whatever it was, lived in my mind. There were no words to describe it. I would see it screaming into my face, its breath worse than the odour of rotting brown marigolds. I knew she was there in the silence of the dark, waiting for me to return to that part of the garden where my father dug out the dead climbing rose.

The thing wanted to steal my breath.

The doctor diagnosed me as asthmatic.

Each time I went into the garden for the remainder of the summer, I sensed it was there somewhere, hiding behind the lilies, lurking in the delphinium, or waiting twined around the base of the mountain ash tree. The Baltimore orioles that sang in the tree's high branches vanished. She, that thing, had driven them away. She was watching me. It was impossible to breathe outside. Lilies wilted before her. I watched them wither and brown as a bugle of earth tubed through the flower beds. The berries on the mountain ash turned black and fell as if drops of poisoned rain.

One morning, I found the orange koi I had named Ramsey floating on his side, his belly torn open, in our ornamental pond near the raspberry patch. His eye reminded me of an eclipse. It stared at a sky it could no longer see.

"It must have been a raccoon," my mother said to console me, but I knew it was the thing beneath the trellis. How could something bring such lovelessness to a garden?

That is when I lost track of eternity. Time came to my childhood garden and the snow fell. The world turned grey. I watched from my window as something slithered beneath the snow, diving in and out of the white drifts as if it was a joy to be among the thorns and dead things. My mother stared out the window at the thing's tracks. "We must have a fox out there, so be careful when you are playing. It might be rabid."

Whatever *it* was, by the following spring I had forgotten *it* existed. Children bury their fears. We moved to a new house, and the garden where there had once been no time became a myth to me, and I grew up.

In my final year of high school, I spent spare periods in the library reading the entire eight books of *The Caxton Encyclopaedia of Art*. In the middle of volume L to P, there was a full-colour pull-out of the ceiling of the Sistine Chapel. I borrowed the librarian's magnifying glass and pored over the page. Each panel, each Sibyl and prophet, was inspired by the centre panel in the ceiling that weighed upon the shoulders of each prophetic seer. The hand of God reached out to infuse a mortal digit with the splendour of life.

In the panel to the left of *The Creation of Man*, Michelangelo painted the moment of human tragedy, *The Fall of Adam and Eve and Expulsion from The Garden of Eden.* There, wrapped around the Tree of Death, handing the Fruit of Knowledge of Good and Evil to the first couple, was the thing I had seen in my backyard.

It had the head of a woman and the body of an iguana, but Genesis 4 tells us God amputated the arms and limbs of the "*subtil* serpent" as punishment for bringing Sin and Death into the world. God tells the serpent that men will tread it underfoot for having wreaked havoc on mankind. The serpent disappears from the Bible, and I began to understand where it went.

Was I fighting off a harbinger of death in a place dedicated to life and beauty when I poked the thing with the spade? Was I a St. George, slaying yet another dragon?

Michelangelo Buonarati was not the only painter to have known that thing. Later Renaissance artists painted the same scene. Holbein gives the serpent in the tree flowing locks. Dürer paints breasts on the beast. No matter how the motif was treated by the Great Masters, the shock and the revulsion of what that creature brought to mankind served as a constant reminder that there was always something horrid lurking beneath the topsoil of a garden. I had met that moment in my childhood. It was my own Fall of Man.

The more I stared at the pictures of Adam and Eve and the serpent in the tree, the more I recalled of that moment in my garden. The thing had a long tail wound around the trunk of the tree as if it would choke life from everything it touched. I started to question whether my horrific childhood memory had been a psychological mask for something else. I had read articles about abused children. I told myself it was not my parents' fault. I had a good childhood. But when I closed my eyes at night and tried to imagine the future, the thing was there shrieking at me with its black eyes. I told myself my imagination had better things to do.

I fell in love with reading and that took my mind off my childhood trauma, whether real or imagined. I went off to university the following September to study literature and see where my imagination, sans thing, would take me.

At the frosh welcome-weekend pyjama party, we were given numbers to pin on our backs and told to go and look for a member of the opposite sex with the same number. It was a means by which the college could maintain its gene pool. I was still very much a virgin, and the idea of meeting someone with whom I might spend my college years cuddled naked in my dorm room was tantalizing. Throughout the evening I danced with girls who caught my eye, but who did not have my number. I should have gotten their telephone numbers or asked them more about what classes they were in. But I was determined to find "my match."

Not long before midnight, a young woman with blond hair, protruding teeth, and a heavy flannel nightgown came up to me.

"We share the number," she said, removing my number from my back and presenting me with hers. Without talk, she motioned me onto the dance floor. When a slow dance started, she pressed against me and whispered in my ear, "I want you. Let's go to your dorm room now."

The worm turned inside me. I suddenly lost control, yet marvelled at the thrill of the experience. She stood between me and my bed and drew the nightgown over her head. Her body was smooth and white and I wanted to touch it. As I stepped out of my pyjama bottoms I saw her left thigh illuminated by the glow of a light from outside. A lump was moving back and forth beneath her skin.

"I hope this doesn't kill the moment, but is there something wrong with your thigh?" I said, and pointed. It was wrong of me to point, but the moving lump inside her leg, like a tongue rolling in the wall of someone's cheek, was putting me off.

She lay back on the bed, tossing her hair to one side, and reaching down, slouching slightly onto her right side, she wriggled out of the lower half of her body, set her legs on the floor beside me, and then pulled the blond wig from her head and spit out her overbite to reveal black teeth. Her yellow and black tail rose up and waved in the air, curling and beckoning me to come closer like someone gesturing "C'mere" with their index finger.

"I thought you had forgotten me," she whispered and began to sneer.

I opened the leaded casement. "'Come to the window, sweet is the night air,'" I said.

"'Ah, love, let us be true to one another.' I adore it when a willing young man quotes 'Dover Beach' to me."

She leapt toward me and I caught her at length. She was just about to wrap her arms around me, her black claws suddenly protruding from the tips of her sham fingers. And at that instant when I held her, the palms of my hands burned and began to blister. I turned to the window and flung her out.

She thumped off a dumpster below and screamed shrilly as her body hit the ground. Then I picked up her wig, teeth, and her lower half, and tossed them after her into the alley. I closed the window and pulled the drapes shut.

My heart was pounding. I washed and washed my hands, put my clothes back on, and ran into the night toward the crowds on Bloor Street. The all-night student hang-outs looked like safe havens by the time I reached Bathurst Street, and I found a bar with its music thumping and a waitress who was only too willing to serve me as many Jack Daniels as I could buy. I came to my senses several hours later in a doughnut shop, a Korean man standing over me with a carafe in his hand, asking me if I wanted more coffee.

I never felt safe in my dorm room after that night. I obtained a roommate named Ramsey who never seemed to leave the room or the concubines he kept there. I did most of my sleeping in the student common rooms between classes. The night of my first attempt at sex was also my last go at it for the next ten years. The thought of having sex with my childhood nightmare was abhorrent to me.

As the leaves turned orange and red around the campus, and the sky burst into that brilliance of blue that can only say "I am dying in the most beautiful way," autumn came to the world of my freshman year. The yellow and purple mums in the planting bowls along the walkways shrivelled and browned. I knew it was her doing. She was lurking in the quads and behind the college walls to suck the life from my world. I stopped giving a damn about worldly things. The only thing I knew I could trust was literature, and I found my passion in Professor Lamoore's class. I heard my new love's voice rolling over and over in my head, its lilting music echoing a power of perpetual spring. "Whan that Aprile where its shoores soote…" Her name was poetry.

By November, when snow was falling in soft, heavy flakes outside a classroom window, I watched as Professor Lamoore leaned against the sill of the window. He was talking nonsense, literally. He spoke about what it meant to craft a new diction and to use it to describe the heroic act of slaying a dreaded beast.

> *Twas brillig and the slithy toves*
> *Did gyre and gimble in the wabe:*
> *All mimsy were the borogoves,*
> *And the mome raths outgrabe.*

Lamoore was an older, plump man who sometimes teetered as he leaned on a wall or propped himself against a desk as he lectured. He had taught my mother during her undergraduate years. His bald head always shone and reflected the brightness from the ceiling fixtures. With his midland accent, the rolled r's and hard consonants took on a lively guttural edge. He leaned over to me as he finished reciting the poem from memory. "Now, what was that?" he asked.

"Gibberish."

"Not quite. It was 'Jabberwocky.'"

The class sat in silence. Some knew the poem and sighed with a 'Let's get this over with attitude.' From under his arm, he produced a copy of *Through the Looking Glass*. Lewis Carroll's book had sat on my bedroom shelf during my growing years, but it was the one volume I could never bring myself to read, and I could not recall why. Perhaps I was frightened by the pictures. Then I forgot it was there.

"The poem is, essentially, a folk ballad in the tradition of 'Lord Randall' or 'Sir Patrick Spens.' We'll talk about the structure and function of the ballad as a poetic form in a few minutes. But there's something unusual about what Carroll does to the poem a few chapters after it is presented in *Through the Looking Glass*. A good poet is like a good magician," Lamoore said, as he thumbed his way through the pages of the little book. "A good magician, a good poet, never explains his tricks or how they work, unless he gives in to great temptation and is trying to prove something. Lewis Carroll must have had a professor or a *grammarian* lecturer at Oxford not unlike me. In Chapter Six, Alice meets a big egg named Humpty Dumpty who relishes in exegesis. Exegesis is the art of explanation. Humpty sits on his wall and professes, and critiques, and insists that everything must mean something. And so, he explains the meaning of 'Jabberwocky' to Alice. Humpty Dumpty recites the first verse of the poem, just as I did, and then he goes on:

"Well, 'slithy' means 'lithe and slimy.' 'Lithe' is the same as active.' You see it's like a portmanteau – there are two meanings packed up into one word."

> *"I see it now,"* Alice *remarked thoughtfully: "and what are* toves'*?"*
>
> *"Well, 'toves' are something like badgers — they're something like lizards — and they're something like corkscrews."*
>
> *"They must be very curious creatures."*
>
> *"They are that,"* said Humpty Dumpty: *"also they make their nests under sundials — also they live on cheese."*
>
> *"And what's to 'gyre' and to 'gimble'?"*
>
> *"To 'gyre' is to go round and round like a gyroscope. To 'gimble' is to make holes like a gimlet."*
>
> *"And 'the wabe" is the grass-plot round a sundial, I suppose?"* said Alice, *surprised at her own ingenuity.*
>
> *"Of course it is…"*

I left Professor Lamoore's class that day with a sudden interest is Lewis Carroll. I knew I had met the Slithy Tove and likely so had the author of *Alice in Wonderland*.

Carroll's illustrator, John Tenniel, depicted the tove in the 1871 edition of *Through the Looking Glass* and got it wrong. The badger suggestion, on Lewis Carroll's part, was a purposeful piece of misdirection. Maybe the author meant wolverine but understood that English readers would not be acquainted with a vicious North American creature. Perhaps Carroll wanted to hunt the tove himself without giving away too many clues of what he was looking for. Why? The tove was more lizard-like than badger-like, but its claws and arms, to say nothing of its foul disposition and its cheesy breath, were *suggestive* of a badger.

But what was Carroll really saying in his strange, Victorian, roundabout way? What was he trying to tell the world about that thing in the garden that appeared from under the sundial, the thing, like a dragon or serpent he had contended with, the source of agony and struggle he failed to defeat? The more I looked at Carroll's writing and his life, the more I understood the horrors endured by Charles Lutwidge Dodgson – Lewis Carroll's real life alter ego.

I believed Dodgson was not only someone who had encountered the creature but who had been plagued by it. I became convinced that the tove hated innocence and happiness. The tove spread rumours. The tove whispered in the ears of those who harboured doubts about others, and who wove those doubts into jealousies. The tove poisoned the world. For years I had been living with the nightmare of the slithy tove. And she was there, on campus, watching me. She was waiting to spoil every good thing I tried to do. I vowed I would confront the creature and in a battle of wills, wits, strength, and skill, kill it or die trying.

When I was kicked off the editorial staff of the college paper without any other reason than that I was constantly distracted and looking over my shoulder, I knew it was the tove that had planted the seeds in the brains of my fellow reporters through some nefarious means. She was persistent. When I went into dining hall, no one would sit with me. I would try to converse but the other students would just look at me and then move their trays. I tried to overcome attacks on my reputation – the sort of college stuff that always happens. I thought that by being a good person, the kind of person who lends notes and offers to buy classmates a coffee, that I could overcome her effects. I thought I had overcome my troubles, but then she struck for real early in my third year.

My roommate, Ramsey, was found dead.

The window was open.

His body was grey and pale as if something had sucked the life out of him.

His hair had turned white just before he died, and his face was aged and lined, even though hours before he was young though slightly overweight. The coroner could not determine cause of death.

I knew it was the tove, but a person can't just go around saying the cause of death was a fictional creature from *Through the Looking Glass*. I told the police I was an insomniac. I had been out all night. I had. I had been putting back coffees in the Korean doughnut shop. The security camera footage from the coffee shop and a variety store where I'd stopped to buy a chocolate bar supported my story. My professors felt sorry for me, and the leniency I received on my final papers helped me to keep my gold medal and win a graduate scholarship overseas.

Lamoore and his wife were proud of me. I was his prodigy. The couple would hold regular teas in their Victorian "house of grace," a gift of free lodging from the college that was a safe haven for ideas and literary talk. I was always invited to their gatherings. Lamoore and his wife, Gamba, would welcome acclaimed authors or renowned scholars as their guests. Just to sit there and listen to the stories the guests shared was a tremendous privilege. The teas were a part of my education that prepared me for my later work. One day, after I had been accepted on a special scholarship to Oxford, Julia Cassidy was a guest at a Lamoore tea.

Mrs. Cassidy was the wife of a strange but troubled professor whose brilliance and temperament had mixed within him in an unusual way. He was kind and generous with his time, but unorthodox in his classroom demeanour. Word around the campus was that he was headed, so it seemed for years, towards a death by alcoholism until one night Professor Cassidy could not get a drink and he hanged himself. His widow, Julia, had the countenance of a suffering angel and an air of wisdom about her. She was someone who carried a very old soul inside. During the course of the tea, Mrs. Cassidy quoted from Rilke's *Duino Elegies*.

"He sounds inspiring," I said. "What's his name?"

The words "Rainer Maria Rilke" sang off her tongue through her flowing Irish lilt. "Have you not read Rilke?" she asked with patience in her voice. I shook my head. "We shall have to see to that." She smiled and went back to her dessert.

The next day, as I was packing the few things I could take to Oxford with me, the porter came to my door with a small package. The outer envelope said simply: "Do not open until you are on your way." I abided by the instruction. Halfway across the Atlantic as the dawn was just beginning, I reached into my carry-on and opened the envelope. It was a copy of Rilke's volume of advice to literary types, *Letters to a Young Poet*. I could hear her voice in the inscription: "In your moment of greatest need, Rilke will provide the answer to your question. Be well and journey bravely, Julia Cassidy."

I settled into my room at Christ Church College. The ceiling was slightly vaulted and the stone doorframe, fireplace, and leaded windows made me feel monastic. As I lay in my cot the first night, I looked up at the vaulted ceiling where it met the cornice. In the nineteenth-century plasterwork a strange bubble bulged that made me think the pipes were about to burst.

I stacked my chair on top of my desk and reached as high as I could to touch it. If the roof was leaking, I wanted to know if I was going to be deluged in my sleep. The moment my fingers hit the surface of the brittle plaster, the bulge burst and a withered grey corpse I mistook for a large cat fell to the floor with a thud. Someone from a nearby room hollered, "Keep it down in there, you bloody sod!"

Despite the fall, the corpse's sinews held the body together. The skull cracked slightly on impact. I could see the remnants of an upper torso with nothing below the waist but a long series of vertebrae tapering to a point. The skull looked partially human, but attached to the sides of the cranium were small horns. The finger bones were tipped with claws. Here was the skeleton of a tove.

I didn't want to touch it with my bare hands. I had seen how toves could suck the life out of a garden and, having flung one out the window of my dorm room and burned my hands, I didn't want those painful blisters again. I put on the heavy leather gloves I had brought for winter, and when I touched the corpse, the palms paled as if the tanning was being drawn out of the dead lambskin. I piled the remains on my desk and stared at the corpse. Here was the proof I needed that the tove existed. But why was it here? Why this room, my room?

In the morning I went to the dean's office, not to tell him about my zoological discovery (which I hid in a paper bag under my bed and transferred to a rental locker at Oxford Station later that afternoon), but to ask who had previously lived in my chamber. I was handed a large black ledger. I poured through the names of previous students who had occupied my room until, under an entry for the Michaelmas Term, 1851, I found the name Charles Lutwidge Dodgson. I was living in Lewis Carroll's old digs.

A number of theories began to run through my head. Had the tove harassed Dodgson throughout his life? Had it come to his dorm room just as it had to mine to claim him as a prize? What if the tove had crawled in through a dove cote in the stone eaves, become entangled in the medieval masonry and died there? Had there been other toves that mistook the absence of one of their own for murder? What if they had sought retribution against Dodgson for the disappearance of one of their own?

In studying Carroll's life, I had been puzzled by his missing diaries. There are four missing Lewis Carroll diaries. The absence of these volumes has been used by his detractors to indict him for adultery and even child abuse. The volumes in question date from 1853 to 1863 and include the years that Carroll spent completing his studies at Oxford and the years when he spent time with the children of a local clergyman, Henry

Liddell. Several Carroll supporters argue that he was in love with the eldest Liddell daughter, but focused on amusing her younger sister, Alice, with his labyrinthine tales of logic and fancy that became *Alice's Adventures in Wonderland* and *Through the Looking Glass.*

The Liddell home is still standing in Oxford. I researched the name of the current owners, a family named Framwell.

Carol Framwell was quite perky and enthusiastic when I called. "Of course I am a Lewis Carroll fanatic," she bubbled. "I adore living here, and we bought the home because of the Liddell connection. I shan't be here, but do come around on Saturday afternoon. My husband will show you the house."

When I arrived, I was greeted by Richard Framwell who wanted to give me a Cook's tour of the interior.

"I'm not really all that interested in the inside as I am the outside," I said, and he looked disappointed. He was a D.I.Y. man and I think he wanted to show off his handiwork. "I want to see the garden."

We wandered around the back and stood in the rain. I had my umbrella up. Richard Framwell is one of those Englishmen who is impervious to water, and he merely tucked his hands in the pockets of his brown oilcloth jacket and remained dry.

"May I ask what specifically it is you're looking for out here?" he asked.

"This is where Lewis Carroll took most of his photographs of the Liddell children, if I am correct." Framwell nodded. "What I need to know is the location of the sundial."

"The sundial? As in slithy toves? You aren't secreting any Stilton, are you?" He looked disconcerted and then smiled with the hope that I would catch his allusion. I laughed, and then realized I had made a very unscholarly if not absurd request. I put my finger up to my lips to motion a hush to him. I did not want the tove to overhear, though I could not tell my host that.

"Do you have trouble growing roses?" I asked in a whisper.

He shook his head, and continued talking in a full voice, ignoring my attempts to keep things in a hush. "I am an ivy man, myself. Holly and ivy. Great Christmas fare. Funny," he continued, "you should ask about the sundial. I found the base of it. We have it in the shed, if you'd like to see it. It was there, about ten paces this side of that old oak, though I suppose in Lewis Carroll's day it was exposed to the light far more. I was digging there several years ago and I had a strange experience. The mud started moving beneath it. You don't suspect it was a tove, do you?" He chuckled. He was testing me. I shook my head.

"You don't mind if I poke around, do you? I want to get a sense of the place."

"Be my guest," he said. "I shall put some tea on, so please join me when you are thoroughly cold and soaked."

I stood gazing at the spot where the sundial had been.

I could hear the birds chirping and the rain pinging on my umbrella. In the patter and the silence, save for a few distant rumblings of motors, I thought I could hear a conversation. An articulate, polite male voice was speaking softly to a young girl. She was giggling.

"*That's enough,*" Humpty Dumpty interrupted. "*There are plenty of hard words there.*"

"*And what are they?*" the child asks excitedly.

Suddenly, she screams and points.

A yellow and black worm slithers from beneath the sundial. It rears its head and snarls at her. The young man grabs the child to shield her. He raises his walking stick and strikes the creature from different sides, grasping the stick lower and lower to put more power into each blow.

Snicker, snack.

The thing with the body of a lizard and the head of a woman screams in pain, but despite the man's best efforts to protect the child the worm is around him in an instant and lunges at the girl.

In the melee the man's box camera and tripod are knocked to the ground.

He thrusts his walking stick repeatedly *through and through.* The beast retreats beneath the sundial.

The girl's white dress is torn. He checks to see if the child has been injured. She is sobbing, and he is sobbing, and neither knows what to do next.

"We have to have evidence of this terrible thing!" he cries to the child.

He sets his camera upright and squeezes the shutter lever. The child looks like an urchin. Her dress is a shambles, and in her empty, lifeless eyes there is terror. "Tell no one of this," he says as the garden door of the house opens.

The commotion in the garden has brought the servants and the girl's mother from the house. They have heard what he has just said.

The girl's mother stops, hugs her daughter to comfort her, then stands and looks at the man. There is a look of dismay and horror in the mother's eyes. She strikes the young man who falls weeping to the ground, and picks up the child and carries her to the house.

Through his tears, he tries to make sense of the shouts and accusations being hurled at him by the girl's father. The young man looks up, and in the undergrowth of the garden's edge the tove is sneering at him through the smile of her black teeth. She has won her victory. Charles Lutwidge Dodgson is ruined.

The young man writes in his diary that he can explain. He records the incident moment by moment. He has developed the photograph of the young girl in the garden. In the lower right-hand edge of the image, because the captured moment has survived the ravages of time and been labelled "The Beggar Maid" by

Lewis Carroll scholars, the bushes are blurred as if something is moving among them. He knows the truth. The girl knows the truth, too. The world refuses to listen.

"Hello, my travelling Canadian friend."

I look up from my moment of imagination. It is the tove.

She has emerged from the spot where the sundial stood. She brushes the dirt from her forehead. She seems surprised that I am not surprised.

"We meet again," I say. "You seem well-travelled or are you an English tove? Was that you I tossed out the window of my dorm?"

"You broke my heart, you little bastard."

"Only your heart? You got off lucky. Had you a pelvis you might not have been so fortunate," I reply, smiling back at her. I refused to let her get the better of me.

"Had I a pelvis you might not have gotten out of your room that night. I could have given you a night to remember."

"I'm sure of it, but such is life. So, what are you planning to do to me now? You seem to have come a long way to join me in my graduate studies. Bored with Toronto, are you? Bring it on. I'm ready for you."

The tove hissed. "You were born on St. George's Day. You are a sworn enemy of dragons, and toves, and beasts of the netherworld. You think you're very brave, cavorting here with your sword or an umbrella, but you are nothing."

"And your point is?"

The tove hissed and looked away as if it could not find a rebuttal.

"May I ask what your name is?"

"Agatha."

"Well, Agatha, I've been charting your progress through history. You have a charm for appearing in great works of art – the Ceiling of the Sistine Chapel, paintings by Dürer, Cranach, Holbein, and so many other old masters. You must be proud of your species. There's a point of literary symbolism that has always puzzled me, however, and I hope you don't mind me asking you now that I have you here, simply because I'm curious about such things, but is the serpent in great works of art Satan, or Lilith, or you? And how many of you are there in your species?"

"Lilith was my sister. She was the one who ruined Eden. She was Adam's first wife – did you know that? He threw her away, though not from a dorm room window. They didn't have second stories back then. She has been a great fascination to great men. They felt honoured to know her, but they all cast her aside. Then the dreadful Dodgson came along and murdered her. She went to him to seek his love one night, and I never saw her again! Do not patronize me with Darwinian zoological categorizations such as 'species.' I would have ruined that laggard Darwin as well, but he just stared at me and started taking notes. A man more interested in finches than rare creatures. Boring sod."

The tove who floated like a gyroscope on her corkscrew tail started to turn away then spun around.

"We stayed alive for centuries by sucking the life from living things. There were two of us. Just me and my sister. It's only me now. I haven't seen her in over a hundred and fifty years. That bastard, that man of two names took her. But I showed him. I ruined him by tearing that little girl's dress then stealing his evidence. He could not defend himself, and so the world ate him. It sucked the life from him. He may have been Lewis Carroll, but polite society called him a child molester. And no matter how hard he tried to bottle that life in every word he wrote, the cloud always hung over him. It still hangs over him. He will spend eternity under a cloud. And I put him there! I put him there! And because you follow in his footsteps, you, the dragon-slayer, the flimsy knight of swords and spears, I will destroy you, too."

"Yes, but I'm not a child molester. I am a celibate. You did me a big favour that night. Clear head, healthy loins, I like to say."

She shrieked: "I will destroy you utterly, not just in this life but for all time. You think you're a young man on the rise. You have not seen what I can do to you. And no matter how hard you may try to put the life of the world into words, you will never succeed because I will be there to pull you down into the shadows where no poetry can protect you."

I determined to stay calm despite my hate for the thing. "Wow. Right. So, exactly what did you do to take his evidence?"

"I stole his diaries! I went to that horridly beautiful little girl as she lay sleeping in her room up there, and I told her, just as he had told her, that if she ever revealed the truth I would destroy her and all her family. The frightened little bitch kept her silence, so I destroyed her, too, by making her hold her own words until she finally choked on her own silence. And Dodgson struggled to tell the truth for the rest of his life, and everyone thought it was fantasy."

"I see. I have a proposition for you, Agatha." I looked the tove in the eye as if I was playing poker. "I have a deal for you."

"No deals!"

"Okay, your loss. You'll never get the bones of your sister back."

"You have my sister's bones! Where did you find them? Give them to me."

"Uh-uh. That is, unless you give me something in return. Something I need."

"What is that?" hissed the tove.

"The missing diaries of Lewis Carroll, a.k.a. Charles Lutwidge Dodgson. I don't think you're the kind of creature that would steal something, other than the colour from flowers and the life from a man's body or soul, only to throw it away without thinking it might come in handy at some point down the line. Well, this is some point. I think you're a greedy tove at heart. You need trophies. All dragons and slithery things need trophies, shiny things to keep at the bottom of a lake or in your nest or wherever you hang out. You're a collector. A creature like you is probably very clever, perhaps a natural hoarder, a cataloguer *par excellence*. Classification is what drives you. It keeps you functional. It keeps you centred. You'd keep something you take so you can use it later and fawn over it in the meantime like a treasure. Well, Agatha, now is later. If you have them, if you have the diaries, I'll make a trade of the body of your sister for the volumes. If you don't have them, well, kiss Lilith goodbye. If that rattles you, then bring it! I'm ready for you. I've spent my whole life preparing for our final struggle. And remember, bones are easily burned or ground-up or, worse, put on display in the Museum of Natural History in London."

"Not the Museum of Natural History! Not that damned Darwin house!"

"Alright. Do we have a deal, then? Diaries for bones? And pardon me if I don't shake your hand to seal the bargain." She humphed and spun round and round, then glared at me.

"Where and when?"

"On Addison's Walk behind Magdalen College at 3 a.m. tomorrow morning. That is where we'll do the hand-over. And remember, no diaries, no tove carcass. And don't plan on pulling any fast ones or Lilith goes to London!" The tove sneered and screamed and burrowed back beneath the spot where the sundial had stood in Lewis Carroll's day.

I got three soccer blokes pissed on multiple pints of Morrell's at a pub halfway down the road to the railway station. I persuaded them to help me roll an empty oil drum all the way to a spot in an area of Oxford known as Mesopotamia where Addison's Walk becomes a patch of wilderness beside the headwaters of the Thames, a river given the ancient name of the Egyptian goddess of the darkness, the Isis. When the chaps rolled off, likely in search of an off-licence, I built a fire in the oil drum and waited.

I stood in the cold, foggy night and watched as the frost etched itself into every crevice and edge of leaf. I gathered some rubbish papers and some kindling sticks and threw them into the flames until I had a nice blaze going. I found a sharp alder rod among the debris and set it aside as my lance, taking my Swiss Army knife out and whittling the end to a very handsome point. I was glad I had brought my heavy leather gloves. I also remembered to bring a bottle of brandy with me to give me strength in the dead of night in case my courage faltered.

Uncorking the bottle, I took a swig and set it open on the ground. I muttered the words "And lo, though I walk through the valley of the shadow of death, I will fear no evil, for Thou art with me." And as I said that phrase, the image of Julia Cassidy popped into my mind. I heard her speak to me in her lilt: "In the moment of your greatest need, Rilke will give you the answer."

What had Rilke said that I was overlooking? I shook it off. I wasn't there to think about Rilke. I had a beast to deal with.

The river whispered in a low *shhh* as it touched the banks and poured over stones in its flow. At my feet, in a bag retrieved from the railway station locker, were the mortal remains of the great seductress, the "subtil" serpent that had brought about the fall of Adam and Eve. Agatha approached out of the fog, winding forward on her yellow and black tail. The tove's head was held high, as if in glory. She had an old blue and gold biscuit tin tucked under her arm.

"That's far enough," I said, my back to the lighted oil drum as I raised my alder lance. The flickering flames illuminated the outline of the tove. Her shadow rose up against the woodland. "Put the cookie box down," I instructed her.

"It's a biscuit tin, you stupid colonial."

"Whatever. That's far enough."

"Show me the bones."

I held up the bag.

"Open it!" she screamed.

I opened the bag, reached in, and held up the corpse. The tove gasped.

"Now show me the diaries." She pried open the tin and her claws made a scratching sound like fingernails on a blackboard, and the purple-covered notebooks tumbled to the ground.

"You know, you really are your own worst enemies," I said as I shook the dead thing at her. "I found this thing in the ceiling of my room at Christ Church. It must have gotten stuck and died in there when it came to torment Dodgson. He did not kill it. It got stuck and died. You've taken your temper out on the world and ruined a man for nothing. You are nothing but rage and hate. So was your sister. What had Eve done other than be like Adam? I can just imagine Lilith, trapped in the space between the plaster and the vault of his room, exhausted, begging for a mercy that would never be hers for what she had done. And she died because nothing can suck the life out of stones."

The tove lunged toward me in rage. I reached down, grabbed the bottle of brandy, and splashed it in her eyes. She screamed and held her claws up to her face, tearing at her brow.

"I will kill you now!" she shrieked as her vision came back to her. I grabbed the corpse and tossed it in the burning barrel.

"No! No! Our deal! Our deal!" And as Agatha leapt up to bite my face with her black fangs bared, I ducked, and the slithy tove went flying over me into the flaming barrel, hissing, writhing, and clutching at the bones of her sister. I reached down and grabbed the bottle of brandy and emptied it into the fire. The brandy ignited her eyes which became two meteors of wrath. I thrust my lance over and over into the tove's belly.

"*Snicker snack!*" I shouted, and watched as blue feathers of brilliant light leapt toward the stars and tindered a green dawn where the river flowed south and east to become Father Thames.

"T'was brillig and the slithy toves did gyre and gimble in the wabe,"…said Alice, surprised at her own ingenuity…

"Of course, it is. It's called 'wabe' you know because it goes a long way before it, and a long way behind it, and a long way beyond it on each side," Alice added.

I watched as the flames consumed the contents of the barrel and the pyre dwindled to ash and embers. As the flames died, I thought I could have made a name for myself with the zoologists, but then again strange creatures that unnerve scientists are usually debunked. The missing diaries were my treasure. When I looked over the lip of the barrel, there was nothing left of the slithy toves.

I had to wait for curfew to pass before I could return to my room. I strolled up and down past Parker's bookstore and paused to look in the window at the latest bestsellers and imagined the book I was about to begin writing there among the Byatts and the MacEwens. But what I saw, as the dawn crept silently through the streets of Oxford, was my own reflection against a display of copies of *Through the Looking Glass*. What had I done? I had killed something primeval that had followed me like a shadow through my life, and I was free and so was Lewis Carroll.

When the porter finally opened the gate, he grumbled something under his breath about blighters being out all night. I didn't catch what he said and I didn't care. In my room as I lay on my cot, thumbing through the lost diaries of Lewis Carroll, I suddenly realized that I was sitting on one of the greatest literary finds of my era. The secret was now mine, and I would redeem my lost author from his century of purgatory.

May 5, 1862

Went to see the Liddells today. I had so much more of the story of the looking glass world in my mind since I last saw Alice. I wanted

*nothing more than to share it with her, to see her face light up with
that rare sense of joy in discovery she possesses. Speaking to her in those
moments was like prayer. One feels divinity is listening back. But as
we were deep in our legend, a terrible thing happened. The creature
that has pursued me all my life, the daemon that destroyed my childhood garden, appeared from beneath the sundial and accosted us. It
tore Alice's lovely dress and frightened both of us within an inch of our
lives. I struck it repeatedly but it would not be beaten. I tried to photograph the thing, but it slithered away, slimy, and lithe, and active.
It was that awful lizard with the head of a woman and the body of
a serpent. Mrs. Liddell was the first on the scene. She assumed the
worst and screamed and struck me. Mr. Liddell arrived and with a
blow grabbed me and cast me to the ground. He bent down as if he
was about to strike me again with his fist, but I kept repeating that I
was only protecting Alice, shielding her from the awful thing.*

I would need to come up with a good story. "Where did I find
these diaries?" I knew I would be asked.

"Oh, well, a slithy tove and I did a deal for the bones of the
serpent that brought about the Fall of Man."

Right. Not good.

I understood Dodgson's predicament.

A week later, I was down in London at the Bermondsey
Market. I'd spent the night at a friend's place and then took a taxi
to the market square just before dawn as the vendors were setting
up in the half-light. I felt as if I was back on the battlefield with
the tove. There, I found what I was looking for.

On a table crowded with silver and bric-a-brac, I discovered
three identically bound Victorian diaries belonging to a lady
who loved mice. Coincidence? I call it blind luck. I got a receipt
from the dealer with an item description and a date of purchase.
In any case, I had my provenance. I'd found them at an antique
market.

I would need to bear out their authorship and provenance, but the handwriting and content would support my claim. The British Library Reading Room is a scholar's best friend. I had made my career and slain the enemy of mankind in one fell swoop.

A year later, the proofs for my groundbreaking biography of Lewis Carroll arrived with the morning post as I was cleaning out my digs at the college. I was on my way to Harvard where I had an appointment in the English Department. The porter was adamant, great breakthrough or not, that I would have to be packed and gone by 10 a.m. for the cleaners and painters to start their business. And there was the matter of the hole in the ceiling. I would have to pay for that. Where would he send the final bill?

That is when I opened my desk drawer and found the copy of *Letters to a Young Poet* by Rainer Maria Rilke hiding behind the paper clips and post-it notes. My eyes fell on Julia Cassidy's inscription and the line "Be well and journey bravely." But what was the question Rilke was supposed to answer for me?

I flipped through the pages of the large type. There is not all that much writing in Rilke's book, but I tell others that it is worth reading. I had never noticed before, but in the same pen as Mrs. Cassidy's inscription there was a tiny star in the margin that caught my eye.

> *"How could we forget those ancient myths that stand at the beginning of all races, the myths about dragons that at the last moment are transformed into princesses? Perhaps all the dragons in our lives are princesses who are only waiting to see us act, just once, with beauty and courage. Perhaps everything that frightens us is, in its deepest essence, something helpless that wants our love."*

Maybe now I could go forward with my life, meet someone I could fall in love with, marry her, start a family, and plant a garden of my own. I imagined walking into a faculty meeting in Boston in the coming weeks where I would be introduced as the man who saved Lewis Carroll and, afterwards, at a stand-up reception, perhaps over glasses of wine and chunks of gouda, I would meet that person. Love is the one thing that human beings have of their own to give. It is the one thing they have of their own to keep. And it is all we have to protect ourselves against the monsters who reside beneath the sundials and other thresholds of time.

I tucked Julia Cassidy's little Rilke book in my coat pocket and put the box of page proofs under my arm. I stepped out the door of my digs, suitcase and future well in hand, and stood looking at the world ahead of me, ready to journey forth to fight more battles. I turned and looked over my shoulder. The orange, yellow, and pink flowers in the porter's small garden patch beneath his lodge's window were blooming brightly in the morning sun.

Frank Westcott

IT WAS A DARK DAY ~ NOT A STORMY NIGHT ~ IN TUCK-TEA-*TEE*-UCK-TUCK

CHAPTER ONE
I LOST MY BALL ~ THE GOLF COURSE ONE

IT WAS A DARK DAY ~ NOT A STORMY NIGHT ~ IN TUCK-TEA-*TEE*-UCK-TUCK. Yu thought I was gonna say FUCK. Tuck-ter-up-tuck or fuck or whatever it was you thot I was gonna say. Like that. But I didn't. I said tuck-tea-ea-ea-up-tuck. Without the exa ggeration on the tee or tea. Tee 'em up sayeth the wizard or wizardette. I can't remember. Was so long ago. *ANY way.* Lost one in the war. Like I said. Wished I could tea 'em up one more time. From the golf course one more time. Would aim straight. Me. Right at the hole. Putter notwithstanding and cold and metallic and clunky especially when the ball dropped into the hole. The clanging thing that clunked. *Cement mixer putt tee putt tee.* Deeply. With Dizzy Gillespie. When your ball dropped. The only one I had left. The other lost in the war. Like I said.

Wished I had another ball to drop. Got distracted by a high flying Bird (Charlie) and remorse and sorrow (Billie) and waved at a wing on a feather and rejoiced forever more and forot my ball in the cup and walked away. The war. You know. Left it there. No tee either. Last one in the bag fell through a slot in the bag where a knife ripped thru the material and the tea bag, no tee bag, teething, fell through onto the course and grass where we walked yesterday. Too. IN the dew. Early. When rains came and washed evidence away from our feet of where we had bin and were going, in this celebratory wonkiness, even if we didn't know how to punkuate and spell out our stories and wanted one more ball...to tea it, *tee-it,* up one more time.

The gymnast, doing back flips on the green, and peeling money out of her pocket in mid-air waving it at me. The money. Honey. Her butt. And wiggling her toes just before landing. She was good. IN this stream of consciousness air she travelled in looking for my ball. The first one lost. The wife. Who ate my ball and squished the life out of me as she raped me with her money grubbing heart. I lost *that* ball. If you get what I mean. Wife who choked on it and killed herself in manic depression and psychotic episodes spreading pablem all over herself instead of the baby. And throwing things at me. And maybe the baby. I hated her for that. Creating the worry. What she might do to the baby. So I stayed home. To protect the baby. And never golfed again. Or played hockey for that matter. Loved hockey. The challenge. The Rocket. The flow. The Belliveau. The ice. Man-cometh notwithstanding LeFleur. And the sound of blades on ice chipping nuance out of movement, supermen dancing like Dina Ross, make that *Diana Ross* in her youth, before she got fat and didn't dance so much. But farted in the song while the music was playing along and her feet not dancing like they used to. She always smiled. At the fart spots. IN a song. But everybody thot she was smiling at the song. Something in the song that made her heart tingle or jingle, or bell ring out of that numace, friendly as it was and only smelling like yesterday's dinner because she digested things slowly. Especially now that she was older. She digested more slowly every day. But she still sang at the same strange tempo for every song in the track of time she reminisced about on the stage of The Venetian where people remembered her as she was, then, before, and saw nothing about the now where she was fat and old and moved differently, but joy-ed in the fact she was still singing, still teeing-it up, and her audiences loved her. Still. IN the memory of time. And me searching for balls on a course long played and lost to and forlorned one more time many times. And she with fingers splayed over the keys of a piano in memory of herself and bowed at the end of the stage performance to reminisce about how it was and never would be again and her daughter and grandchild cried in the stands where everybody sitted in memory or their memories that they had yesterday before the show started.

I looked, of course, for my other ball. Hoping to find it not sunk into oblivion in some desert course where memory linked up with time seeking refuge, nothing important, just a place to rest, and ref, and *uge*, trumping time with the Donald Truming at another hotel in golden Vegas, signs under skies of sorrow and remorse, wondering where the Donald had gone, ducking a quack or too at the audience having lost *his* balls when he played someone else's course and ran for President.

Go figure.

Balls wipe tees of glory out of golf bags wet from the morning dew and this isn't a story, it is a recollection out of time, twisted by memory and tees and tea and Diana Ross dancing on a stage out of home memories where photos and phone booths still existed, and people were not just taking 'selfies' to adorn Facebooks, and internets and surgeon themselves in operations of gold, self-indulging themselves, wanna be's in the making, when only and all they are doing is acknowledging their existence. To themselves. Because nobody else is doing that. Self-seeing their existence. Other than a "like" or two on something they post which gives them credence for more. Posts. Of self. And heart. And start. Starting to reminisce before their time is up. To reminisce what never was. Reminisce: a revenge against the future.

I went searching for that ball. The last one. In an old bag lollipopping out of mind for years in a backroom where I kept it, and found only wife number three and realized I hadn't met her yet. Or if I had I hadn't met her yet as a wife, so didn't know her as a wife. Couldn't. As I say: Can't know something as something before it exists as that something. So, if I knew her as a person, I couldn't know her as a wife if she wasn't. Yet. SO, I left it to the muse and angels, if either existed, to figure it out. To lament. Talking about non-existence. And where we get the where with-all. Somebody asked once where my stories came from.

"Got me…" I said.

"Got you?" she asked.

"You got me here. There. & everywhere," I said thinking of the Liverpudlians and a song they beetled out of nowhere into *Nowhere Man* and wrote *Here There and Everywhere* too, singing forlornly of drums and metro-nones-&-kowns behind the beat, and Paul McCartney had to re-do the track in time with night, when he went back into the studio when no one was looking, and did it right…the timing…and had tea after, and during and set the record straight, back in the day they still made records instead of ituning downloads in cyberspace to your device and ear, wishing you could just hear. Sound clouds be damned. Cloud music sounds like an angel's whisper on a wing of prayer, Aretha Franklin-ing *Respect*, hoping to be a song but too distant in the ear, from the ear, to sound like music or an angel shitting herself, and dropping out of the sky. Then I thought I hoped angels didn't exist, if they started shitting listening to music from clouds, and I clouds, and u clouds, and cybernuts butting their heads against walls of cyber-fabric nuancing nothing, and Taylor Swifting themselves out of old tunes iShaking i-it Off, one more time, and hoping angels didn't know how to shit too. Down a hole. Or if they did, didn't. That'd be shitting bricks for walls of Jericho tumbled down as somebody blew Gabriel's horn, into plasmacy of sound anew, out of old histories making no sense, but sounding like music. And Quincy Jones smiled.

I lost my ball and wanted to Lawrence Welk it and follow the bouncing ball of the tune out of destiny, bring it alive once more. But I culdn't follow it or the tune without the ball. Even if the music played on.

CHAPTER TWO
THE SONG SANG ITS WAY OUT
OF A HOLE ~ A GOLF HOLE

So here we are. WE are. At this point in the story. The non-story that this is. Without a plot. Or spelling. And the plot is a grave you buried your hat in hoping no one would find it. But when they dug you up. They found only your hat and you had left. Already vacated the premises. Rent due. Paid up. Before due. And you left without a word. A typo in the memory of plains and planes flying in and out of Vegas where Angels fear to tred only. When they have their gambling shoed on and forget their wings at hme and look like evrbody else.

There is romance in the novels of form and less formlessness…a thing of the past and future 'cuse it can't be form unless it is formless, and how can formless be form anyway. And if formlessness is a form, then it has to be formless before and after, in its form in the past and future. The present I have trouble with. It sucks. The past I know. The future I forsee. But the now…what the hell is that? You lose your ball in the now, and go looking for it where you *think* you lost it, and hope to find it in the *future*, 'cause you aint got it now. You aint got it in hand. So I wad the streams of the past and future. Wade. That is. But you can wad them if you want. Plug them up. No flow. Just adman the dam of consciousness, so you don't recognize the past and the future, and you think you only lost one ball, but you lost them both. The first wife ate them. And the second wife had none. So the kid wasn't yours. But you treated her like a daughter and her kids as your grandkids. 'Cause there is more to being a father than DNA.

"It aint about blood," the angel said looking like a dream lifted out of a lament in Vegas shoes and glittering gold dresses. She wore more than one at once.

"Why are you looking like an angel?" I asked.

"Because I am," she ansered once and twice, and then again making it thrice. I put more ice chips of nuance in her drink and…to see if that would help.

"You ARE an angel or YOU ARE looking like one?" I asked.

"Both," she said. "It'd be hard to look like one, if you weren't one. And you'd be an impster if you did."

"Impster? You mean imposter," I said.

"No. Imspter. An imp being a playful kind of thing. An imp-ster. New word I invented on my way down."

"Down?" I asked. "down from heaven…the heavens…Le Fleur…a sky thing?"

"Escalator," she answered. "Took the escalator down from the main floor."

"To the casino."

"Well this isn't a spa," she said and jangled black and gold $100 chips in her angel apron. I couldn't know if she was an imposter, impster or angel or what. She looked like all three.

"I dress for all occasions," she said. Thus the dresses. Plural. Fits. Kind of fluffy don't you think?"

"Cloud-like," said I. "Icloud, u-cloud, angel-cloud…some cloud. Cumulus, anyway."

"Always liked cumulus," she said.

"Why?" I asked.

"Makes me think of cumilingus," she answered matter of factly.

"A raunchy angel," I said. Or at least one who's a look-a-like angel-thing-person, doing it up right to look golden. Frailed. I mean finged. Fringed. Beaded. Gowned in sorrow and remorse, angel singing in the background where Diana Ross calls Aretha out in response, out of respect, while she does *Swing Low Sweet Chariot*. Never seen a chariot. Don't know if how they can swing. Swing low. That's it. That's what Aretha and Diana does do in the Monetingmoment, where I listen to sounds of this angel breathing look-a-likes out of her nostrils of heavenly wifts and wafts, she pretends to portend. Maybe she's a which in wolves' angels' clothing. Note the plurals. Angels. She wears three dresses.

CHAPTER THREE:
THE FINAL ONE ~ WOLF BARKING AT THE DOOR ~
LIKE A DOG IN WOLF'S CLOTHING & THREE DRESSES

Back to the beginning. IT WAS A DARK DAY ~ NOT A STORMY NIGHT ~ IN TUCK-TEA-*TEE*-UCK-TUCK. Yu thought I was gonna say FUCK. Tuck-ter-up-tuck or fuck or whatever it was you thot I was gonna say. Like that. But I didn't. I said tuck-tea-ea-ea-up-tuck. Without the exaggeration on the tee or tea. Tee 'em up sayeth the wizard or wizardette.

I was beginning to think this being, this angel in drag, was a glittering cocktail waitress of old, in high heels, dress underwhich she wore a short butt-tight, high-thigh, thong thingy, making her look like a glittering sequined queen of cocktails, cockatoos, cunts, cockadoodle, any-cock'll doo. Didn't lift her dress. Make that dresses. To find out. Can get arrested for that. Even in Vegas. But I looked anyway. Between my teeth. IN the mirror. And watched as she hoisted her dress. Another and another. To let me see she wore cocktail stockings, and a bustier brace that showed her boobs if she bent over, but she didn't and didn't lift her dress, dresses, that high 'cause they, the dresses were tight at the waist. And I wondered if I was tight. At the girth and in alcohol count. 'Cause how'd and wh'd look for golf balls in a casino in Vegas when the course was outside up the street and no swings there where you were in the casino, waging war with an angel look-a-like wanting to gmble her life away, under cigarette trays, Lucky Strike, Cohilas, Camels, in the sky of the old days when you could get hookers, and trays and a smoke all in one pack, standing in front of you in the shape of a cigarette girl with Betty Grable gams.

I looked at her and wondered. "Were you that cigarette girl in another life? Tahoe maybe. IN the seventies? The forties?"

"Yup," she said, spreading her wings like she was with John Travolta in a bad movie and worse costume, the backing by and Paul McCartney's band with Linda, not stuck on this bird look-a-like angel thing, *Wings* doing *Jet* in the 1974 *Band on the Run*-ing it, out of time when this angel-bird-cocktail waitress-cigar smoking, cigarette dispensing, wannabe oldie, rocked in Vegas or Tahoe or both. In the 70s when bands rocked and there was no "CJ," or no "Country Jazz," the "CJ" way…to bring it, music, back to where it belonged. Sounding like a song. Tee-ing it up with respect shown. And there was a wife number one. INStead of some hip-hop disaster, only a clutter of clatter, sounding like subways click-clacking their tracks ~ tracking their tunes, alleged, out of times past when a song was melody instead of the natter we spoke of just now. And I look at this angel wanna be, three dress 'n all, and wonder how I got there. Here. To get there?

"You took the escalator," she said.

I danced a little jig. Two stepped, and East Coast three stepped, and wondered how I learned to dance that way. Hadn't before.

"Early lives," she said.

"What?" I said.

"Early lives," she said. "You learned…knew…how to do that in earlier lives before this one."

"Oh how many lives have I had?"

"Four," she said.

"Four?"

"One, two, three, four…straight ahead…beat. Tap-tap-tap-tap. Four. Beats to the bar. Like that."

"Are you a which. Witch?" I ask.

"Which?" she said.

"What?" I asked for explanation, asking, "Who's on first?"

"That's right! Who is on first. With Abbott and Cosstello. But you asked if I was a w-h-i-c-h, like which way did she go? Then you said witch, w-i-t-c-h, as in with a broom. That flies. And you ride."

"Cool," I said. "I mean the latter one with the broom."

"I take elevators. No…escalators. Take elevators too. But hard to hit the buttons."

"With your wings."

"Yes. John Travolta figured it out. He just stuck his finger through the feathers."

"The Bird flappin' finger or the Peter Pointering flappin' finger?"

"Neither and either. Angels only have one finger when they wear their wings. So they flip birds and point."

"And push elevator buttons."

"Yes," she says. "If you can get yur finger out of the feathers enough to find the button."

"Did you find my golf ball?" I ask.

"Yup. Right here in my wing pocket… Right under my skin. Here. See?"

I reach under her skin. Her feathers. She calls her skin her feathers. Or the other way around. I can't find her pocket. Only hemoroids. Suppossistories.

"My ass!" she says.

"What?"

"You got your finger up my ass."

She inhales and smells of smoke. Cigar and cigarette combined. She farts like Diana Ross in song, and sweet smells Aretha out of a melody in the rafters, where she reaches when she sings gospel. And I wonder where I have been and reach for my balls, and find teo, *two*, and wonder where the one I lost in the war went, and where the two went that my first wife ate, making me ball-less for wife number two, where I fathered the child anyway. Who *does* have my DNA, I found out later. And the grandkids are mine. And so is she. The daughter. The baby.

"So you wanna go golfing?" asks the angel, the cocka-two-itll-doo person, heavy with wings.

"You got balls?"

"No…but you do," she says, bent in sorrow and lament over the hole where a clanging thing had been heard to clunk.

I smile. Go for tea. The pot kind you put a bag in. And purr, pour, from a spout. I linger at the tea table and drink my honey with it, and wonder where she went, the whatever, whichever, witchever, it was, is, I had these conversations with…while trying to get my balls back. Find them. After I had lost them. And I realized I hated balls of the white dimpled variety you smack off your tee, with a club in your hands, when all you need are what's between your legs to swing with, and only one club, not a whole bag full. I know the (?) angel did not/does not exist. OR the witch, if that's what she was. But the wonky story does. Celebratory in the writing. And that makes it all true. Mark Twain said so.

"Tee-uck-tuck. Tea anyone?"

Martha Bátiz

PATERNITY, REVISITED

for Eduardo Pavlovsky

White and blue flag; blue and white sky. It's hard to tell where one ends and the other begins. It's a sunny day – a crisp spring morning that smells of recently cut grass and newborn flowers. Sunday. The surface of the river sparkles like satin with sequin embroidery. The Río de la Plata is bigger than she remembers; it's profound, dark, and endless, like the sorrow it was forced to keep in secret years ago. The park has not changed, and apparently neither have his habits, because he's right there, where she was expecting to find him. Where they used to sit every Sunday morning to watch lazy boats going down the river, eating *medias lunas* and sipping *mate*.

She fights the urge to turn back and run away. Her shaking fingers and the palms of her hands – sweaty, sticky – make her feel weak. Unprepared. Her body has always been wiser than herself. It has always made her vomit or be blinded by headaches at the right moments. An ingrown toenail, she once read, means that you're not ready to move on with your life. As if to punish her feet for playing tricks on her, she spent most of the previous evening scratching around her toenails until they bled – cutting a bit of skin here, a piece of nail there, digging deep into the flesh. Now the improvised bandages are bulky under her well-worn running shoes; walking is painful, and she's forced to let her weight fall on her heels. *Everyone must be thinking I walk funny, like a duck. What would they say if they knew why I'm here? That small boy riding a bike with his father running close behind him; the woman pushing a stroller; those young people jogging…*

The man is sitting on their bench, his back turned against her. She can still leave, but why bother coming all this way only to give up at the most crucial moment? She takes a deep breath and small, careful steps towards the all-too-familiar bench. Stopping a couple of feet behind him, she examines his thick, silver hair. It used to be dark brown once, and she remembers it being soft. But not as soft as hers used to be. What if she found a big rock and hit him in the head with it? One swift, precise movement, an impulse stemming from the depth of her fury. Her purse is heavy on her right shoulder so she switches it to the left, and looks around to see if there are any big rocks nearby. Is anyone looking? Just then, the wind blows her way and the smell of his cologne hits her first. In a flash she's eight again, longing for his embrace – and she freezes. How can her body be such a traitor? And then, as if this were a conspiracy, her shadow betrays her, too, and he turns around. When their eyes meet, he lets out a faint cry.

"Adriana!"

Taken completely by surprise, she adjusts the baseball cap she has been forcing herself to wear for a while now, and which she had hoped would make it harder for him to recognize her. She looks right and left, wondering if running away is still an option, but his eyes are magnets that force her to stay put.

"I knew you'd be here," she whispers.

It takes him a few seconds to react, but once he realizes it's truly her, he immediately stands up, arms wide open, his eyes brewing up a storm. She doesn't reciprocate, but a lump forms in her throat. The air is fresh and clean and yet she finds it hard to breathe. Aware now that a hug is not to be had, he slowly puts his arms down and points to the bench instead.

"Want to sit down?" he asks without drying the tears rolling down his withered cheeks. She clumsily opens up her purse and takes out a tissue packet. After handing it to him, she takes a seat, placing her purse between them. A barrier she hopes he won't cross.

"You know my name is Paula."

He gives her a look like the one she once saw in a dog that had just been run over in the middle of a busy intersection. A dog she didn't stop to help because she was running late for an appointment that was important for her at the time. She has forever felt guilty about leaving the dog there, whimpering. Hurting. It has been years, yet Paula still feels ashamed of herself whenever she remembers. A dog she could have helped but didn't. It still gives her sleepless nights sometimes, her mind running different scenarios around what she could've done differently. Wondering if he, this man sitting on the bench beside her, has ever felt the same way. How such feelings play out when you're talking about human beings and not dogs. Does death by indifference – death by inaction – have a name, other than murder?

"Paula, yes," he says after a long silence. He can't stop staring at her while fidgeting with the tissue, turning it into a small ball between his hands. "You've not changed at all."

Oh, yes, I've changed. You've no idea how I've changed, but instead of saying so, Paula smiles at him without showing her teeth.

"Have *you* changed?" she replies, fully knowing it's a loaded question.

"I never stopped looking for you, Adr...Paula. *We* never stopped looking for you, waiting. Hoping you'd call."

No. Now it's obvious to her that he hasn't changed. He has aged, of course, but remains good at dodging the topics he doesn't want to touch. She wants to say: "I was never yours to look or wait for," but a hummingbird sipping nectar from a beautiful orange flower distracts her for a moment. How many times has she heard people wishing they could fly away and leave everything behind, like birds? But one thing life has taught her is that you can never really leave. That wherever it is you fly away to, you always drag your misery along. Human beings are made up of 70% water and 30% of their past; what is done to them is indelible. This, Paula knows for sure.

"I was very far away. I couldn't…"

He doesn't let her finish her sentence.

"I understand, baby girl. No need to explain. What matters is you're here now! You have no idea how much I missed those blue eyes of yours."

He used to say her eyes matched the flag, and that she should be immensely proud of forever carrying her homeland within her. When she grew up, however, Paula couldn't bear looking at herself in the mirror, so she wore dark contacts. She said they were a fashion statement and liked them because they matched her mood, her fate – and the horror of thinking her eyes embodied everything she had lost, or grown to hate.

"How's Ana María?" she asks, proving she can also dodge a subject that makes her feel uncomfortable. He frowns, and looks down at his shoes. They're clean and shiny. Spotless, as usual. His Sunday shoes. He has probably been to mass early that morning. In contrast, she hasn't been to church after leaving the country. Her ability to pray and to believe is lost: yet another loss for which she has to thank him.

Instead of answering her question about Ana María, though, the man lifts his hand and tries to hold hers. Paula leaps up from the bench as if stung by an electric current.

"I'm sorry! I'm sorry!" he apologizes, looking mortified and gesturing clumsily with his arms.

"Don't touch me!" she hisses, instinctively raising her voice. A man walking his dog stops to look at her. The dog then decides that's a good place to defecate and goes ahead, without a care in the world, taking its time. Paula holds the man's gaze until he's convinced everything is fine. When he notices his dog has finished its business, they both walk away – without him first cleaning up after his pet. *That's why this city has become a minefield, a shit-field.* She had spent the previous day walking around the city trying not to step on dog waste left randomly on the sidewalks, crossing paths with several dog-walkers who, much like the ones in New York or Toronto, were holding up several leashes. But here they were completely incapable of stooping down to clean up, utterly oblivious to what they were doing to their own hometown. *A perfect reflection of what this country is about. Too bad no one else has yet realized that the greatness of a nation can also be measured by how many of its people are actually willing to clean up their own shit.*

"Please sit down again, baby girl. I'm sorry."

She takes a deep breath…and a seat on the bench once more, only this time a few inches farther away from him. He puts the tissue ball inside his pocket and places the tissue packet close to her purse, between them both.

"Ana María died," he says, biting his lower lip. Paula takes in his words slowly; they hurt like stab wounds. She has been hoping to see Ana María. Hear her voice, smell her perfume. *Anaïs Anaïs*, all the rage while she was growing up. A few years ago, she found a small bottle of it at a discount store and bought it. She dabbed a little of it on her pillow and cried. Helpless; alone.

"How did she die?" she gathers the courage to ask, her eyes blue and salty and frail, like glass.

He pauses, looks down at his shoes again, as if that's the place where the right words to say can be found, lifts his gaze and fixes it on the river. A small boat is passing by. Children can be heard laughing.

"You don't need to know. It doesn't matter."

"Yes, it does!" she replies firmly. "I want to know."

He shakes his head, no.

"Tell me! I have a right to know!"

He pauses for a few seconds before releasing the bomb.

"She killed herself."

Paula puts her fist into her mouth and bites it. It's what she does when she doesn't want to scream. She wants to ask why, but can't articulate a single word. He seems to understand, however. He could always read her and knew what she wanted before she could even express it.

"She just never got used to it."

"Used to what?" she asks in a barely audible, high-pitched voice.

"To life without you."

She buries her face between her knees, hugs her legs tight, and cries. Loud, intermittent sobs. Her shoulders are shaking.

After a few minutes, Paula lifts her head, wipes her face with her T-shirt, and when he offers her a tissue, slaps his hand as hard as she can, surprising even herself. His hands used to seem big and strong. Now they're bony and riddled with age spots. He retreats, suddenly afraid of her.

"How dare you blame me?" she justifies herself.

"I don't blame you. I'm just telling you the truth," he replies, rubbing his hand where she hit him. "She couldn't live without you. No: she didn't *want* to live without you. I did what I could to help her, but it was useless. We just missed you so much!"

She rises to her feet and walks towards the river. The water is calm and deep, brownish. Nature's perfect hiding spot. *No wonder they used it to dump bodies.* A colossal oxymoron, this dormant beast in front of her: its water a motherly womb that embraced the dead while still nourishing the hopes and pride of the living. At least of those who still have hope and can feel proud.

"I wish you'd let me explain things to you," he says, getting up as well and approaching her at a safe distance, the back of his hand still slightly red. The park has been slowly filling with people, families having fun, playing. The way the man and Paula used to do in another life, once upon a time. "And you shouldn't leave your purse unattended back there on the bench. This is not Canada, you know? People steal a lot here," he adds.

"So you knew where I was," she says, without turning to look at him.

"Yes," he replies, blushing slightly.

"And you never came to look for me. Instead, you let Ana María kill herself."

He brings his hands to his head. It's obvious to her that he's unable to hide his desperation.

"Adriana, don't be so unfair, I couldn't just go looking for you! And I saved her twice before she finally succeeded."

Funny how he attached the word *success* to the word *suicide* as if it were the most natural combination. *Don't forget who you're dealing with. Why you came back.*

"No, you couldn't just come looking for me, that's true. And my name is Paula!"

He lets out a sigh that sounds almost like a grunt.

"Please. Let me explain."

Paula waits a little; knowing every second of her silence hurts him. She *wants* to hurt him, and enjoys her small power before finally relenting.

"I'm all ears," she says, adjusting the cap on her head, closing her eyes, letting the sun caress her face. Here, on the other end of the continent, the sun feels different – apologetic, perhaps. As if trying to make it up to you for the chaotic state of affairs in the land.

Before starting what he knows will be an even more difficult dialogue, the man walks back to the bench to fetch Paula's purse, flinching, probably at its weight, but he's sensible enough not to ask. He simply places it on the ground close to where they are standing now, and they both can see it. Then he tucks his hands into his pockets, and gazes into the horizon.

"They were shitty times, baby girl," he says finally, after what seemed to Paula like an eternity. A boy runs past them, chasing a red ball. Laughing. Neither the man nor she manages to smile.

"We were at war."

"Tell me something I don't know. And stop calling me baby girl."

He nods, defeated.

"Well, we were at war and—"

"And whose side were you on, huh?" she interrupts.

The man takes his hands out of his pockets and cracks his fingers, one by one. Paula cringes. She forgot this is what he does when he's nervous or upset.

"I love this country. I wanted it to be safe, a country in unity. And there were people doing everything they could to prevent that."

"People like my parents, you mean."

He chooses not to answer.

"They were putting bombs everywhere. Blowing up people's houses, buildings. Creating chaos. If you didn't shoot the hell out of them, they'd shoot the hell out of you. That's simply how it was."

"So that's why you and your friends had to burst into their houses, to kidnap, torture, and kill them, right? It was the patriotic thing to do."

The man is shifting his weight from one leg to the other, clearly not knowing what to say or do. Paula looks at the river and remembers he doesn't know how to swim. She wonders if she could get away with pushing him into the water and letting him drown. Death by drowning is silent.

"I didn't kill anyone, I swear."

She finds it impossible to remain silent.

"You did – just by working *with them.*"

Another boat goes by. People wave. They don't respond, and are booed for their lack of enthusiasm. Someone, a teenager, probably, calls them party-poopers in a shrill voice.

"They always called me after the fact."

"What do you mean?" she asks, genuinely eager to know.

"To tell them if… To make sure they were *dead.*"

A wave of rage takes over her body.

"I was so proud of you when I was little, saying you were a doctor." She pronounces the word *doctor* with contempt, to emphasize her disgust. "Turns out you were a doctor who helped to kill."

"No, I didn't! I just told them…if they were really dead."

Paula closes her fists, hits her hips. Hard. Hard enough for it to hurt.

"And if they were not *really* dead? What then? You stayed there until they had been tortured enough to die?"

She can tell he's irritated by her hitting herself, and gets ready to hit him instead if he comes anywhere near her.

"No! I brought them back to life. I saved them!"

"So they could be electrocuted some more? How kind of you," she retorts, letting out a bitter guffaw. The man takes a few seconds to respond. Paula can tell he's trying to find the right words to say.

"No, I never worked in those…centres."

This time she laughs out loud, without holding herself back. Laughter like a machine gun, shooting at him.

"You're the king of euphemisms. Congratulations."

"Look!" he says, exasperated. "If it helps you to know this, your parents were never tortured. They died quickly, okay? In their own bed. And when I got there, they were already dead."

Paula can't keep herself together anymore. She lets out a scream. A long, intense scream. The man looks around, nervously. People are staring at them, alarmed.

"Why don't we go talk about this somewhere else?" he says. She detects fear in his voice.

"No. I don't want to go anywhere with you. Last time I did, I lost my identity and my childhood." She's crying now, and hating herself for it.

"You didn't lose your childhood. We gave you a wonderful childhood. You were loved, and we took really good care of you."

"Yes. But you're forgetting a small detail: *I-was-not-yours.*"

He can't stay beside her. The weight of her words forces him to return to the bench. It's windy but he feels out of breath; his heart is pounding. His back, covered in sweat.

"I'm old," he tells her from the bench. "I don't feel well."

A little girl who was blowing bubbles is not blowing bubbles anymore, but standing still, staring at them. The girl's mother is keeping guard close to her child, probably wondering if she should intervene, or call the police. Paula picks up her purse from the ground and returns to the bench, trying to feign normalcy. The conversation is not over yet.

"Why did you take me?" she asks, wiping her eyes with the back of her hands, then placing her purse again as a small wall between them.

"I earned you," he says, quietly.

"You what?" She turns to face him, completely in disbelief.

"I *thought* I had earned you," he corrects himself, avoiding her eyes.

"Earned *me*?" Paula makes an enormous, almost super-human effort to remain calm.

"You have to understand. Ana María and I had waited for so long to have a child, so long! And then I heard you crying and there was no one there. Those bastards had done…what they did, and you were next door, in your room, eyes wide-open, crying." His voice is breaking, but he goes on. "You, with those baby-blue eyes I immediately adored, all alone in that room. I panicked. I didn't know what to do, there was no one else, no one I could call, and I couldn't leave you alone there with no one to care for you! I knew of others who had taken babies, or received babies, and I thought, why not us? Why not Ana María and me? We were good people, good citizens, and we were the best parents we could be for you. We loved you so much!"

"So I was your prize? For being loyal to a murderous regime?"

"I already told you I never killed anyone."

"The hell you didn't," she replies, clenching her teeth, forcing herself not to yell. "My father's mother died after he was killed. My aunt, my father's sister, was the one who found my parents dead at home. She killed herself after that, couldn't live with the memory. Can you blame her? It was too much for my grandmother to bear, losing both her children in less than a year. And I was nowhere to be found. She was a widow; she thought she had nothing to live for. I was told she died of sadness, and I believe it. Those deaths are *on you*. And my other grandmother, the one who took me with her to Canada… Who am I kidding here? You'd never understand, obviously. You've never had to endure such sorrow."

"Ana María's sorrow doesn't count? And my own? We couldn't eat, we couldn't sleep after you were gone. Ana María used to lock herself in your room for days on end, sleeping in your bed, surrounding herself with your clothes, crying, screaming, and there was nothing I could do that would soothe her. We all suffered!"

Paula has finally had enough. She stands up, and gets ready to leave. She can't listen anymore.

"*You* suffered?" she says, grabbing her purse. "Did you ever stop to think that I lost my parents not once but twice? That you took me away from my family, and then they took me away from you, and away from here, and I ended up growing up never feeling like I belonged anywhere? Did you ever stop to think about what you had done to *me*?"

Paula takes off the baseball cap and shows him her balding scalp. Her head looks like an abandoned doll's. He's perplexed. Terrified, almost.

"What happened to your beautiful golden hair?" he demands to know, then immediately softens his tone. "Do you have cancer?"

Paula shakes her head.

"I've been pulling it out."

The man's eyes well up again and he stretches his hand to touch her.

"My poor baby girl!" he says. "I'm so sorry! Please forgive me!"

She moves a couple of steps away from him, puts on the cap again, and slides one of her hands inside her purse.

"I have a gun," she says quietly.

The man stares at her in incomprehension.

"I have a gun. If you say anything or you make any suspicious movement, I'll shoot you."

Paula's voice is suddenly deeper than before. The man's body stiffens.

"Take off your shoes," she says.

"But…"

"I said, take off your shoes."

The man does as he is told. His movements are slow. It's hard for him to untie the laces. His fingers are shaking.

"Now, take off your socks."

The man complies while Paula looks around them, making sure no one is watching them anymore. Then, without losing sight of him, Paula picks up the shiny shoes and socks and feeds them to the river.

"You'll have to dive to get them, or walk barefoot all the way back home, where the police are probably waiting for you already. A file has been opened to investigate your role in the killing of my parents and my kidnapping. I'll testify against you, you bastard."

She turns around and walks away. People around her are doing what families do on Sundays at the park. A short woman is selling balloons. Paula buys the lot, and releases them into the air. Then she opens her purse and takes out the brick that's been hiding there since sunrise. She lets it fall on the grass, grateful that it barely makes any sound at all.

Leon Rooke

OPEN THE DOOR

I knew my mother was coming. I did not know she was coming when in fact she came, but I knew she was coming. I could count on her to be there. But she came when I did not know she was coming, which was a thing I did not expect of her. Had she come when in fact she came, if she had said this, I would have been prepared. When people say they are going to do a thing and do it when they have given their word they will do this thing that they have talked about doing, I am on the job. If my brows are arched this minute then already you have the reason. More especially, as she was my mother, which she was, not to make any more bones about that than I would make about her not doing a thing as she had said she would do this thing.

I would not let her through the door. I would not let her in. I made her stand there.

She said, "Gordon, open the door. Open this door now, before I have to put my foot down."

But I was not worried about anyone's foot coming down, since by my lights her foot was not supposed to be there. It was not supposed to be where it was for another hour, and I might want to say that in this instance her foot, or both of them, did not exist. In my mind one foot or two, when belonging to my mother at the unforeseen hour, did not exist.

"No," I said. "Go away and do not come until you said you would."

Thus – thus saying thus-and-so, I went away from the door. As far as I could get from that door I went, and went on with my business. It is not your business what that business was, but I will tell you, since my mood is now, and was then, more generous than you may suppose from what I have told you about this exchange with my mother at my door when she had said she would not be at that door. That I was with someone else at this time, someone my mother would have no business seeing – and would possibly go out of business, or quit the business, or declare instant bankruptcy if she did see – is not germane to the relationship you and I have, although my mother would not see this. To this day, she would not admit this. She would say, "Gordon, you are dreaming," or "Gordon, you are not a lamppost, stop behaving like one." But that is not the same as admitting your admissions. It is not the same as confessing your limitations when it comes to understanding matters you are not designed to understand. To say to me, "Gordon, you are dreaming," or "Sweetheart, enlighten me as to the properties of this dreamland you inhabit" – as she has said to me a thousand times – that is a different kind of testimony altogether.

To this day she feigns ignorance as to why I would not permit her to enter this place where I was that day, when she was at this place when she was not supposed to be at this place. She was to be there an hour later, three p.m. Eastern Standard, that time precisely, when we had mutually agreed to share the results of our mutually agreed-upon presences. At three, fuelled by her wisdom and charged by the loyalties of common persuasion, we had agreed we would sort out the issue to everyone's satisfaction, or arrive, as nearly as we were able, at a compromise that would be acceptable to all, and even mutually advantageous to some. To my mother, I mean, since she was the party who had announced herself grievously wounded, heartsick, faint with shock by what it was I was possibly doing in there, in that place I was in, with the person I was in there possibly doing these things with.

"Oh, sweetheart, Mr. Look Elsewhere, Mr. Make Me Drop Dead, do not imagine your mother does not know of these terrible lies I know you live."

My mother did not precisely know who this person was I was doing these things with, but she knew what her own wounds felt like not knowing who that person was, and how they had come to be wounds wrenching to her very soul and breath. It was the driving urgency of the pains emitting from these wounds, I suppose, that had got her at my door an hour earlier than she had said she would be at my door.

"Gordon," my mother said. "*Boychik*, I do not know this person, but I kid you not: I know everything a mother can know *about* this person. This person is not right for you. An hourglass figure, darling, does not obscure the news.

"Gordon," my mother said. "You cannot possibly be serious about this creature the grapevine has told me you are serious about. This creature is of another *consciousness*, Gordon. A freethinker to excel all freethinkers, according to the grapevine. Her skin and bones are not our skin and bones. Your father and I are enjoying good health, thank you most sincerely, but if this were not the case we would be turning in our graves, darling. The shame, sweetheart! That you would thumb your nose at the thousands of years our people have been on this earth suffering the slings and arrows we have suffered these thousand years. And all for what, darling? So that you can have a good time – what is it that they say? – so that you may get your rocks off with this *shikse*? Talk to a good matchmaker, darling. Talk to me. We will both tell you the same. A schmuck of the first order we did not raise you to be. When it comes to sound and solid thinking, your mind is the hand that clasps at windmills, no literary allusion intended."

"Mama?"

"What? I am not supposed to speak? In my house I can speak. In the synagogue, at my butcher's, at my hairdresser's I may speak, but in my son's hallway, surrounded by people of all and sundry belief, with swastika graffiti scrawled in the very elevator that delivered me here, I am not allowed to speak?"

"Oh, Mama."

"If I were allowed to speak, this is what I would say. All right, have a good time, like you have been having a good time with all the girls since you were old enough to twitch your nose, and be such a trial as the trial you were to me. 'Which one is he knocking up now?' I see a pregnant girl on my street, those years ago, did I not swoon with fear? Did I not grapple with this as with a toothache? A puddle on my doorstep, yes. Yes, darling, my very thoughts through all of those hard years. But marry this one? God forbid, Gordon, that you should look at the scrag twice. If your looking is to lead to more than your rocks getting off, Gordon, then I will beg your father to drive hot pokers into my eyes. Such a waste, darling, of two good eyes. These rocks of yours, what, are you the Great Rocky Mountains which we took you to as a boy? The expense, the worry, I tell you! But wedding bells with this schemer? For this, Mr. Flakehead, I braved steerage? For this, Mr. Hotnuts, I slept on nails? Mr. Dongbrain. For this, your father survived the cauldron? For this I wear socks under my stockings to this day, and my toenails bleed? For this I allowed my other babies to go without shoes? So that Mr. Quickbang can chase his blondes? His Delilahs, his Judiths who would take the blade to his hair? So that he can be Mr. Brave New World, and your father and I Mr. and Mrs. Bathmat?"

"You've flipped, Mama."

"Listen to Mr. Mattress talk. Mr. Waterbed. I ask you, who has flipped, according to the grapevine? A rabbi your father he's not, but even he puts his foot down here. Rocks, yes, darling-pie.

Mr. Sausage Man. But marriage, no. Your father, bless him, Mr. Original Thinker, what help is he to me? The times I have said to him and to you How Can I Go On? How?"

"Mama?"

"Shut up, Gordon. Shut your mouth. Since the burning bush, since Job, since Lenny Bruce and Mort Sahl, not since Shakespeare has daylight seen such a mouthy boy. Is it the practice now in the goys' planet you inhabit that a mother may not speak? Remember at your bar mitzvah? Laryngitis curdles the formerly loquacious boy's magpie throat, and not a word can your father and I hear. We are crowding close, it is all elbows in the face, but can we hear? Not a decibel. Let such horror strike you a second time."

"Mama?"

"So no more funny business, please, Mr. Drive Me Nuts. That these leggie blonde Aphrodite lumps of lust should sleep on your gorgeous chest, it breaks my heart. And what's this, darling? What's this that the grapevine tells me? Your current heartthrob is hari-kari – *No!* – Hare Krishna, this grapevine tells me. *Oy!* Melt my heart, why don't you? Disembowel my bowels."

"Mama?"

"Speak, why don't you? Unsnitch the tongue."

"Mama? Please. Not in the hall."

"So open the door. So let in those you would disown."

"No. Go away."

"Can I believe it, darling? That I raised a son to dabble about in crazy peas? That my womb could cradle a lunatic? Tell me your heart's breath didn't once flop about in dusty sandals and wear white sheets."

"One time, Mama. One time. She had a flat, driving by their temple. She was flustered. She went in, looking for someone to fix her flat. She's inside one minute only, Mama."

"One is too many. More than one minute she is this thing in white sheets, I would give even you credit. Oh, *boychik.* Grab your

kiska and run. Come home. So much better you should get yourself a fine *tchotchke* boasting the sunny disposition of lovelies available – *more* than available, if my eyes are any judge – in your own
neighbourhood. Here's a story, darling. You tell me what it means.
Was once upon a time. Are you listening? Then listen. Once upon
a time, said the very old woman to the very old man seated by her
side. Once upon a time, says this woman, I was a very young
woman. *Oy*, a delectable peach! Did I tell you? Yes, the honey of
honeys, the One and Only. And what does the very old man say
to this statement? How does he reply? What the very old man
says, as he stares with quickening heart deep into the very old
woman's face, is this. Are you listening? What he says is, Must
have been before my time. Yes, before my time. That is the very
old thing that the very old man said to the very old woman
seated by his side. Did I laugh? No, I did not. Rodney Danger-
field, Shelley Berman, your father is not. I ask you, Gordon, what
does this wonderful story mean? It is the story of a happy marriage. It is a story about choosing your life's partner wisely, about
sticking with the tried and true, by which I do not mean getting
your rocks off with snake-legged tiger-lipped blondes. Oh, getting
them off, yes, if you must be such a bad boy, but not the other
thing. Not wedding bells. Are you listening to me, Mr. Rock City?
Mr. Gravel Pit. If this is not what the story means, then you tell
me what this story means. It means tranquillity, it means choosing your life's partner with attention to the scorched bones your
own bones have replaced. Listen to your father. Hasn't he told you
this? It means wearing your skullcap where skullcap was invented
to be worn. God forbid you should wear it in bed. Gordon, I
should have to stand here on my varicose veins, in my bloodied
heart, in my wreath of tears, repeating to you the nasty reports
reaching my ears through the grapevine. You don't wear the
safety mitt when you sleep with your latest flopover. So the
grapevine tells me. So your father hints. A knife in my heart, that

thought, Gordon. A knife. Procreation with bunnies, God save us. Two percent our people are percentage wise on this continent and look at you, tending your own hot fire, contributing nothing to our percentile.

"Here's another story, Mr. Innocent As Lambs. Also once upon a time. Was once upon a time a darling boy married outside his faith a Miss Sandalfoot and many little Sandalfoots soon were running through their ankles. But did these offspring honour their father or even know his name? No, these blondie hell warriors spoke from secret code books, they wore white sheets and panhandled the good peoples' money on our boulevards and avenues. The luckless father died alone and forgotten, mewling like a stringy cat, crying 'Mercy, mercy,' like to with the ending of Mr. Bernard Malamud's excruciating book of the title that this second eludes me, and about which I have grave reservations having to do with the shock value, but wherein mercy is begged for one hundred and fifteen times plus, for good measure, once in the Hebrew. Yes, for good measure, once in Hebrew. You have read this celebrated work, I assume, and if so you will recall mercy has taken a Florida holiday. You can call for mercy a million times, in all the languages, but it is too late if mercy is in Miami and not punching the clock. What is my point? My point is that the stringy cat in this story is never to know the bliss known by these very old people in the wonderful other story, which was a story overflowing with the bountiful meaning the mewler in this one refused to heed."

"Mama. Please quit. Please go."

"So. So, a reaction. A reaction of any kind from Mr. Blind and Cannot See, I can live with. I will tell you yet another story, not once upon a time. This is a present-day story."

"No more stories!"

"Quiet. I will skip to the good part. A son whose heart was a locked chest came to look at a house. With him also to look is his mother, and on her arm the neighbour's daughter, a tootsie so hot all agree pavement melts beneath her saintly feet. Such a nice house, a *family*-type house, and look there, a bustling synagogue mere doors down the street. But will this hardhead listen to his mother? Will he so much as glance at this tootsie of all tootsies, who would give him a drove of babies come each snowfall?"

"A tootsie, was she? You don't, by chance, mean that dumbo Ethyl?"

"So, all right, Bette Midler Ethyl wasn't. So she hung onto you like wallpaper and gushed like a fire hydrant anytime you patted the top of her head. Unlike the string beans you not once let your parents set eyes upon, because, the grapevine tells me, they wore shoplifted underwear, had toenails and eyelids a foot long, and couldn't keep their knees together since day one.

"So, what's the moral of this story, Mr. Wiseguy? The moral of this story is two morals. One, this son was not wise to his values and had a low opinion of his birthright. And two? Two is he was not a nice person. He was a *secretive* person, Gordon. That locked chest he called a heart was filled to capacity with secrets kept from his mother, kept even from the grapevine. What happens, Gordon, once that chest is open? We find mice, all these years, have been inside that heart's chest, chewing away at those secrets how they will chew at corncobs, so that all the naked eye perceives is what once were *shikses* in there numerous as eggs in a henhouse have been nibbled down to nothing but ragged toenails. You tell me: Is that a nice person? Is that a person respects his mother?"

"Dear God, Mama."

"Don't 'Dear God' me. Listen, Gordon. Listen, my love's potion. If ever you have opened your ears to a mother's tongue, then open them now. You want God. I'll give you God. What God said is this. Are you listening? God said, *Worry Only If Darkness Falls Before You See My Likeness A Second Time.* I worry,

Mr. Hate Us All. The darkness is falling, Mr. Kick Us In The Teeth, and one day you will look for me, as you will look for others who once constituted your prime pieces and parts, but I will have kicked the bucket. And these others who trek and haunt Diaspora will be sightless to you, as you are sightless to them, as for all intents and purposes your present-day actions prescribe that they can kick it too. I worry. I worry. In your own elevator, *what?* – it's night, your fuehrer friends are confused? They think they are spraying their evil shit on a synagogue?"

~

That is what my mother said when she arrived at the time she said she would not arrive. Her remarks above are abbreviated, skimmed, highlights only, in recognition of your busy schedule, and do we all not require time to putter about in house and garden, motivated to accomplish this and that neglected task, or yet demand additional moments in life's timetable to partake of leisure fruit? Believe you me, she is still at the door, on her two p.m. call. It is two o'clock, I tell you, and she is kicking her expensive shoes against the door. She has not yet said all these things narrated above. That is her three o'clock speech, and her two o'clock speech borrows only a few of these lines.

"Hold on, Mama," I said. "Mama, you just stand tight."

That is what I said, to hold her there, while I raced to the other end of that place I was inhabiting, and said to my co-inhabitant, "Let's try the window. Let's see if we can get you through this window."

But my cohabitant was having none of this. Inasmuch as the space we were occupying was on the thirty-seventh floor, she was having none of these attempts to force her out the window.

What she said was, "Gordon, please, please, this once, stand your ground."

To which I replied like so: "Do you hear her banging on the door? Do you know she has packed extra shoes, to bang them on that door? Do you know what she will *do*, what she will *say*, should she come in here and find us in here together? Do you? We will both of us wish we were dead, and my mother will wish it, too, and wish, furthermore, that she had brought us to that condition."

The person I was sharing these accommodations with then said: "You must face the music this time, my love."

But the music she is talking about is not music I wanted to face. My mother is shouting, "What is going on in there? What are you doing? *Mitt*, darling!"

She is at the door, she is early, but she does not yet have her three o'clock artillery fully unpacked.

"Don't think I don't know what is going on there!" she shouts. And I am shouting back, although I know it is useless, for my mother is the last one to hear people shouting. If a hundred people are yelling *Fire!* she will turn up her collar under expectancy of rain, and go on her way, pretending fire is not yet an element among the four elements Einstein or Solomon have yet got around to inventing.

"Think *precaution*! Think *mitt*, precious love!"

And I am yelling back what it is people yell back when they have been caught amiss.

The other party in question, she has calmly put on her clothes. She is arranging her beautiful hair. Now she is lighting the weed, she is twisting the gold band on her finger, she is having a sit-down.

"Open the door," this vision is saying. "Let your mother in."

But I notice she is not opening the door herself. She is brave, I have figured that out. She is Godiva on the horse, but she is not a woman as would open the door and face my mother's music.

What my mother says is this: "Open the door, Mr. Sneaky Leak."

"Open the door," the other one, the beloved one, says. "Tell your mother the terrible thing you have done."

"You could hide in the closet. You could hide under the bed."

"I will not. She will look in the closet. She will look under the bed."

"Who's that?" my mother says. "Who are you talking to in there? Are you trying to kill me, Gordon? Are you trying to give me heart attacks? Think *mitt*, darling. *Mitt!*"

She will not be returning at the appointed hour. My beautiful wife is opening the door.

Norman Snider

HOW DO YOU LIKE ME NOW?

In the episode we're shooting next week, the President of the Galaxy Federation is just a small role which only requires a day player. Following instructions from the network, I write her as a woman. One of the actors auditioning to play the part turns out to be the legendary Nica Graham.

It's a morning in April. I drop my boy Liam off at daycare. His nanny will pick him up later in the afternoon. Then, an hour later, I walk up the stairs to the studio. A retooled power plant, it's a long drive from downtown.

Liam's mother and my wife, Anne, is busy with her on-camera television job. She's on a flight from Buenos Aires to Paris. I'm doing my best to cope with raising the little guy. So I need to keep my own job writing science fiction episodes for network television. Showbiz, you have to love it.

My boy misses his mom. I remember when he was only a baby. I had just written the number one movie in America. We were all three happy. I used to tote him around on my chest dancing to a blues tune. Then Anne and I danced alone, close.

A year ago I was writing a feature for a studio. It was an adaptation of a British crime series, *Calculated Risk*. The project vanished suddenly like a stage magician's assistant from the box. The director walked away from the movie one month before shooting. The picture walked away with him. One second, the studio's howling with enthusiasm for you, the next you can't get anybody to return an e-mail.

And no explanations.

The producer's woman assistant stops me in the hallway. She asks me if I can take a casting session. The show is falling apart. People are getting fired every day. I see them walking past my office door, cardboard box full of belongings in hand.

Bruno, our producer, is hungover or just gone crazy. He's been getting more erratic as the series continues to fail in the ratings. The bosses back in Los Angeles are getting less enthusiastic about their U.S.-Canada-France-Germany co-production and continually cut back the budget.

There are a dozen actresses waiting in the hallway; nervous, expectant. The audition room looks like a humble classroom. It's just a makeshift desk, some beat-up chairs and, on the ceiling, unforgiving blinding lights. The sides are strewn around the table, all pink paper, orange or lemon-coloured.

It's a bleak place – lives and careers are decided here, not to mention car payments and grocery money. And there she is, Nica Graham, tall with wild red-blond hair, thin delicate wrists, a throaty voice, and womanly hips.

Nica Graham.

The star of *Closer to Midnight,* indie masterpiece, where she played the heiress's doomed sister, auditioning for a small part in a network science fiction series. That movie meant everything to me. Nica's performance struck true amidst so much mainstream sentimentality and falseness. Her character reminded me of an old love, the sort of helplessly perverse woman you never saw portrayed on screen. The director had stepped up to major studio projects. But there wasn't a big market for the Queen of the Indies.

Nica wants nothing more than for me to like her. If I was just some meatball she had met at a party – specs, skinny – she would keep conversation to two seconds and a tight smile.

But, Nica Graham needs this job and she thinks I can give it to her. So I get the bright smile, a blast of warmth. But I can see dark shadows under her grey-green eyes. Beneath the smile, the exquisite features are pinched, panic lies not far underneath the pale skin. The very fact she's going for the job shows either bad management or desperation.

I sip mineral water from a can while she runs the lines with Vera, the jumbo-size middle-aged casting director. She has to be three hundred on the hoof. She has some obscure medical condition that causes her to gain and lose weight. One week she's a sickly looking fragile creature; the next, she's as big as house. Vera's young male assistant runs a digital camera. Bruno and the director will look at all the clips on their laptops and make their decision. Bruno probably just checks them out on his iPhone. Nica Graham, yes or no?

But then Nica and I have a conversation. The star of *Closer to Midnight* and the writer of *The Stars My Destiny* have a theoretical discussion about the nature of power. She fiddles with the silver bracelets on her wrist.

Nica is, after all, going to play the President of the Galaxy Federation. Power. Women and political power. How power changes character.

I listen to Nica's observations, her references to Catherine the Great and Elizabeth Taylor as Cleopatra. And most importantly, how Nica Graham would play a woman President of Outer Space.

I see her as very strong, yes? But there's something dark pulling her, too. Are you familiar with Jung's concept of the "shadow?"

Yes, I say, I've read Jung.

Her shadow is black and it's dense but it's the source of her power. Art, she says, often comes from a dark place. Have you read Foucault?

Sorry, I haven't.

Nica 's observations are a little pretentious for science fiction television. But indie actresses read heavy books. It's curious that she brings up Jung because Nica Graham herself is the archetype of The Actress. You could see her on Broadway in the 1920s, or in the West End in the 1890s. She was five hundred years of The Drama in one flame-haired package. And drama is my obsession, as well as my bread and butter. In these parts, it's a solitary one. Sure, there were lots of local industry folk about but none of them had ever been part of a film like *Closer to Midnight* and I couldn't tolerate them.

Under the table, after the Jung and Foucault stuff, where only I can see, good old Vera makes a loose fist and moves it back and forth. In the world of episodic television, Jung and Foucault equals jerkoff.

I also want to say that I'm the possessor of a couple of killer credits and only the ups and downs of showbiz have landed me on this space opera. But that doesn't come up until later, when Nica and myself are in pillow talk mode, and she's telling me that science fiction television is actually an advanced form and one she's dying to work in.

I know, I'm a married man. The cheating husband is the worst villain imaginable. Despised on all sides. Ask any woman. Worse than a murderer, probably. Doesn't matter that just as often it's the female of the species that's got that evil glint in the eye, especially with men with celebrity or power. And, on the other hand, men aren't going to stop chasing women. It's like trying to stop Niagara Falls.

Ordinarily, I don't have a chance with a beauty like Nica Graham; she's way out of my league. I know she likes me, even if she just thinks I can get her acting jobs. I'll hate myself if I don't yield to temptation just this once. Besides, I'm lonely.

Let me say that I despise the casting couch. I would rather piss blood than have some no-talent actor mess up my story, in even the smallest part. I know plenty of horndogs who have put their hopeless actress girlfriends into a movie, then give her two lines as a flight attendant or secretary. Doesn't matter some poor hack's spent years of his life writing the flick and the girl will fuck the scene up for him good and proper. They don't care any more. I still cared. I was doing my level best on *The Stars My Destiny*. And even the legendary Nica Graham wasn't going to mess up my work.

Long and short of it, Nica Graham doesn't get to play the President of the Galaxy. She's a bit too young for the part, really, way too sexy, and Bruno, the prick, goes for a better-known, older, and more stately actress.

Anne calls me at home. She's back in Paris. It's good to hear her voice but she's in a hurry. And it's a bad connection. Call home is probably number three on her to-do list. It's not that she doesn't love Liam or love me, she has a job to do and that comes first. I don't resent her dedication; I envy it. Whole-hearted absorption in the task at hand.

I can see the Eiffel Tower from my hotel room, she says.

You're on the Right Bank?

The office booked the hotel, she says. It's some kind of convention centre with a terrific bistro a couple blocks over.

Hideo Kitagawa, her favourite cameraman, was a terrific shooter. He was as lithe as a samurai, glossy hair tied in a man bun. There are many attractive people in the world. It's hard when you're on the road so much. Nobody likes to stay home alone. Makes it difficult to stay married. Goes with the territory. Occupational hazard. But Anne and I have been together more than twenty years.

I tell her about Bruno, the show; the shop talk of two television professionals. When I ask about her shoot, Anne changes the subject. She's good at directing conversations. It's one of her strengths as an interviewer. She has battled her way up from the local news to doing the big international stories. You have to respect that accomplishment. I'm proud of her.

How's Liam? she asks.

He misses you.

I hope he's eating properly.

Just as long as I give him fried chicken.

Can't you try something else?

He loves my fried chicken.

It just isn't healthy.

I'm doing my best. I have a job too. Maybe you know?

If you're going to be like that, I'm going to hang up.

Liam wants to talk to you.

Put him on then.

After they talk, the conversation is over. I toss and turn all night, unable to sleep. I had worked for years on the story that made my screenwriting career possible. For Anne's friends in broadcast journalism, I was the deadbeat husband, even though I was behind her every step of the way. A deadbeat she foolishly kept around when she could be married to a higher-level guy. But Anne had hung in. Then, once it got going, my success seemed an outrage to the pecking order. Her friends all thought I must be related to some powerful guy in Hollywood. All the same, there was no way Anne was giving up the job she had worked so hard for and move home and hearth to the fleshpots of L.A.

Throughout the summer, I start to run into Nica around the city. At a book party or shopping for groceries. Then, one night, she's sitting opposite me in a restaurant on a tree-lined boulevard. I'm with a buddy, Waldron, a lawyer downtown. Anne's shooting a doc in Finland. Liam's with his nanny. The food is excellent. I order caviar. We finish the meal, the battered remains of the Brie and grapes lying in the middle of the table, the soiled linen napkins lying carelessly tossed. I have a cognac and I'm thinking about having another.

Across the room, Nica is with a guy maybe thirty years older than herself. The Beauty and the Beast doesn't begin to tell it. Sandor Kovacs, for that turns out to be the Beast's name, is one of those emigré Eastern European real estate developers with old world charm and right-wing opinions. Shopping malls and condos. Sixty-ish, knitted sweater and cords, a huge gut, and thick white hair combed straight back. His face is oddly misshapen. And for some crazy reason I notice he has extremely large feet. Kovacs had had quite a time of it as a child, first under the Nazis then under the Soviets in charming old Budapest. Probably that's where he got the misshapen head. And I could all too easily see him trotting around to the secret police to hip them to what bad shit his mother and father are doing.

Nica looks my way, waves, then returns to her conversation. She's wearing an aubergine-coloured cowboy shirt, dark pants and heels. It doesn't look like she and Kovacs are getting along too well. He doesn't look too happy with her, I'd say.

Nonetheless, after I check my cellphone for messages from Liam's sitter, I heave myself over to their table to make nice. She makes the introductions. Right away I can see the wheels turning in his head. Those wheels have been turning rapidly for decades, and to the tune of millions.

Can I get Nica a continuing part on the show, he wants to know.

Don't put the poor man on the spot, Nica tells Kovacs.

It's some Old World tradition at work here, Vienna, champagne, cigars, rich men, and actresses. But I'm blandly noncommittal. Season coming to an end, blah, blah, blah. But it's true enough. *The Stars My Destiny* is over and it's not coming back. I shouldn't really be ordering caviar.

But before the night's over, Nica excuses herself to the ladies'. My eyes follow her and once again I remark on her voluptuous hips.

When I look at my cellphone in my parked car half an hour later I see she's sent me an e-mail with her phone number. At home, later, Liam fast asleep, I check out all her performances on YouTube. I stare at the screen as Nica plays Caldwell in *Closer to Midnight*. She's sensational. Elegant, delicate, tragic.

We meet next afternoon for coffee. Italian café off Bloor Street, a patio with potted ferns. Heavy-set executives with briefcases speaking corporate jargon to one another at the next table. It is a beautiful afternoon. Nica's arms are remarkably slender in her persimmon-coloured sleeveless shirt. Later on, she refers to this coffee date as "that time you proposed to me." Actually, it's more like I propositioned her straight out.

Right away, we're two conspirators. We speak about things and places we both love: Piazza Navona, Bill Evans, the beach at Puerto Escondido, the films of Nicholas Ray, the oyster bar at Grand Central, Book Soup in West Hollywood, Gloucester's blinding scene in *King Lear*. Nica seems to know more about each of them than I do. We're both feeling lonely and friendless. I don't actually say, Let's fuck, but that's the gist of the matter. Nica takes a sip of her espresso and says, I suppose it's inevitable. I'm a little surprised at how eager she is. When we leave the café we're in a big hurry to get to a bed, any bed.

Walking out on the street with Nica Graham is interesting. The sun is reflecting off the glass and steel buildings. Men's heads snap around to get a better view of her, every few strides. One guy even snaps her picture with his phone. Nica's head, proud beauty, tilts upward. She's untouched by their longing. Sometimes, she tells me, it's an ordeal for her to walk to the corner to get a carton of milk. Some hard-on is always going to try his luck. I even had the feeling that a couple fans were trying to follow us.

I'm sick of this town, she says. I wish I was back in L.A.

Nica 's condo is opposite the museum on Bloor Street. One of those buildings where there's one unit per floor. Startling view of the city skyline. Chinese vases and Francis Bacon lithographs. Books piled everywhere. Opera plays softly on hidden speakers. She keeps the place way too hot; right away I start to sweat.

I put my arms around her. The first kiss is tentative, reluctant. For a moment, she looks fearful. I guess she is thinking of the possible consequences of sleeping with me. A doubtful look creases her features. It seems like she's going to back out at the last second. Then, she runs her long fingers through my hair.

I've been wanting to do that, she says.

In her narrow bed, Nica's skin is pale and marvellously smooth. Small breasts. Right away, we can't stop fucking. One furious go after another, interspersed with the recitation of life stories, her head nestled on my belly.

Dad was an oil patch lawyer out west, privileged childhood, lots of horses, riding. Drama school in New York, modelling days, fall from innocence. You on the pill, sweetheart? asked the pot-bellied fashion tycoon, before her first day on the runway. But it's a paycheque while she takes courses in Feminism and Film Theory at NYU.

Then, the indie scene in lower Manhattan. One film after another for five years. Marriage to a Brit theatre actor lasts a year before he comes out of the closet. A breakdown. Stint in L.A., then *Closer to Midnight.* Overseas festivals, PR junkets, the whole nine yards. This success leads to a part in a big picture with the Big Star. On set he made a move, she refused, bang, he edited her scenes out of the picture. Thanks for nothing, Mister Big Shot. Bang, back to Canada and scuffling for roles in television.

I was about to launch into my own life saga when her iPhone rings. It's Kovacs. Nica's expression turns grim. His voice is loud. I can hear it but I don't understand anything he's saying.

You're driving me nuts, she says.

Nica tries to stall but the developer's a steamroller. She hangs up and gets out of bed, her hair awry. Nica sobs, then ceases with a hand to her mouth. She puts on an orange silk robe, and says, You better go.

Couldn't you put him off?

Hurry, he's five minutes away. You have to leave.

Don't tell me it's going to be better than what we've just been doing.

Poor Sandor is an old man.

But you don't deny him his pleasure? Whatever he can manage?'

Who do you think pays for this condo? she says.

That shuts me up. Nica Graham with all her airs and graces, Queen of the Indies, is having her rent paid in exchange for sex like a Russian stripper.

Don't look so stunned, she says.

I reach for my clothes. I looked up to see Nica staring at me.

Well, she says. How do you like me now?

Less, I say.

This is just lust, says Nica Graham. If it was love I'd treat you much worse.

I can't help but laugh.

I've been exploited for sex, I say.

Haven't we all, she says.

As she shows me the door, Nica apologizes.

I'm so sorry, she says. I just can't handle being poor anymore. It's so *uncivilized*. You're a lovely guy. Think about it and you'll get it.

I said I understood her arrangement with Sandor Kovacs. But I was lying. I wanted no more of Nica Graham. She'd seen the last of me.

Anne comes home with the autumn. And I'm happy to see her. She brings me Scotch from duty-free, Liam a French rugby jersey. My housekeeping leaves a lot to be desired, even with the cleaning woman once a week and Anne lets me know about it. But once again we're borne along in the slow, narcotic currents of a long marriage. There's no underestimating the vectors of affection and need that bind us together.

One Saturday evening, we have dinner with a physicist husband and wife couple who, like Anne, continually circled the globe, banding together against the parochial locals. Anne is looking especially lovely. She's tall, big boned, full-breasted. She has a new hairstyle, and her straight blond hair curves in a wing over her face. For some reason, all the eating utensils are tiny, hard to manipulate. It must be a new design fad, a fashion thing. The decor in their house is remarkably like our decor at home. Our hostess, like many of her friends, adores Anne, and copies her in most everything.

At the table is a woman who had had an affair with an Exxon executive in Houston. He had lent her half a million dollars to help buy a three-bedroom condo. Now she had returned to an old lover. The oil executive wanted his money back. The woman thought she could sweet-him out of it. She was wrong. She had just received a very tough letter from a prominent Houston law firm. They weren't kidding around with her.

Women overestimate the power of the pussy, says the physicist husband, stroking his bushy beard. The physicist looks like a tie-dyed Birkenstock hippie but he is maybe the top guy in his field in the country. He also has a shrewd eye for stocks. He's infatuated with Anne but too timid or bourgeois to do anything about it. He's not alone; Anne gets plenty of heavy-breathing fan mail.

Remind me of that later, says the physicist's wife. She's from New Delhi via Berkeley. An actual nuclear scientist.

Anne pours herself her third glass of white wine. She smiles at the woman with the oil exec lover. She's indulgent of self-destructive behaviour – not in either of us, but in other people, who she keeps at a firm distance.

What does Mark say? she asks.

Mark was the erstwhile boyfriend. He was an unemployed art director in advertising. I felt for the guy. Been there.

Mark doesn't know a thing, says the woman. He's completely in the dark, poor lamb.

That sounds like transparency in a relationship, says Anne.

Which you believe in passionately, I say.

The truth is essential.

When did you find Jesus? I ask. Anne was the champion of the diplomatic lie; usually to save others embarrassment.

Can we drop this, please? says the physicist's wife. She twists the rings on her short, dark hands.

You're wrong about me, says Anne. I hate secrets and I hate liars.

After that evening, the dinner invitations slow. I lie awake at night and debate myself about Nica. Somebody very smart once said, If you want a woman, ask yourself what you want her for.

It's a good question.

As the windows turn grey with dawn, I can't stop remembering those hours she and I spent in bed. But I don't want Nica for a wife. I don't want her for, what? A girlfriend? A bit on the side?

Nica Graham is trouble.

I don't know what I want her for. I just want her.

Now, I'm without a writing assignment. But I'm trying to work on a script in my studio at home. It is based on the story of David Goodis, the crime novelist whose book was the basis of Truffaut's *Don't Shoot the Piano Player*. After a short-lived career in Hollywood, Goodis had gone home to Philadelphia to live with his elderly parents and write novels for pulp publishers for chump change. He liked to be beaten by fat, ugly black prostitutes. A couple of the novels were classics. My interest in Goodis betrayed my character. The script would take ten years to get made, if ever.

Nobody outside showbiz understands these downtimes. Old time actors in the West End of London just say they are resting. As far as the world at large is concerned, you are just another layabout bum. As the leaves fall, Nica Graham and I, out-of-work writer, out-of-work actress, are making love in the afternoons like doomsday is coming.

Long hours of desire that render me breathless, unable to speak, lying beside her afterwards. Whatever happens, I don't give a rap, Nica's been worth it. I consider the virtues of shamelessness; just doing the hell you want, whatever the consequence. Spent, we listen to music and hold hands. Nica likes show tunes, Broadway's best from Cole Porter to Stephen Sondheim.

Let's do it.

Let's fall in love.

I'm happy when I pick Liam up from daycare, happy when I take him home and read him stories until Anne comes back. I'm without regret when she speaks to me only when absolutely necessary. I'm left alone to watch YouTube clips of Nica on my laptop.

Then, Nica Graham becomes difficult to reach. I phone three times, only get her voice message each time. I try to stifle my confusion and panic. It keeps rising. Radio silence, the standard method of saying goodbye in these times. Also, in business. And business has a nasty way of leaking into personal relations.

One afternoon after work I'm having a Scotch on the rocks in my favourite rooftop bar, looking out the window twenty stories above the streets. I like the formal service here, the caricatures of dead celebrities framed on the wall. The first snow is beginning to fall, melting just as soon as it hits the pavement. A basso voice just behind my shoulder intones, May I buy you a drink?

Sandor Kovacs, materializing out of nowhere. Don't vampires do that? He's wearing a baggy suit. He sits down before I can object. He's trapped me. He is carrying a slim zippered briefcase. Kovacs orders a bottle of wine. He puts on a pair of rimless spectacles and takes out a printout from the briefcase. His law firm has hired an investigator. Kovacs knows everything. I suspect he is more intelligent than either Nica or myself.

You're a very talented man, he says. In other circumstances, I'd want you as a friend.

I wish I could say the same, I tell him.

Kovacs eyes narrow.

You are cruel. It would be a pity if you suffered a setback. A major setback.

You're not threatening me?

Let me finish, he says.

Kovacs consults the investigator's report. A waiter pours some wine. The glasses go untouched. Then, absently, he removes a Luger pistol from the briefcase and absently places it on the table, as if it were of absolutely no account. When he's certain I've seen it, he puts it back in the briefcase. He's a rich man. Easy to have me killed. Or maybe do it himself. Then Kovacs tells me how it's going to be. I'm lucky, he's going to give me a break.

I don't think Anne would look on your little adventure with much pleasure. You would certainly lose your family. You seem very fond of your boy. What's his name, Liam? This is what is going to happen. Nica is not going to see you any more or take your phone calls. You are not to see her again in any circumstances. You are going back to your life and I shall go back to mine.

There are plenty of other women besides Nica who'd like you to pay their rent.

Kovacs' big hands turn outward in supplication.

Of course, but I can't live without her.

For a second, I have a moment of pure detestation for Kovacs and all his shopping malls, his Old World manners and the totalitarian ethic that has worked well for him in the free world.

Tell you what? Take your piece, insert it between the lips of your rectum and pull the trigger.

Kovacs laughs, claps his hands, delighted.

Oh, excellent. Capital! Free-style! I love to play that way!

I get up, wine untouched, and leave.

Next day, I lie in wait like a stalker for Nica in the parking garage of her condo, wondering how my life has taken this humiliating turn. Nothing comes free and I am paying a high price for all that deep desire. After an hour, Nica appears and after a glance, blows right by me. She wears a track suit with a triple white stripe down the leg and has her hair pulled back tight under a blue L.A. Dodgers ball cap, and she looks so pale she seems to be suffering from a rare wasting disease. Camille dying in a public ward somewhere. All her beauty at this moment has vanished. When I fall into step, she increases her pace, trying to get away from me like I am one of those hard-ons who stop her on the street.

Can you at least talk to me?

It just wasn't meant to be, you and me. Let's leave it at that.

No, I won't leave it. You're staying with a man who has you followed? How do you think that's going to end?

Nica reaches her green SUV and gets in. I scramble beside her into the shotgun seat.

As opposed to staying with a man who's so scared of his wife he won't even take me to dinner.

That isn't fair.

You're a coward!

There are empty soda cans, years-old fashion magazines, Starbucks' coffee cups, everywhere in her car. A bomb site. Suddenly all the lights in the place go out. Some kind of power outage has left us in darkness. Nica has given me a couple of months on the cuff. Now it's time to talk turkey. Like Sandor Kovacs, she tells me how it's going to be. She has it all planned. I would move out and leave my wife. She would leave Kovacs who isn't as tough as he thinks. We would shake the damn snow off our shoulders and set up house in sunny California.

What about Liam?

Leave it to the lawyers. Custody can always be worked out.

If you want to live like that.

Jesus! Everybody lives like that.

Doggedly, Nica returns to her theme. We aren't a real couple, we never leave her condo. Even though she's in love with me, she can't even phone me at home. We never even go for a walk. All we do is fuck. Even Kovacs enjoyed a nice stroll down by the lake.

At this point, if I had a brain in my head, I would have stepped out of the vehicle and left Nica Graham to Sandor Kovacs or Fate, whichever one would finish her off first. But it was something else that was meant to be. But I agree to the walk in the park, as a holding measure. Now, there's two women about whom I have a bad conscience.

It's December now and I find myself too often walking snowy streets. Too many homeowners neglect their walks. You have to watch for ice if you don't want to slip and fall. The snow is settling in a mournful way. It will stay, dirty and muddy, for months. I favour the side streets and back ways where I can miss the press of humanity on the sidewalks.

I'm playing Russian roulette with my life. I think I'll just drop Nica Graham. I don't want to lose my family. I don't want to lose my son. Neither do I want to leave them in the lurch. And I can see now what life with Nica would be like. Demand upon demand. High maintenance? The category was invented for her. But how to drop her? Silence? A frank discussion? Picking a terminal fight with Nica would be easy.

These dark thoughts are interrupted by the ringing of my cellphone in my coat pocket. It's my agent, Ted, calling from Beverly Hills. He's neglected me for months. So right away I know it's good news. You have to chase agents down to get bad news.

Hey, says Ted, Showtime picked up *Calculated Risk*. Charlie Sheen wants to play the lead.

What?

He identifies with the hero's drug problem.

Oh, man.

Don't complain. They want it for next fall's schedule. They're gonna put it in production right away. They're cutting you a big cheque. They're talking you up for other projects. You're getting steam, my friend. Feel good.

After Ted rings off, the falling snow doesn't look so bad to me. Kind of like a cheery Christmas scene. The sun even comes out from behind the clouds for the first time in weeks. My sojourn in episodic television is over. Nica is just the kind of company you keep when you're on the downswing. I will do my best to patch things up with Anne. Maybe a Caribbean beach holiday. I will outfit the basement with a home gym, really get in shape. It will be a new life.

When I walk in the front door and give Anne my good news about *Calculated Risk,* she seems less than overjoyed. If anything, the deep freeze has descended about ten degrees.

I want to show you something, she says.

I follow Anne into her immaculately neat office. She picks up a manila envelope and hurls it at me, blue eyes blazing.

You cretin!

The envelope bounces off my chest and spills open. Half a dozen glossy photos fall to the floor.

Nica and myself, almost naked. Going for it in the park by the lake.

They delivered these to me at work, says Anne. FedEx. Imagine the humiliation.

There are some things you just don't want to see yourself doing. In the photos, my ass, seen from above, is large and pale. Nica's expression is one of lunatic frenzy. Together, we appear to be a pair of copulating barnyard animals.

I want you to get out, says Anne. Right now.

You're hysterical, I say. Let's talk this over rationally.

You're not ever going to see Liam again. I've already talked to a lawyer.

You're not exactly one to talk.

Just leave, okay?

Anne hurries out of the room, leaving me to ponder the photos.

An hour later I pack a small bag and make a hotel reservation. Even though it's snowing again, I decide to walk. Heavy clouds blot out the stars.

I put in a call to Nica on my cellphone.

I can't talk, she says, Sandor is here.

Do you know what that bastard did?

I can't really talk.

Well, when will you be able to talk?

Never, probably. Sandor's leaving his wife. We're going to get married.

Then, she's gone.

The snow gets heavier. The few pedestrians plod on, heads down, invisible to one another. It's a cold town, I think. Chilly weather, chilly humans.

I stop off at a bar. It's a kind of low-level student drinking place. I order a double Scotch. Beside me are two guys, some kind of Eastern Europeans. Russian? Bulgarian? They're huge, like nightclub bouncers or Olympic wrestlers. One turns to me with a smile.

When you pay me dollars you owe?

You've got the wrong guy, I say.

No, I have right guy.

We have right asshole, says the other, stepping to my other side.

We go outside then discuss, says the first one.

I recognize the accent now. Not Russian or Bulgarian – Hungarian.

Outside in the alley, they proceed to lay a crunchy beating on me. A fist like a ham to the gut. A stunning kick to the groin. Then, the nut, right into my nose. A football stadium head butt.

I collapse to the pavement. The pain is nothing I've ever experienced.

Sandor didn't need to do this, I say. I get the picture.

Is not Sandor, says Hungarian Number One. She pay us, the actress.

Nica? Nica did this?

There's no response, just silence. Snow, gently falling. Then, they're gone, disappeared.

How do you like me now?

Bleeding, in pain, I get to my feet and I trudge through the snowdrifts. The weather's turning into a blizzard and it's getting more difficult to see more than a few feet in front of me, the tall buildings getting indistinct. But I see something very clearly. My life in this city has come to an end. I don't belong here. Tomorrow, I'll book a flight to California. It has to be warmer there.

Matthew Heiti

FOR THEY WERE ONLY WINDMILLS

Orson shifts his bulk forward, resting elbows on thighs, squatting on the toilet like some great idle god. The white robe flutters open, his belly rolling down to touch the cold lip of porcelain. Bathroom door flung open to a long tiled corridor ending in a door flung open to a blue expanse, the smell of seaweed and beach foam drifting in.

Orson looks in the mirror above the marble countertop, catching the growing darkness under his eyes, the grey spidering out through his beard. He pulls the robe closed in embarrassment or maybe fear – the pink of his loose skin a kind of confession.

His forehead heaves, a concentration. Another push. Nothing is exhumed.

Orson lies in bed, staring up at the painted wooden ceiling. He traces the spiral pattern, following the mosaic of colour and line as it curls inward like a labyrinth, but he keeps losing the thread, his eyes imploding toward the centre – this unreachable thing. His arm grasps for the mosquito netting, pulling it closed around the bed, the fading light going honeyed through the gauze. Rhythm of ocean pulling him into some perversion of sleep.

Fitful dreams of a gaunt man in a suit of armour. Some kind of conquistador. Riding across a wide, empty plain. Flash of lightning. A rainstorm, a biblical flood. His armour rusts, silver going brown, flaking away, leaving him naked and pink under a universe of water. A chorus of devils raise their voices in screeching agony.

Orson surfaces to the sound of someone screaming in German. Incomprehensible noises, like a cornered animal, accompanied by a pounding on the wall, heavy thud of furniture, glass shattering, a final vicious shriek – silence.

The moon hangs swollen in the open window. This heat never-ending. Orson strains over the edge of the bed, reaching under to grasp the cool leather handle, pulling out the case.

It sits on the floor, a dark hunched shape, clasps winking in the half-light. He runs his hand along the black shell, sliding his fingers into a pouch and coming out with a hard circle of glass. He holds it up to the moon, light bending in the cavity of the lens, then returns the case to its spot below.

Orson lies back, drawing a book from under his pillow. The volume is thick, binding cracked, pages marked with hundreds of tiny shreds of paper. Opening to the first page. He reads the first sentence over and over like a mantra, letting it drag him to morning.

Padding down the hallway into the parlour to see chairs upended, cushions torn and cindered, broken bottles, pale glass the colour of the sky above the surf. Wrapped in a tapestry is some large shape. A tuft of greying hair peeking out one end, a swollen foot poking out the other. Flies buzz above a bowl of figs.

Orson grabs one end of the tapestry and pulls, groaning with effort as the fabric unfurls, disgorging the great naked body of Marlon, flopping to the floor like a beached whale.

Orson rights the divan and settles onto it, sinking deep into the cushions. Marlon scratches his testicles and rolls away from the light.

"What happened here?"

Marlon lifts his head and cracks one eye. Seeing Orson, he lies back again.

"What the devil—"

"Please," Marlon's hand lifting in weak protest. His voice mumbles out like an insect, lips pursed around the words. "Gotta at least wait til I've observed Mecca."

He rolls to a kneeling position, resting with hands on the floor, forehead touching the tile, almost in prayer. Then he shifts his weight forward, the muscles in his back quivering in every direction as he grunts and snorts.

"What are you doing?"

"Handstand." Words squeaking out like a balloon losing air and then Marlon gives up, somersaulting forward with a crash, knocking the bowl and sending figs rolling across the floor.

Orson slips his hand into the pocket of his robe, fingering the glass lens. "Is it your acrobatics that have laid waste to the entire room, dear boy?"

Marlon pulls a stringy lock of thinning hair back from his face. He reaches out and grabs a fig, biting into purple flesh. "I was in charge, I'da burned the place to the ground. Was that kraut."

"Klaus?"

"Something about a wife or a prostitute or money, or maybe it was character work. I dunno, honey, I went to sleep and let him work it out." Marlon reaches under himself and brings out a damp sheet of paper. "This came under the door – bill for last week."

Orson takes the piece of paper and shoves it into his robe without looking. "You read the book yet?"

"Yeah. Sure. Quick read, real gas."

"We should rehearse."

"Later, kid. First, I'm gonna lie here a while." Marlon draws his arm across his eyes to block out the light. "Then I'm gonna make myself some mimosas."

After a moment, his breathing gets heavier. Through an archway, Orson sees the sandstone balcony and beyond – the blue unbending sea. Orson pulls the lens from his pocket and holds it up, closing one eye. The image distorts, the ocean leaking across the floor to buoy Marlon up, carry his body out into the wastes.

The hash smoke clings sweet to the roof of his mouth as Orson lays the tube down on the nightstand. Most of the shisha is made from hammered brass, but the base is a glass jar, partially filled with clear water, fog curling thickly in the space over the liquid. Placing his lips around the spout, he inhales once more. The fog stirs, dragged up the tube, and just as Orson thinks he sees something there – he's exhaling, the jar filling with smoke again.

He lies back, tips of fingers and toes humming, head stretching away from body, connected only by a thin membrane. His eyes again drowsily follow the path of the design on the ceiling. The disc spins and reels above him.

When he opens his eyes, the fog in the shisha jar has been swept away like a curtain. Leaning forward through a cloud of hash smoke, Orson sees something – a small dark shape – a man – suspended motionless in the water. Rusted armour.

The gaunt man.

Orson watches as the body slowly sinks to the bottom of the jar. He reaches forward, fingers brushing the glass, and the eyes of the figure pop open. He jolts back and the glass cracks, lines wrinkling across its surface. Then an explosion. An endless rush of water fills the room. The bed rises toward the ceiling. A great wheel spins madly above him.

When he wakes, the shisha is lying on the floor. Ash, broken glass, a pool of water. His book is on his chest, pages creased open to an etching of a windmill.

Orson struggles first with the slacks and then the shirt, giving up when it's clear he no longer fits them. He cinches the belt of his robe, jams into his oxfords and sets off down the windowless passageways feeling as if he is bending toward the very bowels of the house. An obstruction, a constipation, never to emerge. But eventually he finds himself in a dusty courtyard, down a set of stairs and at a wrought-iron gate.

The sun hasn't risen yet, and Orson stands outside the walls of his rented flat on the dirt of a narrow medina. A mule tied to a post glances his way, tosses its tail, lets loose a stream of shit onto the street. If only it were so easy.

He walks the webwork streets until dawn breaks, finally resting at a coffeehouse, sucking black coffee from a small cup. A pair of men in brown habits and fezzes squat on embroidered cushions, drinking fresh mint tea and smiling encouragingly at Orson in his dirt-streaked bathrobe.

He pulls a few coins out of his pocket, some combination of francs, rials, pesetas – he doesn't know – places them on his table and pushes through the curtain into the hot slap of sunlight. Spire of church, dome of mosque, column of synagogue. The square overflows with men and women of all shades and dress rubbing up against one another on the way to prayer or market.

He crosses the square, shaking his head at the vendor who tries to sell him a bowl of pickled lemons, brushing away the children tugging at his robe for change, and enters the cramped dim office of the Western Union.

The agent with thick glasses doesn't speak any English, so Orson twists Italian words into snatches of Spanish. His last traveller's cheque is exchanged for a pathetic number of bills and after much gesticulating from the agent, Orson gathers that the wire transfer from his German investors has not arrived.

Standing back on the square, preparing to submerge once again into the crowd, Orson hears his name and turns to see the agent stumbling out of the office, waving an envelope, blinding white in the sun. Orson takes the letter, tearing it open immediately, expecting the transfer and finding a telegram instead:

ALL FAVOURS CALLED IN STOP ALL BRIDGES BURNED STOP ALL HOPE AND MONEY LOST STOP LOVE ILYA STOP PLEASE STOP

Orson feels a tug at his sleeve and turns to see a small child holding a pinwheel up for him, the toy blades humming a rainbow in the breeze.

Sundown, Orson rides a mule up a series of switchbacks to the plains above town. He purchased the animal from his neighbour and it is disagreeable and lazy, stopping periodically to take in the sights, to chew on the drifts of grass growing along the trail. Orson raps it on the head and the mule turns, snapping at his hand, trying to sever it from his wrist.

Finally, they crest the ridge and Orson slides off the mule, landing in a heap. He looks out at the empty landscape. This great expanse, this brimming void inside his body. A gust of warm air sweeps by, swirling handfuls of dust. A faint humming sound, like the wings of insects, reaches his ears but he cannot place it. He tries to remember what he is doing here – the excitement of a new start, the buoyancy of ideas – everything gone stale under paperwork and finances and the endless denials of shaking heads, closed doors. He tries to remember what it feels like to be something.

"Just give me a second chance."

The mule tilts its head, coal eyes shining wet in the sunset, blinks in reply. "How many second chances do you need?"

The humming insect suddenly pitches upward and the air seems to vibrate. He squints into the distance, shading eyes with hand. The warmth is sucked out of the breeze and a surge of cold air hits Orson, sending him back a step.

The fading sun catches it first – a cloud rising over the mountains, coming down the slopes in a dark froth, then across the plains, swallowing the sky.

Staggering back, Orson looks for cover he cannot find and ducks behind the mule, peering over its flank at the wall of dust. The mule, suspecting that Orson might try to mount it again, watches him and snorts. Within seconds the dust storm rushes over them, grains of sand tearing across skin, air snatched from lungs, Orson's screams joining the howl of the wind.

Shutting his eyes tight, Orson draws the glass lens from his pocket, jamming it against his left eye like a monocle, staring down the throat of the storm. From its depth an iris grows, a speck of light dawning over him. In the centre something takes shape. A spinning disc, a white tower. A windmill on the plain.

When he wakes, the storm has passed and the mule is pissing on his shoe. Orson looks up at the stars. The wail of a hyena in the night, calling to him, "Last chance…last chance."

Marlon is in the courtyard fountain with two beautiful Arabian women when Orson comes through the gate, dragging the mule behind him. One of the women has a bar of soap, the other a cloth. Marlon is in the middle, spitting water playfully.

"Climb on in," Marlon spreads his arms invitingly, then drags the giggling women closer. "But your lady friend's gonna have to wait her turn."

"Her name's Rosy." Orson ties the mule to the gate and climbs the stairs. He stops on the landing, sucking in his gut and standing like a captain on the prow of his ship. "Need you up early tomorrow."

"Sure thing, kid. You know me – early to bed, early to rise."

"Before noon."

Orson pulls the case from under the bed, setting it on the mattress. Sarcophagus puff of air and wrench of metal as the clasps snap open.

This ragged idol. Precious treasure. This maker of dreams. Black beetle shell, gold-rimmed lens, 35mm magazine, clockwork mechanism. The Caméflex. This child's toy.

He scrubs his hands in the basin, picking the dirt of the streets from under his nails – the way he watched an old dervish in rags wash his hands before touching his Qur'an like a careful lover.

He lifts the separate limbs of the camera out of the case and lays them down on the bedsheet. Taking a piece of silk, cleaning each part before snapping it together. These dissembled pieces becoming something whole. Finally reaching into his pocket to pull out the hard curve of glass, screwing the lens into place.

"*Il mio bambino*," he lullabies with the camera gentle in his arms, the candles dying to dark and sleep.

He's up by three, head and groin buzzing, excited. So much to do before first light. Down the hall, cracking a door to whisper "Marlon."

Pushing open wider to show a great slab of Marlon, head resting on the soft thigh of a stranger, two more women draped across him like blankets, another curled up at his feet.

"Need you up soon, we're shooting at first light."

Marlon mumbles, "Sure, honey, sure."

On his way out, Orson calls the International and leaves a wake-up call for Klaus.

Marching the night streets, kicking clouds of dust at rats peering from alleys, two drunks laughing as he passes – "*Camisón! Camisón!*" they sing after this fat man in his bathrobe – finally arriving in the rectangle of yellow pouring from the doorway of the Café

Hafa. He grabs a cup of tea from the toothless gentleman behind the counter and heads for the terrace off the back.

No moon in the pitch black and his hand finds the flaking paint and rust of railing, Orson can't see the water but he hears it sigh up the rocks. He sips the cold sweet mint and is just about to decide he's wasted the trip, then catches the sound of ripping paper off to the side.

"William?"

Another rip.

"William, that you?"

Rip.

Scratch – and the match goes up in a whiff of sulfur, the brief light showing dark shapes around a table. *Scratch* – and he sees William's trench coat, other trench coats with him, a white pillar of paper. *Scratch* – and Orson pulls a cigar from his pocket and lights it, puffing.

"William, I've come for the script."

Rip. "Can you wait?"

Orson puffs, the cherry on his cigar throbbing with each inhalation, him imagining this cigar is the only light left in the city, across the black water there's a Spaniard wondering what the hell that red speck is. A dead continent coming alive.

Orson puts his hand on William's shoulder, brittle, like touching a deathbed grandparent, "You're losing weight."

Rip. "I'm losing everything – it's my new profession."

Scratch – and Orson leans over the table, the other trench coats leaning away from the light, William leaning over a mound of paper with a razorblade. *Rip* – the paper splits into two. *Rip* – into four. Black.

"William, are you tearing up my script?"

Rip. "Ain't tearing it up, Slim. Wrote the sonuvabitch, but it was radioactive, so I'm liberating it...real script'll expose itself when I tape it back together. You got any tape?"

"We're shooting in two hours."

"Or glue. I could use glue. I'd eat glue. Pawned the type-writer for some eukodol. You got any bennies? Think we smoked all the hash in the city – all the hash in Arabia. Time travelled and smoked all the hash in the history of the world. You got any morphine? Jesus, I could use some cocaine. Nutmeg. You got any demerol? Nembutol? Anything left at all? The only thing left is people – the only drug left. Let's snort people. Suck that blood, shoot it vein for vein. Smoke pubic hair. Find me a truly beautiful person, a god, tear the flesh away, grind the bones down to powder and snort it, snort all that beauty in and shit out all the ugliness in your guts. I just need something. Something that'll make me dream again. Can't dream anymore."

Orson gently pries the razor from his hand. William's face turns up at him in the early blue, a sack of bones in a trench coat.

"You got any tape, Slim?"

Orson watches the mess of paper scraps blowing off the table in the wind. "I'll get you that glue. I need you and your friends to build something for me."

The door cracks and the dawn light hits a bulge of white surrounded by brown skin, a chorus of groaning in the sun. The great planets of Marlon's ass have become pillows for a half dozen Arabian princesses.

"Where's Klaus?"

Marlon farts, vibrating the princesses. "What's that, honey?"

A crash as Orson dumps an armload of metal on the floor. "Put your costume on and meet me in the courtyard."

Sitting on the lip of the fountain, Marlon squirms and grunts his way into a breastplate, "This armour was made for a dwarf."

Pacing, cigar puffing, "You were supposed to lose weight."

"Unh! I did lose weight, kid, but it found me again and it…Mnhuh!…brought some friends along."

"He's emaciated, in the book – it's symbolic – he's wasting away."

"Guh! I'm wasting away too," – pats the bulb of his belly – "just in the other direction."

Orson peers down the medina, "The hell's Klaus?" The mule, unhappily still tied to the gate, rips the pocket off Orson's bathrobe and he stubs it with his cigar.

Splash – and he turns.

Marlon's thrown the breastplate in the fountain and is all white rolling flesh except for underwear and sandals. He picks up a rusted iron cap and plunks it on his head.

"Fits."

The shrivelled raisin of a clerk at the International babbles at Marlon in some loose imitation of French.

"The kraut's not here," Marlon translates for Orson, with questionable accuracy.

"Where the hell is he?"

"He dunno, but there's blood all over his room and a dead pig in the bathtub."

"A pig?"

"Yeah, and someone shit on the bed."

They find Klaus at the jail, rolling on the floor in his own piss and shrieking at the gendarme who has just finished pulling off one of his fingernails with a pair of pliers. The sweat-stained officer waves the bloody flake in his prisoner's face and yells, *"Espía! Espía maldito!"*

Klaus spits and pisses and bleeds and shouts *"Ich bin Jesus Christus Erlöser, ficken sau!"*

"Espía de mierda!"

Peering in the doorway, Marlon tugs at Orson's sleeve. "What's going on?"

"They think he's a spy."

"Why?"

"Not sure. Something about climbing the walls of the Sultan's palace and rubbing himself against a palm tree."

Klaus and the gendarme have finished screaming and are both now looking at the two fat men in the doorway. Orson clears his throat. "This man isn't a spy. He works for me."

"No es espía?"

"He's an actor – *è un attore.*"

"Qué?" The gendarme kicks at Klaus, who is busy trying to bite his captor's leg. "Un actor?"

Orson puts the black case on the floor, snaps the lid and lifts out the Caméflex. The gendarme looks at the camera, Orson, and then at Klaus, something dawning over him.

"Ah!" He smiles, gold molar shining. "Humphrey Bogart!"

The smile fades. He looks down at the fingernail, embarrassed. He wipes it on his pant leg and offers it back to Klaus.

A dusty plateau crouching on the skirts of the Sierra Morena. Backlit by the sun, the silhouette of a man on horseback comes over the hill into view. Armour white and shining he sits atop his steed, his squire at his side. These figures like statues, carved in shadow and light, these ghosts of pastoral Spain.

Next to them, a drunk on a bicycle pulls up.

"Holy fuck." Orson brings the camera down. "Get him out of there!"

The drunk looks up at the naked fat man with the pot lid on his head, looks down at the man with the bulging eyes in poncho and sombrero, looks at the drooling mule. The drunk falls off his bicycle laughing. Klaus throws his sombrero on the ground and stamps on it, cursing and spitting.

"Please don't wreck the costumes, Klaus."

Marlon pats the mule and watches Klaus hurl the bicycle down the hill. "Say, what're we doing here, kid?"

"You and your squire are just setting out – leaving everything behind."

"Right, right…and where're we going?"

Klaus points at Orson, yelling, "Ficken sau!"

"That's good, Klaus. Going? You're…going to lead a life of chivalry."

"Ah. This a period piece?"

"Marlon – have you even read the book?"

"What book?" Marlon pulls something from his nose and wonders at it. "Just write my lines out and I'll pin 'em to the mule."

"We're not recording sound. Say whatever – just move your lips."

Klaus flings his poncho at Orson. "*Wo ist mein geld?*"

"The costumes, Klaus – please. Look, we're losing light – can we shoot this?"

"Lemme see the script."

"I can't."

"*Mein geld, ficken sau!*"

"What d'you mean, you can't?"

Klaus is so close Orson can see the spittle pooling at the corners of his mouth. "*Ich wünsche mein geld!*"

"There's no money. There's no script. All right?"

Marlon groans, Klaus can only stare, a vein bulging in his vast forehead. Orson sits on the camera case and pulls a cigar out of his robe.

"Look – we've been here I don't know how long – weeks – and I've paid for your hash, I've paid for your booze, your food, your women – all for nothing. Marlon, you're obese, you're balding and your last good picture was ten years ago. And Klaus, what can I say? You're shitting on beds and molesting palm trees. This is rock bottom, gentlemen."

Marlon slithers off the mule. "So...what're we doing here then?"

"We're making a movie. Last movie in the world. Last chances all around," Orson lights the cigar, blowing smoke rings. "And tonight...we shall have last rites."

The paint on the façade is flaking, the street deserted, but inside the Gran Teatro Cervantes is full of colour and light. Marlon and Orson sit together in the empty theatre watching a woman wrapped in silk wiggle her belly while the jangly strings of gypsy jazz come pouring from the horn of the gramophone set on stage.

Orson watches Klaus, down in the pit, elbows on the stage, snatching at the dancer's skirt, her trying to stomp on his hand. "This theatre used to be one of the grandest on the continent. Now it's a sewer."

"I think it's great."

"The begging I've done for little bits of money...you do something ugly to make something beautiful." Busted springs squeaking, Orson squirming. "Same damn thing every time I make a picture. Don't know why I do it."

Marlon sucks his cheap brandy. "So, what the hell's this movie about, kid?"

"You're this sort of knight errant, on this mission to help people. You want to make things better. Only you're not really a knight, you only think you are, you're actually delusional and nobody wants your help and you die alone without making anything better for anyone. Even yourself."

"I don't do comedy, honey, you know that."

Orson watches Klaus trying to lick the dancer's foot. "You know the worst thing you can call someone?"

"Dunno – John Wayne?"

"A genius." Orson stretches and yawns, palms rubbing eyes. "It's a dead word – like knight errant. It's what they call dead men."

"Whattaya talking about, kid?"

"Waste."

They watch as Klaus chases the dancer off stage and smashes the gramophone into pieces, smashing these into even smaller pieces. Orson yawns again.

"La Mancha…you know '*mancha*' means stain? A wet splotch – some mark you can't wipe off. But '*al-mansha*' is also the Arabic word for dry land. I'm barren. Haven't been able to shit for a week."

"*Ich bin die stille.*" Exhausted, Klaus turns toward the audience, eyes sparking with some black rage, but then his voice comes out all slippery and smooth. This unexpected tenderness. "*Ich bin die stille…Ich bin die stimme…Ich bin der schrei…Ich bin der strom…Ich bin der sturm…Ich bin…Ich bin…*"

The voice falls into whisper, *ich bin ich bin*, a dying rhythm. A purr, *ich bin*. Orson's eyes droop, *ich*, head falls forward, *bin*. Rebounds.

He is alone in the theatre. Silent, a tomb. Then a *clank clank* in the distance. *Clank clank* getting closer. Some kind of pressure pushing down on his chest. *Clank clank* coming from somewhere backstage. *Clank clank*.

The curtains part. A gaunt man in a suit of armour clanks to the middle of the stage.

A laugh from the back of the theatre. Orson tries to turn, but he can't. Another laugh, off to the side. Another. And another. The theatre vibrates with laughter, pitching up and out of control. The gaunt man raises the visor on his helmet and Orson sees some old, grey, lifeless thing.

The face of Orson.

He tries to stand but he's being pressed back into his seat and he realizes – he's wearing the suit of armour. He can smell the rust. His body too fat for this cage, trying to burst out but the scrap metal bears down on him, crushing him, snatching his breath.

A groan from the stage and the wooden planks bulge upward, then splinter with a crack. From the hole, a white tower sprouts, reaching for the dome of the ceiling, bending over him. The blades of the wheel twirling, dragging him up, sucking him closer and closer to the grinder.

A blast of hot light on his face and a voice above it all – clear – *"Ich bin der Erlöser!"*

And he thinks, I am saved.

He wakes to the morning sun on his face. Marlon asleep on the chair beside him, Klaus still standing on stage – silent and staring. Orson grabs the black case from the floor, gives Marlon a shake. "Awake, dear boy – we're going to shoot the catastrophe."

They climb the switchbacks, the mule carrying the camera equipment, Marlon holding on to its tail, dragging his sweating nakedness up the incline, Klaus silent and stalking after like a panther, and Orson in front, cigar smoking, bathrobe brown with dirt, a monk's habit, leading his tribe to the promised land.

Orson can feel his heart hammering, something in his chest – exhaustion, excitement or hope. And when he finally reaches the plateau, he sinks to his knees in its presence, his voice clutching out in a whisper, "It's perfect."

A white tower, standing tall on the plain, disc spinning in the breeze – a windmill. A sentinel, the last stronghold between hope and the void.

"The fuck is that?" Marlon wheezing beside him. "That paper-mâché?"

A bunch of black trench coats are piled at the base of the tower, William standing next to them holding an empty bucket of glue, bits of paper stuck all over. "Built your dayus ax mackerel, Slim."

Marlon groans. "I hate fuckin' beatniks."

"Gentlemen, this is our day of reckoning." Orson starts unstrapping equipment from the mule, setting up the tripod. "Marlon, I'll need you on Rosy – you'll be charging at this windmill here."

"That's a windmill?"

"No, it's a giant, it just looks like windmill."

"Giant? It's five feet tall."

William rubs his nose with a glue-soaked hand. "That's all the paper we had."

"It's a symbol, Marlon."

"It's a giant, it's a windmill, it's a symbol. Make up your fuckin' mind."

"The entire film rests on this." Orson's hands on Marlon's shoulders, leaking cigar fumes. "You fighting the giants."

"Okay, but it's paper-mâché and I'm taller than it."

"Look – every useful thought I've ever had has been pissed on or trampled over. Marlon, this is my sword," lifting the Caméflex. "It's rusty, and nobody wants to see a fat knight kill the dragon anymore – they're in love with the dragon, they want the dragon to eat the knight and shit him out in Technicolor. But this is all I have. After this, you can go back to your goddamn penthouse in Vienna or Tokyo or wherever and pick up a cool million here or there doing crap films and spray all your integrity down the toilet, but today – today you're getting on that fucking mule and you're going to bring that giant down and obliterate it."

"But…" Marlon clears his throat, murmurs. "He doesn't – in the book, he doesn't. He just falls on his ass."

"Thought you didn't read it."

"Read a bit this morning on the shitter."

"Well," – Orson tilts the camera up, looks through the viewfinder, the tower a white god in the desert – "this isn't the book. This is mine."

"Maybe…you should take a break, kid."

"I don't need a break!" Orson throws his cigar, sending the mob of trench coats scurrying. "I got just enough film in here to shoot this one scene, to shoot it once, and that's it."

Marlon laughs. "One scene ain't a movie, honey."

"All my films are in this one scene. Everything." Orson takes a deep breath, looks up at Marlon – letting himself be an aging fat sick irrelevant constipated failure. "Please. I need a saviour."

"Kid, I'm not…" Marlon looks embarrassed. "I'm just not."

"Ich bin…"

Everyone turns to look at Klaus.

"Ich bin der…" He stands, strangely calm, holding Orson's cigar in his fist, like a torch. *"Ich bin der Jesus Christus."*

"The hell's that crazy kraut saying now?"

"I'm not sure."

"He just say something about Jesus?"

Louder – *"Ich bin der Jesus Christus."*

"Listen, you crazy kraut, I told you already – you're not Jesus anymore, that was your last show. You're the sidekick in this one, more like Judas."

Klaus opens his mouth and screams a throat-ripping, larynx-shredding animal sound, and runs shrieking at Orson, who stumbles back covering his face, Klaus trampling over him and rushing for the windmill – the hundred yard dash, dodging the trench coats reaching out for him, slapping William with a backhand before he can tackle him, vaulting over Marlon's wide, squat body and standing before the white tower.

He looks back at Orson. *"Ich bin der Erlöser."*

He jams the cigar into the tower. *Whoomp* and the layers of glue ignite, a blue aura of flame leaping out from the windmill. Orson staggers toward it, voiceless, knocked back by the heat, throwing handfuls of sand at the fire. He's finally dragged back by Marlon to watch the pages, the scraps of paper, curl in flame.

"Give it up, kid – the Kaiser here killed your giant."

Orson shakes Marlon off and crawls to the Cameflex, lifting it, sighting the tower in the viewfinder. Black, it's all gone black, everything going black and dead.

Click. Button pressed. *Whirr*, the reel spins. Recording.

Marlon says things to him, tugs at him, but the world's gone silent for Orson, unable to pull his eye from the lens, documenting this death in motion. The fire exhausts itself, but the tower still stands. A dark husk.

Marlon is the first to go, shrugging his great naked shoulders and turning away, then William and the trench coats shuffle down the trail chasing a fix, then Klaus the Destroyer runs off into the hills screaming, then even Rosy the mule snorts indifference and clop clops back to town. Every soul gone.

Through the lens, Orson watches the tower stand and stand. A memory, a premonition. This constant enemy blowing him back. Sucking him in. Him tilting without any ground to stand on.

Then, slightly, a breeze. Lazy, it brushes by the tower with a shiver, a shake. Something touches Orson's cheek, reaching to pull a flake of ash from his beard. A gust and the tower wavers, coming apart like dandelion seed, millions of black particles taking to flight. Within seconds, there's nothing left.

He lets the reel spin on until it ends with another click. The film safely inside the canister, dark and quiet. A witness.

Slowly, Orson puts down the Caméflex, returns it to the case. But before he closes it, he removes the canister with a snap. He rolls onto his back, the canister pressed to his chest, and stares up at the night sky spackle. He waits for the release. Waits for a movement deep down to signify he has overcome something here. He waits for the desire to shit. But nothing. His guts hold on.

He feels an ache, something digging in, and he reaches behind to pull up a plastic rod, a flowered bulb. A child's pinwheel, just beginning to spin. Round and round, round and round it goes.

He twists the canister in his hands, the lid turning off. The reel of film coiled inside like a black snake in its den. Later, when he can find the money to post it, the reel will go to a lab in some low-rent studio and some low-rent producer who won't speak any language he can understand will cut it into little bits and add other little bits that have nothing of Orson in them and, later on still, a handful of people will watch this film that is not his film in some low-rent theatre, and someday someone will ask him about all that potential and what happened to it.

He's pulled the snake from its hole. Grabbed hold of the oily film and unwound it from its reel. It's flapping across the sand, uncoiling, venom coming out in a black river and in the morning sun it will be gone and so will Orson. A waste, what a great waste.

Born in a meteor crater, Matthew Heiti is an author, playwright, screenwriter and teacher, living, loving and working in Sudbury, Ontario. He has published a novel, *The City Still Breathing*, and a play, *Black Dog: 4 vs the wrld*. He is currently serving as Playwright in Residence for Pat the Dog Theatre Creation, and completing his second novel. www.harkback.org

Helen Marshall is a lecturer of Creative Writing and Publishing at Anglia Ruskin University in Cambridge, England. Her first collection of fiction *Hair Side, Flesh Side* won the Sydney J Bounds Award in 2013, and *Gifts for the One Who Comes After*, her second collection, won the World Fantasy Award and the Shirley Jackson Award in 2015. Previous to winning this year's Carter V. Cooper Award, she appeared in *Book Three* and *Book Four* with shortlisted stories as an emerging writer. Helen is editing *The Year's Best Weird Fiction* to be released in 2017, and her debut novel will be published in 2018.

Diana Svennes-Smith of Eastend, Saskatchewan, is a graduate of the Iowa Writers' Workshop where she was a teaching-writing fellow and recipient of the Glenn Schauffer New Zealand Fellowship. Her work has been published in *Maisonneuve, Turbine, The Fiddlehead, The Asham Award Anthology, Reconstruction, Cosmonauts Avenue* and *Room*. A recent Michener-Copernicus Fellow, her debut novel *The End of Steel* is forthcoming with Doubleday in May, 2018.

Sang Kim of Toronto is a restaurateur, chef, food literacy activist, and writer. He coordinated innovative approaches to literary events, such as COOK/BOOK, literEATure, and the Parental Guidance Not Required Reading Series which focuses on presenting the work of young teens and prodigies. He is currently at work on two story collections, *Spoiled Rice* and *Woody Allen Ate My Kimchi*, a food memoir.

A.L. Bishop writes fiction and non-fiction. She is a recent graduate of the Humber School for Writers who lives in Niagara Falls. This is her first published work, and it will also appear in *ELQ/Exile Quarterly* in 2017.

Katherine Govier has published 10 novels and three collections of stories. Her latest novel is *The Three Sisters Bar and Hotel*. After the 2010 release of *The Ghost Brush*, it was translated into Japanese, Spanish and French. She is a winner of The Toronto Book Award and the Marian Engel Award. Katherine has been President of PEN Canada and Chair of the Writers' Trust. She founded and is director of *The Shoe Project*, a writing and performing workshop for immigrant women writers. She lives in Toronto, and Canmore, Alberta.

Sheila McClarty of Oakbank, Manitoba, has had her short fiction appear in *Grain, The Antigonish Review, Crannog* and *The Fiddlehead.* In 2011 her collection of short stories, *High Speed Crow,* won the Eileen McTavish Sykes Award for Best First Book by a Manitoba author. She is a graduate of The Humber School For Writers.

Caitlin Galway is a Toronto-based writer whose first novel, *Blackbird,* came out in 2013. She has been published in *Riddle Fence, The Broken Social Scene Story Project, enRoute,* and online for the CBC. She has won cthe CBC's Stranger than Fiction Contest and Riddle Fence's Short Fiction Contest, and was among the long list for the Carter V. Cooper Competition in 2012.

Bruce Meyer is author of more than forty-five books of poetry, short fiction, and non-fiction. He is professor of Creative Writing at Georgian College in Barrie, Ontario, and an Associate of Victoria College of the University of Toronto. Always looking to push his boundaries, he has edited for Exile Editions *The Goethe Glass,* an anthology of Climate Fiction stories, due out in 2017.

Frank Westcott of Alliston, Ontario, is an author, poet, short story writer, lyricist and musician, and a former teacher with Special Education certification. In 2011 he won the Carter V. Cooper Short Fiction Award/Best Story by an Emerging Writer category, for "The Poet." In 2014 his poem, *And She Lay Herself Down*, was a finalist for the Gwendolyn MacEwen Poetry Award.

Martha Bátiz of Mexico has lived in the Toronto area since 2003. She has published articles, chronicles, reviews and short stories in Mexico, Spain, Dominican Republic, Puerto Rico, Peru, Ireland, England, the United States and Canada. Her first collection of stories was *A todos los voy a matar*, and her award-winning novella, *Boca de lobo*, will be released in translation, as will a new collection of stories, by Exile Editions in 2017. In 2015 she was selected a Top Ten Most Influential Hispanic-Canadian.

Leon Rooke has published seven novels, 19 short story collections, two poetry volumes, several plays, and co-edited – mostly with John Metcalf – seven influential anthologies. Some 350 of his stories have found print, many anthologized. In 2016 *Fabulous Fictions and Peculiar Practices* (stories arising from sketches by artist Tony Calzetta) came out in a lavish trade edition, as did *Swinging Through Dixie* (two novellas, three stories), while his applauded 1990 novel *A Good Baby* was simultaneously reissued. Awards are numerous. He is a member of the Order of Canada, and is also a painter. Now 82, his best is yet to come...

Norman Snider of Toronto is a screenwriter, author, journalist, and professor. He has published *How to Make Love to a Movie Star* and *The Roaring Eighties and Other Good Times* (Exile Editions), *Smokescreen: One Man Against the Underworld*, and *The Changing of the Guard*. For film, he co-wrote – with David Cronenberg – *Dead Ringers*, and most recently *Casino Jack*, starring Kevin Spacey (also brought out as a book with Exile Editions).

Exile's $15,000 Carter V. Cooper Short Fiction Competition

FOR CANADIAN WRITERS ONLY

$10,000 for the Best Story by an Emerging Writer
$5,000 for the Best Story by a Writer at Any Career Point

The 12 shortlisted are published in the annual *CVC Short Fiction Anthology* series and *ELQ/Exile: The Literary Quarterly*

Exile's $3,000 Gwendolyn MacEwen Poetry Competition

FOR CANADIAN WRITERS ONLY

$1,500 for the Best Suite of Poetry
$1,000 for the Best Suite by an Emerging Writer
$500 for the Best Poem

Winners are published in *ELQ/Exile: The Literary Quarterly*

These annual competitions open in October & November
details at: www.TheExileWriters.com